W9-AYF-416

ECHOES OF TERROR

ECHOES OF TERROR

MARIS SOULE

FIVE STAR
A part of Gale, Cengage Learning

GALE
CENGAGE Learning·

Farmington Hills, Mich • San Francisco • New York • Waterville, Maine
Meriden, Conn • Mason, Ohio • Chicago

GALE
CENGAGE Learning®

LIBRARY OF CONGRESS CATALOGING-IN-PUBLICATION DATA

Names: Soule, Maris, author.
Title: Echoes of terror / Maris Soule.
Description: First edition. | Waterville, Maine : Five Star Publishing, [2017]
Identifiers: LCCN 2016041609 (print) | LCCN 2016049830 (ebook) | ISBN 9781432832810 (hardcover) | ISBN 1432832816 (hardcover) | ISBN 9781432834746 (ebook) | ISBN 1432834746 (ebook) | ISBN 9781432832674 (ebook) | ISBN 1432832670 (ebook)
Subjects: LCSH: Women detectives—Fiction. | Missing persons—Investigation—Fiction. | BISAC: FICTION / Thrillers. | FICTION / Mystery & Detective / General. | GSAFD: Mystery fiction. | Suspense fiction.
Classification: LCC PS3569.O737 E28 2017 (print) | LCC PS3569.O737 (ebook) | DDC 813/.54—dc23
LC record available at https://lccn.loc.gov/2016041609

First Edition. First Printing: March 2017
Find us on Facebook— https://www.facebook.com/FiveStarCengage
Visit our website— http://www.gale.cengage.com/fivestar/
Contact Five Star™ Publishing at FiveStar@cengage.com

Printed in the United States of America
1 2 3 4 5 6 7 21 20 19 18 17

ACKNOWLEDGMENTS

My thanks to Sergeant Ken Cox of the Skagway Police Department for taking time to answer my questions—both in person and through follow-up emails—about how the police department would handle a missing teenager report and for giving me a tour of the police station. Also, my thanks to National Park Service ranger Jacqueline A. Lott Ashwell for taking an hour before she went on duty to talk to me about her job and training. I do want to state that none of the characters in this novel is based on Sergeant Cox or Ranger Ashwell; however, both Cox and Ashwell helped me better understand their jobs and the area. Any mistakes in procedure are strictly mine.

A big thanks to my long-time friends David Curl and Ardyce Czuchna-Curl for taking a day off from their summer jobs at Skagway to drive my husband and me up the Klondike Highway to the summit and back, over to Dyea, and all around Skagway. They put close to 200 miles on their car that day. Months later they also took the time to read the rough draft of this novel and suggest corrections.

My critique partners—and friends—Julie McMullen and Dawn Bartley have lived—off and on—with this novel for years, finding errors, making suggestions, and giving encouragement. Thanks so very much.

And, finally, a lifetime of thanks to my husband, Bill, who willingly supports and encourages my passion to write.

CHAPTER ONE

7:25 A.M. Thursday

"That guy is a frickin' idiot."

"Who's an idiot?"

Brian Bane glanced at the girl sitting next to him before again splitting his attention between the twisting road in front of his Chevy Blazer and the tailgating Ford Explorer. On their right the roadway dropped over a thousand feet. As much as he liked excitement, this Internet-born adventure was not starting out as he'd imagined.

"The guy behind us," he said, keeping a tight hold on the steering wheel. "He came up out of nowhere. Now he's all over my ass. Like there's any way for me to go faster up this grade."

Misty—or Miss T as she was known on ChatPlace—twisted in her seat to look behind them. Her wild, blonde curls brushed her shoulders, and her miniskirt showed a teasing view of her inner thigh. "Shit," she hissed through her teeth.

"What?" Brian said.

"He sent Vince."

"Who sent Vince?"

"My dad."

"Your dad?" Brain didn't like the sound of that. "So, who's Vince?"

"He's a guy Dad knew in the Marines. He's supposed to do computer security for my dad's business, but he keeps acting like he's my bodyguard. I can't do a frickin' thing without him showing up."

She flopped back against the seat, and crossed her arms over her chest. The fact that her old man had sent someone after her, and the way she was pouting, didn't bode well. For the first time since he'd picked Misty up in Skagway, Brian wasn't so certain she was the eighteen years she'd advertised.

"How old are you, Misty? Your real age, I mean."

She glared at him, and then looked away. "Age is meaning-less."

Meaningless, my ass, he thought. *Damn, I'm so screwed.* He was about to take an underaged girl into Canada. No wonder some steroid filled ex-Marine with an over attachment to the boss's daughter was after him. He'd be lucky if he wasn't arrested as an international felon.

"Do you think—?"

A thump to the back corner bumper sent the Blazer into a fishtail, and Brian gasped, clinging to the steering wheel as he fought to bring the car back under control. "Jeez, Misty, your dad's buddy just rammed us."

"Then step on the gas," Misty ordered, giving a quick glance behind them. "Outrun him."

"In this thing?" The old Blazer was tired iron. The first part of the Klondike Highway, from Skagway to White Pass and the Canadian line, was a twisting, turning two-laner that rose from sea level to over three thousand feet. The steep incline was already taxing the engine. They'd be lucky to outrun a snowplow through this stretch.

Again the Explorer rammed into them, this time lurching them straight toward the guardrail as the road turned. Misty yelped and grabbed at the door. Brian swung the wheel. The sensation of the front right fender grating on metal vibrated through the steering column. When they came out of the turn, the Explorer was nearly touching the Blazer's side.

"Your dad's buddy is nuts! He's going to kill us."

"Just go faster!"

"I'm going as fast as I can."

The powerful Explorer began squeezing them closer to the guardrail. Jaw clenched and muscles taut, Brian struggled to keep his SUV on the pavement. Adrenaline pumped through his body, a bitter taste rising to his throat.

And then his heart nearly stopped.

Just a few hundred feet ahead, the guardrail turned into a twisted, jagged strip of metal that hung limply to the ground. Open air replaced protection. One bump from the Explorer as they passed that broken section of guardrail, and they'd definitely be going over the edge, tumbling down the mountainside.

"That's it, Babe."

Brian pulled his foot from the gas and began to brake.

"What are you doing? Don't slow down!"

"Forget it," he said in disgust. Man, his friends had been right about this whole hooking up on-line thing. They'd tried to talk him out of it, but all Brian had been seeing was a summer traveling through Canada with a hot chick. Instead of lots of sex and partying, after this ex-Marine got through with him, he'd be lucky if all of his body parts were intact.

Brian brought the Blazer to a complete stop, his entire body shaking. The Explorer angled in front of him, preventing a forward escape. With a sigh, Brian shifted into park, and then turned toward Misty—the beautiful, sexy Miss T.

The beautiful, sexy, underaged, Miss T, he mentally corrected. "Wouldn't you know I'd hook up with jailbait."

She glared at him. "So, it didn't work out. Stop whining. Vince isn't going to do anything to you."

"Oh yeah?" Brian sure hoped that was true. "So, what was this, just a little joy ride for you?"

"What it was is none of your business." Once again she looked away, out the side window.

Brian stared at her for a second, kicking himself for being such an idiot, then he stepped out of the car. As he looked toward the Explorer, he wondered if he should act angry—after all, Misty had duped him—or guilty, because he should have known she was underage.

The other car door began to open, and Brian called out, "Listen, man, I had no idea she was—" He broke off as the man straightened and faced him. He almost laughed when he saw the bear mask . . .

Then he saw the gun.

CHAPTER TWO

3:00 P.M.

"Poppa, do you have any idea where Phil might have gone fishing?"

Katherine Ward watched her grandfather straighten his lean body, his gnarled, age-spotted fingers still gripping the hoe he was using to dig the weeds away from a rose bush.

Russell Ward shook his head. "Phil? Haven't seen Phil in weeks."

"He was here just yesterday, Poppa."

Brown eyes, once keen as an eagle's, gazed at her through clouds of early cataracts and mental confusion. "He was?"

"Yes. You were telling him about a great spot to fish for lake trout . . . somewhere off the Chilkoot trail."

"Yesterday, you say?"

"Yesterday morning." Normally she would let the subject drop, but today she needed information. "It's important, Poppa. Phil hasn't checked in. Gordon is getting worried, and so am I. If Phil went fishing, it would really help if we knew where."

"Could be he went to Black Lake," her grandfather said, then shook his head. "No, not Black Lake. Maybe . . . ?"

His words trailed off, so she tried another angle. "How about the other guy, Poppa? The one Phil mentioned he's been fishing with lately. Do you remember his name or where he was staying?"

Again, the look in her grandfather's eyes told her the answer

11

before he shook his head. "I'm sorry, Katherine. I . . . I just don't remember. You sure Phil was here yesterday?"

"I'm sure, but that's all right. We'll find him."

Her grandfather glanced at her uniform and the Glock holstered at her side. "You leaving for work?"

"Since Phil hasn't shown up, Gordon asked me to come in a little early. But don't worry. Sarah will be here at four. She'll fix your dinner."

The bushy white brows on her grandfather's weathered face came so close they almost formed a straight line above his eyes. "Little Sarah Wilson? She's coming to dinner?"

Katherine smiled. "Poppa, little Sarah is now fourteen years old and as tall as I am. She's coming to fix *your* dinner."

"I can fix my own dinner."

"I know you can, but Sarah needs the money. And she'll be company for you while I'm at work. Just the other day you said it got lonely when I worked the late shift and you had to eat alone."

Katherine didn't see any sense in telling him the other reason she'd hired Sarah. The night she came home and found the burner on, Katherine knew the time had come when her grandfather needed additional care. Someone to cook his dinners when she wasn't around. Make sure he didn't wander off. The house they called home might not be as fancy as some of the newer homes being built around Skagway and off the road to Dyea, but it had stood on this plot of Alaskan soil for a hundred years, and her grandfather would truly be lost if anything happened to it.

"Your roses are looking good," she said, noting the buds would soon burst into an array of red and yellow blossoms. "Going to enter them in the flower show again?"

"Depends." He looked back at the plant in front of him. "I might not be around in August."

"Why? You thinking of going somewhere?"

He frowned at her. "You know what I mean. This old body's ready to go."

They'd been through this before, and Katherine hated it when her grandfather talked about dying. He was the last of her family. When he went, she would be alone . . . truly alone.

"You'd better plan on sticking around for a long time," she said and gave her grandfather a quick hug. "If you happen to remember where Phil might be fishing, call the station. Okay?"

"You'll be here in the morning?"

"I'll be here," she promised. Lately her grandfather had become more concerned about having someone around when he woke. Her assurance seemed to satisfy him.

"Take care of yourself," he said and went back to his weeding.

"Always do," she responded softly.

Katherine left him there, working in his rose garden, and got into the Tahoe she'd been issued when she joined the Skagway police force. As she pulled out of the drive, she noticed a red Explorer parked across the street and two houses down. A dented front bumper and broken headlight marred its finish. She considered leaving a note on the windshield, warning the owner to get the light fixed, then decided she didn't have time. It wasn't until she was at the corner, and happened to glance into her rearview mirror, that she noticed someone—or something—in the Explorer's driver's seat.

She stepped on the brake. Crazy as it seemed, it looked like a bear sitting behind the steering wheel.

Shifting into reverse, she started to back up for a closer look. She was barely a car length away from the Explorer when the ring of her cell phone made her stop. Katherine knew who was calling.

"You on your way in?" Sergeant Gordon Landros asked as

soon as she answered.

"Be there soon," Katherine said, glancing back at the Explorer. Whatever she'd seen was gone.

"Well, make it fast. We have a missing teenager."

CHAPTER THREE

The six-block drive to First and State shouldn't have taken more than a couple of minutes, but tourists crossing the streets impeded Katherine's progress. A sea of bodies bobbed in and out of souvenir and jewelry shops, clear evidence that a cruise ship had recently docked.

Gordon had ended the call before Katherine had a chance to ask if the teenager disappeared while onboard a cruise ship or if it was a local. She didn't even know if the teenager was male or female.

All she knew was Gordon wanted her at the station . . . and fast.

The moment Katherine entered the side door, the motherly voice of Alice Bowers, their middle-aged clerk/dispatcher, vibrated down the short hallway between the front office and the booking area. "Ma'am, Sergeant Landros *is* the officer in charge."

Although she couldn't be seen, Katherine nodded in agreement. Just Monday the chief had been rushed to the Bartlett Memorial Hospital in Juneau with a ruptured appendix. While he was recuperating, Gordon Landros was the senior officer of their small force and therefore in charge of the station.

"In that case, do something!" a woman demanded, her voice unfamiliar. "I'm telling you, she's been kidnapped."

Katherine frowned.

"Kidnapped" was a totally different situation from "missing."

15

Simply hearing the word put her on edge.

And, now she knew it was a female who was missing.

That also put her on edge.

Quickly, Katherine headed for the reception area.

"Now, now, Mrs. . . . Mrs. . . . ?" Gordon said as Katherine reached a spot where she could see the sergeant, Alice, and the woman.

"Morgan," a striking blonde snapped. "Crystal Morgan."

Gordon and the woman stood on the visitors' side of the counter that divided the entry area from the clerk and office section. His back to Katherine, Gordon asked, "And why would someone want to kidnap your daughter, Mrs. Morgan?"

"She's my stepdaughter," Crystal Morgan said firmly. "And they would want to kidnap her because her father has money. Lots of money."

Heavy makeup made it difficult for Katherine to tell Crystal Morgan's age, but she guessed the woman to be in her late twenties or early thirties. The woman looked familiar, but Katherine wasn't sure why. She definitely wasn't a local. In a borough as small as Skagway, the police got to know the year-round residents.

The blonde lifted her left hand, and a monstrous diamond flashed. At the sight of the ring, Alice Bowers raised her eyebrows and mouthed a silent "ooh." Gordon, on the other hand, didn't seem to notice the wedding ring or the fact that the woman was half his age. His gaze had slipped to the woman's chest.

A form-fitting pink sweater accentuated a bustline that would make even a Barbie doll envious, and Katherine wondered if that was also the result of a healthy bank account. Money did have its advantages. "How old is your daughter?" she asked.

The blonde turned toward her, gave her a quick up and down glance, and smiled, evidently assured by Katherine's dark-blue uniform, gold badge, and the Glock in its sidearm holster that she had the right to ask. Or, maybe Crystal Morgan didn't care who she told. "Misty is my stepdaughter," she repeated. "She's sixteen. Stubborn, spoiled, and impulsive."

"Katherine. You're here. Good." Turning toward her, Gordon nodded. "This is Mrs. Crystal Morgan. As you heard, Mrs. Morgan believes her daughter is missing."

"Not daughter. Stepdaughter." Mrs. Morgan ground out the words. "And, I don't think she's missing. I think she's been kidnapped."

"Kidnapped. Yes." Gordon moved over to the door that divided the front-desk area from the rest of the office. "If you'll follow me, Officer Ward will take your statement."

That Gordon was giving her the case surprised Katherine. Usually he managed to pick up the ones involving beautiful women, leaving her to handle the drunks and domestic violence complaints.

As the blonde came through the door, Katherine got a full view of the woman's outfit. The skin-tight sweater topped a beige miniskirt and espadrilles with three-inch heels. Katherine figured Crystal Morgan must have arrived on one of the cruise ships. The heels weren't something a camper would wear. They weren't even appropriate attire for the boardwalks of Skagway . . . unless being a streetwalker was what she had in mind.

Katherine stepped over to their one and only interview room. Her demeanor didn't change when she looked through the doorway, but she had a feeling she knew why Gordon wanted her to conduct the interview. The room was a mess.

For the last week, the telephone company had been using the space to store materials while they rewired the office. Well, Gordon might not want to spoil his "in-charge" image with a little physical labor, but Katherine wasn't opposed to dealing with the situation. She quickly moved a set of tools off the table and a spool of wire off one of the two chairs.

"Go ahead and sit down." She motioned for the blonde to take the chair farthest from the door. "Would you like some coffee? Tea? Water?"

"Maybe water," Crystal Morgan answered and fanned her face with her hand. "Yesterday, in Juneau, I was freezing. So, today I wear a sweater, and now I'm roasting."

"That's Alaska for you," Katherine said and stepped back. "I'll just be a minute."

She asked Alice to get the water, and then went looking for Gordon. She found him in the far end of the building, at his desk. "Okay, what's up?"

He looked up from his computer screen. "What do you mean, 'What's up?' "

"You actually want *me* to interview Miss Blonde Bombshell?"

A slight blush colored his face, and he cleared his throat. "I, ah . . . We didn't exactly hit it off. I think maybe she thought I was coming on to her."

Katherine suppressed a smile. *Thought he was coming on to her?* More than likely he was.

"She asked if there was a woman officer who could help her."

"And being the only woman on the force . . ."

"I called you," Gordon finished for her. "Besides, look at all the paperwork I have to finish. I don't have time to look for a spoiled, rich kid off doing her own thing. My bet is she'll show up when it's time for the ship to leave."

CHAPTER FOUR

3:30 P.M.

Charles Bell dropped the bear mask on the kitchen table, glanced at his watch, and then walked over to the refrigerator. He had plenty of time to return the Explorer to the campsite, switch vehicles, and drive back. Plenty of time for a beer.

He popped the tab and took a long draught, sighing as the cold liquid ran down his throat, leaving a tingling sensation. Drinking beer was one of the pleasures he'd renewed right after his release, and soon he would be renewing another pleasure.

He smiled at the thought, his erection almost painful.

He hadn't expected this bonus, but the moment he saw her, he couldn't resist. A weaker man would have given into temptation as soon as he brought her here, but he couldn't satisfy his needs and listen to the radio at the same time. Besides, she was still groggy. He wanted her to know what was happening, wanted to see her reaction . . . hear her screams.

He glanced at the police radio lying on the table next to the mask. *Damn.* By now someone should have seen the Bronco. It didn't go that far down the side. By now someone should have noticed how the tire tracks went over the edge of the shoulder. So why wasn't anything being said?

A buzzer went off, and Bell tensed, looking toward the front of the house. Was there nothing on the radio because they knew where he was staying, where he had her?

Holding his breath, he hurried into the living room and

pushed aside the drapery . . . just enough to see outside. Although a narrow slit of light now pierced the darkness of the room, Bell stayed in the shadows. From his position, he could see a portion of the front yard, the driveway, and the trees surrounding the house. A red Explorer sat in front of the garage door, its front bumper dented and headlight broken, but so far no other vehicles were in the yard.

He waited, watching for a police car to arrive, for any sign of movement in the woods, for any indication that his hideout had been discovered.

He'd placed the electronic eye close to the main road so he would know if someone drove or walked up the driveway. So far the buzzer had gone off a half-dozen times, each alert putting him on edge and causing his heart to race, but so far the only thing that had wandered up to the house was a bear. And that was his fault.

He shouldn't have dumped all that meat in the garbage compound. Maybe the bear couldn't get to it, but it was obvious he could smell it.

Stupid, stupid, stupid, Bell chastised himself, but it was too late to do anything about it.

A full minute passed. Two. Finally five. Nothing came into view. No car, person, or bear. With a sigh, Bell allowed the drape to fall back into place. One more false alarm. But it was a warning, and one he would heed. He needed to get the Explorer out of the yard.

CHAPTER FIVE

Katherine entered the interview room and saw that a pitcher of ice water, two glasses, a pad of paper, and a pencil now sat on the table. Mrs. Morgan was staring at her fingernails.

No hysteria, Katherine noted. *No signs of anxiety.*

Over the years, both when she was a uniform with the Kalamazoo Department of Public Safety and during her three years on the force in Skagway, she'd discovered mothers reacted in different ways when a child went missing. Some cried, some got angry, and some were stoically silent, as if afraid to believe what was happening. It seemed Crystal Morgan was going to be the stoic type. Then again, Crystal Morgan was the stepmother, not the birth mother, and her detached behavior might be a good indicator of the stepmother/stepdaughter's relationship.

Katherine closed the door behind her.

The moment she did, she wished she hadn't. In the short time she'd been away, the overpowering scent of Crystal Morgan's perfume had filled the small room. "Sorry for the delay," Katherine choked out and cracked the door back open.

"Are you all right?" the blonde asked, giving a slight smile.

"Yes, fine." Katherine cleared her throat and sat down. She picked up the pencil and pulled the pad of paper closer. "As a start, I'll need some basic information. Mrs. Morgan, is your first name spelled with a C or a K?"

"With a C, and do call me Crystal." She brushed a lock of blonde hair back from the side of her face. "Your secretary said

21

your first name is Katherine. Do you go by Kathy . . . or Kat?"

Katherine frowned. Although they were informal at this station, and she didn't mind the woman using her first name, the idea of anyone using a nickname—especially Kat—made her cringe. "I prefer Katherine."

"I'll try to remember. It's just that years ago I knew someone named Katherine, and we always called her Kat . . . or Kit Kat. I'll bet your folks also called you Kit Kat."

Katherine tensed and studied the woman seated across from her. "Do I know you?"

"Know me?" Crystal Morgan smiled smugly. "No, I don't think so. I'm just guessing, but I don't believe we travel in the same social circles."

"I'm sure we don't." Katherine doubted they had anything in common; yet there was something familiar about the woman. Maybe one time in their pasts . . . "When you were a child, did you attend school in Michigan?"

Crystal's smile disappeared. "Katherine, do you really think where I attended school is important? My stepdaughter has been kidnapped, and I want to know what you're going to do to find her."

The woman's attitude irked Katherine, but she had to admit Crystal was right. A missing teenager—even if she'd simply wandered off—was far more important than why Katherine felt she knew the blonde. With a nod, Katherine asked, "What is your stepdaughter's full name and age?"

"Misty Marie Morgan. Age sixteen going on thirty. My husband, Misty's father, is Thomas J. Morgan, president and major stockholder of Tomoro Industries. You *have* heard of Tomoro Industries, haven't you?"

"No. Should I have?"

The look Crystal Morgan gave her said she should have.

"Tomoro Industries is involved in alternative energy projects.

22

Today's future. It's been in all of the papers lately . . . and on TV. The company is one of the Fortune 500, and Tom was even profiled in the April issue of *Forbes.*"

Katherine put down her pencil. Now she knew why this woman looked familiar. "The article included a picture of you with your husband, didn't it? You were wearing a fur coat or something."

"You saw that picture? Here?"

"We're not exactly in the back woods." Katherine didn't add that it was only by chance that she'd seen the picture, that the magazine had been left on the counter by one of the seasonal employees who'd stopped by the station asking if they knew of any apartments for rent.

"Tom got a lot of flak from PETA about that coat." Crystal sighed and poured water into the glass in front of her. "I'm not allowed to wear it to any more public events or anywhere we might be photographed."

"I didn't read the article," Katherine confessed. "Was your stepdaughter's name mentioned?"

"Yes, dammit." Crystal scowled. "You can't trust reporters on anything. Tom told the one who did the article for *Forbes* not to mention Misty, but she did. Both Misty's name and age. And a few weeks ago, when I was interviewed for a newspaper feature, I know I told the woman not to include anything about this trip to Alaska. But, what did she do? She not only wrote that Misty and I were taking the Inside Passage cruise, she also named the cruise ship, and when we were leaving."

Katherine understood what Crystal was saying. A potential kidnapper might have seen the information, would have been able to look up the cruise line's schedule, and would have known exactly when Misty was due to dock in Skagway.

"Where is your husband now?"

"In China. He's there on business." Once again, Crystal

smiled smugly. "For the president . . . of the United States."

Though impressed, Katherine considered it beside the point. "Does he know his daughter is missing?"

"No." The smile disappeared, and Crystal lowered her gaze. "I haven't told him. Not yet. I . . . I didn't want to worry him."

Husband not contacted, Katherine wrote. *Wife didn't want to worry him.* Possibly a good excuse, but she wondered if there might have been another reason. "Mrs. Morgan, did your stepdaughter leave any kind of a note? Anything that might make you suspect she's run away?"

"She has *not* run away," the blonde said emphatically. "She's been kidnapped."

"How can you be so sure?"

"I'm sure because we were supposed to meet for lunch at noon, and she didn't show up."

"Maybe she forgot." Katherine remembered how short a teenager's memory could be . . . how short hers used to be.

"That's what I thought at first," Crystal said. "I figured she went back to the ship or was somewhere in town, shopping. She's been upset with her father lately, and nothing I say seems to help. I figured she just needed some time by herself. But that was almost four hours ago, and I can't find her anywhere."

"Perhaps she took one of the shore excursions the cruise offers."

"No." Crystal leaned forward. "Listen to me. She did not take any shore excursions. She did not run away. Misty has been kidnapped . . . and *you* need to find her."

Katherine quelled the urge to tell Crystal Morgan just what she thought of her attitude, and, instead, focused on the woman's insistence that this was a kidnapping. There had to be a reason she was so certain. "Have you been contacted by someone?"

"No." The blonde sat back again. "Not yet, at least. But if

you were a kidnapper, wouldn't you figure this was the perfect time to kidnap the daughter of a rich man? I mean, from here she could be flown to some remote area and never found."

That was a possibility, but Katherine hoped Crystal was wrong. "From what I've heard, we've never had a kidnapping here."

"Well, there's always a first."

Katherine silently agreed. No one knew for certain where or when a kidnapping would occur. If they did, she doubted she'd be sitting here interviewing this woman.

"You don't believe me, do you?"

Katherine blinked. She'd let her mind wander. Truth was, she didn't want to believe a girl had been kidnapped. Not here in Skagway. "I'm sorry, I—"

"You think I'm overreacting, don't you?"

"No, not at all." If anything, Crystal Morgan's reaction was quite appropriate . . . maybe even a bit delayed. "I do understand your concern."

"Then do something!"

"I . . . We need to be sure before we take any action." Katherine forced herself to think logically. "Did you and your stepdaughter have an argument?"

"Argument? No. Look, she—"

Katherine interrupted her. "What was her attitude this morning?"

"It was good. Real good. She was up and dressed before the ship even docked. I'd just gotten into the shower when she knocked on the door and said she was going to do some exploring. I told her to meet me back at the boat at noon for lunch. I'm sure she said okay."

For the first time, Katherine saw a hint of emotion besides anger. Crystal Morgan started blinking rapidly and sniffed a couple of times. "I didn't even get a chance to hug her good-bye."

Although Katherine didn't actually see any tears, she found a box of tissues behind a spool of telephone wire and pushed it toward Crystal. "So, she left the ship early this morning."

"A little after seven. Right when they started letting people go ashore." Crystal took a tissue, dabbed at her eyes, and then sighed. "What was I supposed to do? Insist she wait for me? She's sixteen. She doesn't listen to me. Besides, I thought she'd be fine on her own."

"And you're sure she's not onboard the ship, simply avoiding you?"

"Yes, I'm sure." Crystal glared at her. "Why would she try to avoid me?"

"I just need to make sure."

The blonde gave a shrug. "Okay, if you need to know everything, I talked to the ship's director . . . or whatever his title is. He said she hasn't come back since she checked out this morning. They know this because they've got a computerized scanning system you have to go through whenever you get off or on the ship. It shows she got off. It doesn't show her getting back on. But—"

She pointed at Katherine. "Just to be sure, I looked for her. I walked all over that damn ship, went to all of the spots where she likes to hang out. None of the other teenagers had seen her today."

Katherine had to admit, it did sound as if Crystal had thoroughly checked out that possibility. There was, however, one other reason the girl might have disappeared. "Do you think she might have taken this opportunity to run away from you and her father so she could get back with her birth mother?"

Crystal stared at her for a moment, and then snorted. "Let's hope not. Misty's mother is dead. She died five years ago."

"Oh." Katherine wrote, *mother dead,* on the pad of paper. She wanted to add *stepmother an arrogant smart ass,* but she didn't.

Katherine focused the rest of her questions on getting a comprehensive physical description of Misty Morgan, including any identifying marks and what the girl was wearing that morning. When Katherine felt she had everything she needed, she stood and said, "Do you have a picture of Misty with you?"

"I have her school picture and a copy of her passport. She has the original with her, but they told us we should do that . . . make copies and keep them separate. That picture's not so great. Misty hates it."

"I'll need the picture and the passport copy, at least long enough for Alice, our clerk, to make copies we can show to the tour agencies."

"Tour agencies?" Crystal looked confused.

Katherine tried to explain. "Your stepdaughter could have easily hooked up with Dyea Dave or one of the other tour companies on shore. You must have noticed the sales booths on the way into town. They're set up on the dock so they can catch people coming off the ships. Your stepdaughter may have decided to go to Liarsville . . . or hike over to the cemetery and up to Reid Falls."

"Jeez, haven't you listened to anything I've said?" Crystal ground out. "Misty has not gone on a tour or a hike. My stepdaughter is not into tours or hiking, not unless it's a tour of a shopping mall. How many times do I have to tell you? She's been kidnapped."

CHAPTER SIX

4:30 P.M.

Charles Bell waited until the garage door was down before he stepped into the house. Although the sun would be shining for another eight hours, the moment he closed the door behind him, he was in semi-darkness . . . a warm semi-darkness. After all, a hive needed to be warm.

It was the media that nicknamed him The Beekeeper, not only because he had hives in his backyard and told the reporters he liked honey, but because he'd kept her for almost a year, hidden away in his personal hive. He read what they printed about him, and watched the videos made during the trial. "Lock him up" was the verdict. "Let *him* see how it feels."

So they did.

They locked him up in a hospital where doctors poked and prodded, gave him shock treatments, and prescribed pills. He told them what they wanted to hear, and he learned—about tranquilizers, how to give shots, and what dosage to use. They fired nurses when medicine went missing. They never appreciated his intelligence or how careful a beekeeper has to be.

They shook his hand before he walked out the door and told him to keep taking his medicine and that he had to report to the police on a regular basis.

Report to the police. He smiled as he slowly walked down a short hallway. What should he say? *"Guess what? I'm back."*

Bell stopped in front of a closed door.

28

Just as before, he'd planned ahead. He'd changed the traditional bedroom door knob so it couldn't be opened from inside the room without a key. He hadn't been sure if he'd find what he needed in such a small town, so he'd brought the lock with him. As it was, he could have purchased a similar lock at the Skagway hardware, but the lock wasn't the only item he'd brought with him, and it was better not to arouse suspicions. He didn't want anyone remembering his face.

Slowly, quietly, he unlocked the door and turned the knob.

When he first arrived at the house, he pulled all of the shades and closed all of the drapes. With this bedroom he took his precautions one step further. Insulation torn from the attic covered the windows, held in place by sheets and blankets tacked onto the frames. Not exactly soundproof—not as good as the cell in his first hive—but the location of the house almost guaranteed no one would hear any screams.

Bell snapped on a flashlight, its beam creating a narrow band of illumination. He aimed it at the nearest twin bed and let it travel over the occupant he'd so carefully lashed to the old-fashioned metal frame. He'd been lucky. They didn't make beds like that anymore—strong and sturdy.

The girl's eyes were closed, her blonde hair fanned out over the pillow, and her breathing slow and regular. She looked to be sleeping.

No signs of stress.

That pleased him. He'd been nervous that morning, worried about the dosage. Too much and the tranquilizer might have stopped vital functions, would have ruined everything. Too little and she would have made a fuss. So far his calculations had been right. She was probably in that half-world of sleep and awake. Groggy. Not quite ready to face reality.

Soon, however, she would know what was going on.

CHAPTER SEVEN

"She's convinced her stepdaughter has been kidnapped," Katherine said the moment she reached Gordon's desk.

"And, what do you think?"

"I don't know." But the possibility bothered her. "Mrs. Morgan said there have been newspapers and magazines printing pictures and articles about the girl's father and how much money he's worth. Someone might have decided he'd pay well for his daughter."

Gordon pointed at the table on the other side of the room. "I finally recognized her. Remember the magazine that worker left here?"

Katherine walked over to the table where the two-month-old copy of *Forbes* magazine lay next to a half-empty coffee cup. The magazine had been opened to the picture she'd remembered: a full-length snapshot of Crystal Morgan wearing a fur coat and a slinky, low-cut cocktail dress. The tall, good-looking man standing next to her wore a tuxedo. Together they made a striking couple.

"I'm surprised you didn't recognize her immediately," Katherine said, glancing back at Gordon. "You and Phil were drooling over that picture."

"We were not."

Katherine smiled and returned to his side. "Mrs. Morgan also said a recent newspaper article mentioned that she and the girl were going to take this trip, including the name of the ship."

"Damn." Gordon shook his head. "That means anyone with a docking schedule would know when the girl would be here."

"I think you'd better take over this case." Simply thinking that Misty Morgan might be the victim of a kidnapper made Katherine uneasy.

"Oh, come on, don't tell me a cop from the big city of Kalamazoo can't handle a kidnapping."

"I was a uniform, not a detective." *As if he didn't know.* "You need to handle this." *Please,* she almost added.

He looked at her, and for a moment she thought she was off the hook, but then he shook his head. "No, Mrs. Morgan's all yours. But I'll make you a deal. If you decide this really is a kidnapping, we'll call in the State Troopers and hand the case over to them."

"Okay." At least that way she wouldn't have a girl's fate resting in her hands.

"But, I don't think this is a kidnapping," Gordon said. "I mean, why just take the girl and not the wife, too?"

"The girl did get off the ship before her stepmother."

"So, this kidnapper sees an opportunity and takes it? No, I think she'll show up before the ship's ready to leave. But, just in case I'm wrong, have Alice get the girl's picture to the cruise line agencies and to the Canadian border station."

"Alice is already on that. She's also contacting the train station, ferry terminal, and Wings of Alaska, and having ship security check their video logs, just in case the girl did slip back on board."

"Good." Gordon looked back at the computer he'd been working on. "I'll help when I can, but I'm not getting very far on this paperwork, and still no word from Phil."

Which reminded Katherine. "I talked to my grandfather. I'm afraid he couldn't even remember that Phil was at our place yesterday morning, much less where he told him to go fishing."

"Well, if he does remember . . ."

"I wouldn't hold my breath. He's forgetting more and more every day."

A look of sympathy touched Gordon's eyes. "That's got to be rough on you."

"I can handle it." She wasn't about to tell him watching her grandfather slip away, bit by bit, was tearing her apart. "When was the last time you heard from Phil?"

"Tuesday. He said he was going fishing with a buddy and, if they had a good day, he'd have a fish fry this weekend, and we'd all be invited. Any idea who this 'buddy' is?"

"Someone he met recently. I know my grandfather's met him."

"But, you haven't?"

"No; I've always been at work when Phil and this 'fishing buddy' stopped by." She tried to remember if her grandfather had mentioned the man's name, but didn't think so. "You know Phil. Anyone who loves fishing is his buddy. Have you tried calling Phil's cell?"

"Cell. Home phone. Radio. I even stopped by his house. No sign of his car . . . or of him."

"Something must have happened while he was fishing. Have you alerted the park rangers?"

"About an hour ago." Gordon sighed. "Darn it all. This just isn't like him. I'm hoping nothing's happened to him."

She felt the same way. "Let me know if you hear anything."

"I will. Meanwhile, we do have Doug out on his bike. Have Alice call him in and give him a picture of the missing girl."

Doug Pierson was their community service officer, a seasonal position with the force. Mostly he rode his bicycle around town, answered questions, and kept an eye on the tourists. Simply having an officer on the streets often averted trouble.

"I'll drive around, too," Katherine said. "And, I'll take Mrs.

Morgan with me. She might spot her stepdaughter faster than Doug would."

"If you think it's necessary. Or I can call Jim in."

"No; don't do that." Jim Preto was also a seasonal officer and, less than two months before, he'd also become a new father. Ever since the birth of his baby, Jim had been moaning and groaning about how little sleep he and his wife were getting. Though Katherine would admit the young officer looked like a walking zombie, she was tired of hearing his complaints and being forced to admire baby pictures. "Unless something else comes up, I'd just as soon be out, doing something."

"What a time to be shorthanded." Gordon ran his fingers through his thinning hair and looked back at the computer.

Katherine felt sorry for him. Most days their small force of four full-time officers and two seasonal officers could handle the petty crimes and disturbances that occurred in Skagway. But today wasn't shaping up like most days. Today they didn't need a missing teenager. Especially not the daughter of some rich, influential businessman.

She started to leave, but Gordon stopped her. "Oh, one more thing. If you do drive Mrs. Morgan around and get over on the Dyea Road, keep a look out for a white bear. Crazy Cora was in here this morning. She said she saw a spirit bear over near the Graysons' place."

"Oh, yeah?" Katherine chuckled. "And she's sure it was a white bear, not a light-colored cinnamon?"

Mrs. Cora Tremway, known by the year-round residents as Crazy Cora, had lived in Skagway most of her ninety-plus years. Over those years her hearing had gone bad, and her eyesight was worse than a nearsighted moose's. She was constantly coming in to report "sightings." Or, she would call at night—often when Katherine was on duty—to report strange noises. Getting the woman off the phone was a chore, but was better than going to Crazy Cora's house.

"You know Cora," Gordon said. "She insists it was a spirit bear. Says it's here for a reason."

"Yeah, to find food."

Katherine had heard stories about the white bears the people of the First Nations called "spirit" bears. According to the Native Americans, the white bears were supposed to be good omens and have magical powers. Katherine, however, preferred the scientific explanation. DNA testing had proved the bears simply to be a variation in color of the black bear. Nothing magical about them.

"According to Cora," Gordon said, "seeing a spirit bear means something is about to happen, and she felt it her duty to tell us."

"What it probably means is the park rangers are going to have to catch it and move it away from here before it has a confrontation with some tourists. Why was Cora at the Grayson place? Are they back? Have any idea where they went?"

"No idea." Gordon shook his head and grinned. "And that had her upset. In Cora's opinion, we should know where every resident is at all times."

"Oh, yeah?" Katherine chuckled. "And, if we kept tabs on people like that they'd say this was a police state. Still, it's strange the way the Graysons took off without telling anyone."

"Maybe they did tell others, just not Cora. This trip must have been something they planned. They did cancel the paper and put their mail on hold."

"True."

"Oh, and one other thing." It was Gordon's turn to laugh. "Cora said she saw a bear driving an SUV. Can you believe that?"

"A bear?" Katherine repeated. "Where? Where did she see a bear driving an SUV?"

Gordon stopped laughing and frowned. "Over near the Chilkoot Trail. Her granddaughter was driving her to Dyea."

"Did Cora say what color SUV?"

"No." Still frowning, Gordon studied her expression. "I didn't ask. What difference does the color make?"

"Because as crazy as it sounds, I thought I saw a bear in an SUV near my grandfather's house just before I came to work." And, now she wished she'd taken the time to check out that vehicle. "It was parked down the street a ways, but I'm pretty sure it was a Ford Explorer—a red one. What I noticed—more than the bear, if it was a bear I saw—was the vehicle had damage to the bumper and headlight."

"Hmm. I thought she was crazy." Gordon said nothing for a second, simply chewed on his upper lip, then nodded. "Have Doug ride his bike over to your place and check it out."

"I will," Katherine said, but knew before she involved Doug she would do a little investigating on her own. "Meanwhile, don't you go around telling people I thought I saw a bear driving an Explorer. I'm sure both Cora and I simply saw some bearded, bushy-haired guy who, from a distance, looked like a bear."

She heard Gordon chuckle as she walked the short hallway back to the front-office area. Once there, Katherine used the phone in the reception area to call her grandfather. He answered on the sixth ring.

"You okay, Poppa?"

"Katherine? Is that you?"

"Yes, Poppa. Just checking. Is Sarah there yet?"

"Sarah?"

She heard the confusion in his voice, and she repeated who Sarah was and why she would be coming.

"No. She's not here."

"Is there a red SUV parked across the street? It has a broken headlight."

He didn't answer right away, but through the receiver Katherine could hear her grandfather shuffling over to the kitchen window. Finally he spoke. "No vans parked on the street. No cars at all."

"Okay, that's good," she said, somewhat relieved. "One more thing. Do you remember the name of the man Phil was going fishing with?"

"What man?"

"Phil's new fishing buddy. You said Phil brought him over to the house the other day. Do you remember his name?"

"I . . . Ah, I . . ."

Katherine heard her grandfather clear his throat and could picture him struggling to remember the name . . . or even the memory of meeting the man. Finally, she spoke up. "That's all right, Poppa. It's not important. Sarah should be there soon, and I'll see you in the morning."

She decided there was no sense in having Doug check on her grandfather if the Explorer was gone. Their energy needed to be directed toward finding Mrs. Morgan's missing stepdaughter and discovering what had happened to Phil.

Alice was off the phone, so Katherine asked, "When was the last time you tried Phil?"

"Ten, fifteen minutes ago."

"Both his phone and his radio?"

Alice nodded. "I know Gordon stopped by Phil's place earlier today, but I had Doug stop by again. He said Phil's cruiser still isn't there, and when Doug peeked through the windows, he couldn't see any signs of Phil. This isn't like him, Katherine."

"I know he forgets the time when he's over at our house exchanging fish stories with my grandfather, but I can't imagine him forgetting to show up for work. Something must have happened to him."

A grin softened Alice's age-weathered face. "You sure he goes to your house to talk to your grandfather?"

"Alice . . ."

In spite of Katherine's warning tone, the older woman's grin grew wider. "Honey, I do believe that man is interested in you."

"If so, he's wasting his time."

"Aw, come on, Katherine, give the guy a chance."

"Sorry." She'd been over this with Alice too many times. "Not interested."

"He's a nice guy."

"I don't get involved with fellow officers."

"Far as I know, you don't get involved with anyone," Alice said, eyeing her closely.

Katherine refused to respond. Alice might want to know what went on in Katherine's private life, but she wasn't going to hear it from her.

Finally, Alice dropped her gaze and once again picked up the phone. "Guess I'd better keep at these calls. So far the tour agencies are a negative. You going to be in there with her?" She nodded toward the interview room.

"For a little while longer. Why?"

Alice motioned her closer and in a hushed voice said, "That perfume she's wearing makes this place smell like a brothel."

CHAPTER EIGHT

Crystal Morgan had a cell phone out, but the way she was glaring at it, Katherine had a feeling something was wrong. "Problem?" she asked as she closed the door behind her.

"Battery's dead. I told Misty to plug it in after hers was charged. Obviously, she didn't. That girl . . ." Crystal looked at Katherine and shook her head. "Well, at least I don't have to face my husband's anger for a little while longer."

She stuffed the phone into her leather handbag, and Katherine once again got a strong whiff of perfume. She grabbed a tissue before she sneezed. "Once we finish here, you can use the pay phone just outside the entrance."

Crystal glanced that way, then sighed. "He's going to be so upset. Last night I told him he had nothing to worry about, that Misty was fine."

"Did your husband also talk to his daughter last night?" Katherine wondered if he'd said something to upset the girl and make her take off.

"Yes. She called him. That's what prompted his call to me. He said she sounded strange, and she told him she loved him."

"And that was unusual?"

"For Misty, yes," Crystal said. "She and her dad have been banging heads lately."

"What else did she say . . . besides her loving him?"

"Something about how this trip was going to be really rad." Crystal shook her head. "Why he thought I would know what

38

she meant by that, beats me. Most of the time she treats me like the enemy. As far as she's concerned, when her mother died, her father should have taken vows of celibacy and never looked at another woman."

"How long was it after her mother died that you and her father married?"

"A couple years." Crystal's eyebrows rose. "And, no, we were not having an affair before his wife died. I worked for him, that's all. We didn't go out until a year after she died. I think that was more than a reasonable enough time."

Katherine had no idea how long was reasonable, but she was curious about the dynamics of the relationship. "If you and Misty weren't on good terms, why are you on this cruise together?"

"I thought it would help us get along better." She forced a laugh. "I honestly thought when Misty changed her mind and said she wanted to go, that spending a week together might make us friends."

"But that didn't happen?"

"Not so you'd notice." Crystal straightened in her chair and her gaze drifted toward the closed door. "I wonder if the kidnapper has sent Tom a ransom demand yet. I guess I really should call."

"If your husband's in China, how would the kidnapper know how to contact him?"

"How should I know? Email. Text message. Or maybe the kidnapper would contact Tom through his office."

"If your husband or someone at his office was contacted, wouldn't you be called . . . to make sure it was true?"

"Yeah, probably." Crystal Morgan frowned, then smiled and held up her handbag. "But how are they going to call if my phone's dead?"

"They could contact the ship."

"Last time I checked, I had no messages." The blonde glanced toward the door. "But maybe I should check again."

"We'll do that," Katherine said. "Also, wouldn't a ransom demand prompt your husband to call us or the FBI?"

Crystal scoffed. "Not Tom. He'd call his buddy Vince. Vince the wonder man who can solve all problems."

"And this Vince is . . . ?"

"Vincent Nanini. He used to be Tom's captain or something when they were in the Marines. He now runs a computer security company, along with another guy. Tom has them check his computers at work, as well as the ones we have at home. Tom's paranoid about viruses and hackers. He's always worrying that someone's going to steal one of his projects before he gets it patented."

"Well, if this is a kidnapping, this Vince had better let us handle it."

" 'If'?" Crystal forcefully repeated. "You still don't think Misty's been kidnapped, do you?"

Katherine knew she had to be careful how she answered. The Skagway Police Department didn't need an irate tourist complaining about the treatment she'd received. "What I'm saying," she began, "is we are doing everything in our power to find your stepdaughter, but until you or your husband is contacted, and we know for certain this is a kidnapping, we cannot label it as such."

"But, if she has been kidnapped, and the kidnapper asks for a lot of money, it's going to take Tom a while before he can get it all together."

"I'm sure a kidnapper would realize that."

"And, you can bet no kidnapper is going to contact me. I have no money. It's all Tom's."

"But would a kidnapper know that?"

"No . . ." She seemed to think about that. "No, I guess he wouldn't."

"And, you do realize there are reasons other than money for kidnapping a teenager." Just thinking about the possibility made Katherine tense. "Have you noticed anyone watching your stepdaughter? Maybe someone on the boat? Anyone made friends with her that seemed too friendly?"

Crystal didn't answer right away, and Katherine waited, watching the woman. The blonde looked away, and for a moment her features tensed, but then she shook her head, and looked back. "No . . . nothing like that."

Katherine let out the breath she'd been holding. "That's good."

"Look," Crystal said, staring directly into Katherine's eyes. "I know Misty didn't run away. She couldn't have. Neither of us is traveling with a lot of cash, and Misty is smart enough to know her dad would track her down if she used her credit card to rent a car or buy a ticket."

"But you said she took her passport with her when she left the ship."

"We always do." Once again Crystal Morgan held up her handbag. "I have mine in here, but that doesn't mean I'm planning on running away."

"Maybe your stepdaughter met someone here."

"That's what I've been saying. Someone recognized her, saw his chance, and grabbed her. Hell, kids are kidnapped all the time. Especially rich kids. They've even made movies about it. It was Mel Gibson's only son in *Ransom*. With Tom, it's Misty, his only daughter."

Crystal Morgan gave a frustrated sigh. "Damn, Vince wanted us to take a bodyguard along with us; now he's going to be telling Tom this is all my fault. But, wouldn't you think a cruise ship would be safe?"

Katherine wasn't sure about that, considering how many people had died on or fallen off cruise ships in the last few years. However, as far as she knew, the ships that stopped at Skagway seemed to have good security in place. "What did the ship's security officer say when you notified him that your stepdaughter was missing?"

"Well, I didn't exactly notify anyone," Crystal admitted, looking down at her untouched glass of water. "I mean, I asked if she'd returned and, as I said, according to their computer, she hadn't."

"So, once you discovered she wasn't onboard you came here?"

"No; I looked around town for her, then I came here."

"So, it's been a while since you've checked on board." Katherine hoped that meant this interview was a complete waste of time. "Your stepdaughter might have returned by now."

"That would be wonderful," Crystal said, but her expression didn't convey much hope.

CHAPTER NINE

A heavy, lethargic sense of exhaustion weighed down Misty Morgan's eyelids, the effort to raise them almost more than she could muster. When she did, darkness greeted her. A total, inky blackness that made her blink twice to make sure she actually did have her eyes open.

She started to move, only to discover something wrapped around her wrists bound her arms above her head, while similar bindings around her ankles limited how close together she could draw her legs.

Panicking, she struggled, lifting and pulling on the restraints, but no matter how hard she tried, she couldn't bring her arms down to her sides or bend her knees more than slightly. She was flat on her back, arms tied above her head and her legs spread wide apart. She was also naked. She could tell that because something heavy and rough covered her from her shoulders to just below her knees, and the material scratched at her skin, rubbing against her nipples and hips. She lifted her head slightly, bringing her chin toward her chest. A musty, moldy smell filled her nostrils, and she let her head drop back.

Staring into the darkness, she tried to make sense of where she was and what had happened. She recognized the feel of a mattress beneath her body and figured she was covered with a wool blanket, but why was she tied to a bed?

Before her mother became ill, she used to take Misty to visit her grandparents. The bedding at their house had the same musty odor as the blanket on top of her now. The moment they stepped into her grandparents' house the smell was there. But Misty knew she wasn't at her grandparents' house. They were dead . . . and so was her mother.

So, where was she?

What had happened?

And why was she so tired?

She remembered meeting Brian as they'd planned. She'd been relieved to see he looked like the picture he'd posted on ChatPlace. She'd half-expected he'd be some pimply-faced geek or middle-aged pervert. If so, she never would have gone with him. She wasn't stupid.

Brian's smile had indicated his pleasure in seeing her, and he didn't question her age—not then—so she figured taking the time to put on makeup had paid off. She'd hoped the people at the border wouldn't notice the change she'd made in her birth date. She didn't want to have to explain why an underage American citizen was going into Canada with an unrelated adult.

He had wanted to stay in Skagway and get some breakfast. He said it would give them a chance to get to know each other. She'd argued that she wanted to get on the road while it was early; wanted to start their adventure right away.

The way he kept looking at her, like a tomcat staring at a bird that had just offered itself to him, she knew she'd taken his mind off breakfast, and they would be safely across the border before Crystal finished her shower, put on her makeup, and got dressed. It would be afternoon before her stepmother even realized she was gone.

Gone. The word sliced though Misty with icy clarity. *Brian is gone.*

In the pit of her stomach, she felt the same panic she'd experienced when Brian's vehicle lurched forward. Looking over the edge and seeing how far they would fall if he didn't stay on the road had made her dizzy. Yet, she'd been sure it was Vince following them; sure he wouldn't do anything to hurt her.

She'd been angry when Brian stopped the Blazer and stepped out. Angry with him for not making a run for the border, and angry with Vince for spoiling her plans. Her dad was the one who should have come for her. Not Vince.

She could still picture Brian standing by the Blazer's open door. She'd expected to hear Vince's voice; instead she heard a loud crack that echoed across the valley.

She couldn't see Brian's face at that moment. She didn't understand what had happened, not until Brian crumpled to the ground.

She should have screamed. Not that anyone would have heard her, but still . . . She should have tried to get away, should have moved faster. But, no; she'd sat there, staring at Brian . . . or where Brian once stood. Stared and didn't do anything until her door was jerked open, and she saw the face of a bear and the body of a man.

Even though his facial features were hidden, she knew it wasn't Vince. The height was wrong. The width of his shoulders.

"Who . . . ?" she'd managed, before she felt a pain. Like the sting of a bee, the prick was quick and unexpected, and, before she could react, a warm sensation started moving away from the spot, flowing up her arm and through her body. She might have also said "Why?" though she wasn't sure. All too quickly her eyes grew heavy, and a humming sound lulled her to sleep.

A soft groan—not a hum—pulled Misty away from her memories. She turned her head toward the sound. "Who's there?" she asked, the knot of fear in her stomach growing tighter.

Another groan was her only answer, but it told her one thing . . . she wasn't alone.

CHAPTER TEN

Katherine stepped out of the interview room first. "Any word?" she asked Alice.

"From Phil or about the girl?"

"Either."

"No word from Phil, and I talked to the security officer on the *Holiday Festival.* He said they're checking the videos, but he's sure the girl hasn't returned to the ship. The other cruise lines have been notified, along with the tour vendors. Doug's taking the girl's picture to each of them, and I've faxed her picture to Canadian customs, along with the missing person report."

"I think I should go back to the ship, see if Tom has called," Crystal said, leaning against the door frame. "I'll need a ride."

The police station was only a short distance from where the cruise ships docked, and Katherine was about to say "tough" when she remembered the blonde's three-inch heels . . . and that Gordon wanted Crystal Morgan to feel the Skagway Police Department was taking her report of an alleged kidnapping seriously. Katherine also knew going along would give her a chance to talk to the ship's personnel, get their take on the situation.

"Let me tell Sergeant Landros," she said, "then we'll go."

As soon as Katherine slid into the Tahoe, she rolled down the windows; nevertheless, the moment Crystal Morgan unzipped her leather bag, the overpowering smell of perfume filled the air, and Katherine sneezed. Three times.

"Are you catching a cold?" Crystal asked.

"It's your perfume."

"Oh. Sorry. The bottle spilled in my bag." Crystal pulled the zipper closed and looked toward the docks. "While I'm on the boat, I'll grab another handbag."

Katherine sneezed again and headed the Tahoe for the docks.

"God, how can you stand to live in a town this small?" Crystal asked, looking around.

Katherine remembered her thoughts the day her grandparents told her they were moving to Skagway. As far as she'd been concerned, she was going from one prison to another. It took years before she understood the wisdom of that move.

"I like it here," she said, meaning it. "Besides, Whitehorse isn't that far away."

"Like how far?"

"A hundred and twelve miles."

Crystal stared at her. "And you call that close?"

"Close enough." Katherine acknowledged dock security and parked the Tahoe as close to the cruise ship as she could before she turned off the engine. "Most people who live here year round like the isolation."

"I'd go crazy," Crystal said. "My God, what do you do for fun?"

"Fish. Hike. Snowshoe in the winter."

Crystal shook her head, and looked down at Katherine's hands. "You married?"

Katherine figured her lack of a wedding band pretty much answered the question . . . if it deserved an answer. Feeling another sneeze coming on, she opened the Tahoe's door and stepped out. "When we get to the ship, we can double-check if your stepdaughter's returned."

A handful of passengers was leaving the massive, block-long cruise ship when Katherine and Crystal arrived at the security checkpoint. "I'll check for any phone calls and get rid of this handbag," Crystal said and held out her ID card to be scanned. In a moment, she'd cleared security and disappeared into the belly of the ship.

Katherine showed her badge and questioned the men monitoring the flow of passengers on and off the ship. "Miss Morgan has not yet returned," the man by the computerized screen said.

A distinguished-looking, middle-aged officer, standing slightly back from the doorway, stepped up and identified himself as Hans van Vermer, Executive Officer. "The young lady was among the first to leave the ship. I was here when she did so. We're scanning the videos now, but I'm quite sure she has not returned."

"Did she leave with a tour group?"

He shook his head. "I've checked with our tour director. We have no record of Miss Morgan or Mrs. Morgan signing up for any tours at this port."

"So, you're sure Miss Morgan is not on board your ship right now?"

"Positive." He smiled. "With that girl, my staff and I would know if she were."

"Why do you say that?"

He sighed. "In just a few days, she's made her presence known. She—"

Van Vermer's cell phone rang, and he paused to glance at the screen. "If you'll excuse me a moment," he said, "I need to take this."

He stepped a few feet away, and, keeping his voice low, answered the call. Katherine picked up a bit of his conversation, a "You're sure," and "I'll talk to him later." Finally the officer ended the call and came back to stand in front of her.

"That was in regards to Miss Morgan," he explained. "You asked why we would be aware of her. Just last night one of the guests complained about a young lady skinny dipping in the pool on the top deck. It seems Miss Morgan bribed the man assigned to watch that area into leaving his post."

"Are you harping on that again?" Crystal asked, coming up beside the officer. "I thought we had that little incident resolved."

The look van Vermer gave Crystal Morgan was a study in self-discipline. "Indeed it has been, Mrs. Morgan," he said, and then nodded toward Katherine. "That crew member swears he has no idea where she might have gone."

"Why would she tell the guy anything?" Crystal asked. "He could barely even speak English."

Katherine had a feeling van Vermer would like to say something about Crystal's comment, but he kept his response official. "My staff and crew will continue to search for the young lady, but if she's not back in an hour, I'm afraid we will have to leave without her, we can't—"

"Yeah, yeah," Crystal interrupted. "This boat waits for no one. I got it." She held up a canvas bag for Katherine to see. "I dumped the other one. Oh, and I did have a message on my room phone. My husband *has* been trying to call me. I didn't want to keep you waiting, so can I use that pay phone at the station?"

CHAPTER ELEVEN

5:30 P.M.

"Hey, Kat—" Crystal Morgan shouted through the open doorway that connected the covered entryway to the police station's reception area. "What time is it here?"

"Her name is Katherine," Alice said coolly from her position behind the counter. "Officer Katherine Ward. And it's five thirty."

Katherine gave Alice an appreciative nod. Their dispatcher had never questioned why Katherine insisted on no nicknames. No one in Skagway had ever called her Kat; at least, not to her face. Which was why the folded and taped scrap of paper Alice had handed her when she returned with Crystal bothered Katherine. Clearly written on the outside was *KAT.* "Who gave this to you?"

"A kid I've never seen before," Alice said. "He delivered it just before five; said some guy gave him the note earlier today, and asked him to deliver it to you at exactly five o'clock."

"Exactly five o'clock?" Katherine glanced at the clock on the wall. "Did he say why it had to be at that time?"

"The kid said the man told him you'd understand the significance of the time."

"Really?" Katherine tried to think of what she might have had scheduled at five o'clock, especially with a man.

"The kid was really upset that you weren't here. He said he didn't want the guy mad at him. Only when I assured him I'd

50

give you the note as soon as you returned would he give it to me."

"Do either of you know what time it is in China right now?" Crystal asked, easily heard through the open doorway.

Katherine grabbed a pair of scissors from Alice's desk. If she remembered correctly, China's time zone was way ahead of Alaska's, but how much ahead was another matter.

"It's ten thirty," Alice answered.

"Night or morning?" Crystal asked, echoing Katherine's thoughts.

Alice had the answer. "Morning. Tomorrow morning."

Crystal muttered "Crazy," Alice grinned, and Katherine smiled. Alice was a constant source of trivial information. It was no surprise she had the International Date Line down pat.

One snip of the scissors cut the tape sealing the note. Katherine carefully unfolded the paper and stared at a crude, childlike drawing of a clock. The circle filled most of the sheet's inner surface—the hour hand pointing at the number five, the minute hand at the twelve. Beneath the drawing, crudely printed in pencil, were the words *YOU HAVE TWENTY-FOUR HOURS*.

"Alice . . . ?" Katherine turned the paper so their dispatcher could see the drawing. "Do I have anything scheduled at five tomorrow?"

"Not that I'm aware of."

Alice reached for the note, but Katherine held it back. "No. I've already contaminated it by opening it. In case we need to get fingerprints, we shouldn't touch it any more than necessary."

"Really? You think it's a threat or something?" Alice frowned as she stared at the piece of paper. "You know that looks like a kid's drawing to me. Even the writing looks like a kid's."

"And maybe that's all it is." Katherine hoped so.

"Darn it all." Alice shook her head. "I'm sorry. This has to be

a prank. Something the kid or one of his friends came up with."
She kept shaking her head. "I should have known."

"Known what?"

"That it was a prank. After all, the kid said the man who gave
him the note was wearing a bear's head."

" 'A bear's head'?" An uneasy feeling crept over Katherine.

"Yeah, that's what the kid said, and then he pointed toward
the National Park Service visitors' center. He said he met this
bear-headed man there." Alice frowned. "You think there's
something going on there at five tomorrow?"

"Not that I'm aware of."

"Maybe that new ranger is trying to set up a date with you."

"Well, this is a strange way to do it." Katherine looked at the
note again. "No, I don't think this is about a date." There was
something too ominous about the wording.

"Sorry," Alice said. "I should have had the kid wait; then you
could have questioned him yourself. But, I didn't know how
long you'd be gone."

"I didn't know we'd be back this soon," Katherine said and
nodded toward Crystal, who was still out by the pay phone.
"She had a message from her husband."

Alice also looked in that direction. "You think he knows
something about his daughter's disappearance?"

"I don't know." Again, Katherine read the note. "The kid
said I was supposed to get this at exactly five o'clock?"

"Exactly," Alice repeated.

Twenty-four hours. Katherine stared at the drawing of the
clock. *What was supposed to happen at five o'clock tomorrow
afternoon?*

Crystal Morgan's voice cut into Katherine's thoughts. "Call
me," she said. "Your daughter is missing."

Katherine realized the blonde must be leaving a message on her husband's voice mail. She also noticed that Crystal hadn't used the word "kidnapped."

CHAPTER TWELVE

"Shouldn't we put Misty's picture out there by the phone, along with the other pictures of missing children?" Crystal asked, coming in from the covered entryway and pausing in front of the bathroom door.

"We will if we don't find her soon," Katherine answered, hoping that wouldn't be necessary.

"Good." Crystal opened the door beside her. "I'm going in here. If my husband calls, let me know."

Katherine nodded and waited until the blonde had closed and locked the bathroom door behind her. Then she asked Alice, "Any luck with the calls?"

"Nothing positive, but something unexpected. Constable Wiffle called in response to the picture I'd faxed. He said they already had Misty's picture; that some guy who works for the girl's father called them this morning and said to be on the lookout for her, and to stop her if she tried to cross the border."

"Someone called the Canadians this morning?" That they knew Misty Morgan was missing hours before she'd even heard about the girl confused Katherine.

"That's what they said." Alice thumbed through several odd-shaped slips of paper on her desk, all the while grumbling about needing a new message pad. Finally she pulled one slip out of the pile and handed it to Katherine. "This is who they said called."

Vince Nanini. Katherine recognized the name and nodded

toward the bathroom Crystal had entered. "She mentioned him. Did you get a phone number? Some way to contact this guy?"

"No. I didn't think to ask."

"What time did he call them?"

A sheepish look crossed Alice's face. "I didn't ask the time, either. Howard just said, 'this morning.' "

Considering her own aversion to detailed reports, Katherine knew she'd better not say anything to Alice about her lack of details, but the dispatcher must have read the look of disappointment on Katherine's face. "I'm sorry," Alice hurried to explain. "I was busy issuing a driver's license when the call came in. This place went crazy after you left. That kid with the note for you came by, the phone kept ringing, and two people wanted driver's licenses. I think we got a new batch of seasonal workers."

She reached over and picked up two more slips of paper. "These are for you, too. The top one's from Jane, over at the bookstore. She said the security alarm's been fixed and shouldn't go off again, at least not accidentally. Second call may need a follow-up."

"I sure hope that alarm's been fixed," Katherine grumbled, taking the messages Alice handed her. In the last month, there had been two false alarms at the bookstore during her shift. "Jane needs to get a new one."

"New ones cost money," Alice said, as if Katherine didn't know that. She might have added more, except a college-aged boy stepped into the station at that moment.

"Is this where I can get a driver's license?" he asked, and Alice automatically handed him one of the forms they kept on the counter, along with a clipboard and pen. As she explained what she needed from him, Katherine glanced at the second message. It included a telephone number, a man's name, and the make of a vehicle. Alice's handwriting was close to a scribble, a series of unrelated words—*dent, hiking, light,* and *front*—along with seven numbers.

"What's this mean?"

Alice turned away from the counter, and reread what she'd written. "Oh, yeah. Sorry about that. He called right while I was taking a guy's picture." She pointed at the numbers. "That's the number to call. He's over in Dyea. He said someone ran into the front of his Ford Explorer; that he's been gone for a week, hiking the Chilkoot Trail, and, when he got back, he noticed one of his headlights was broken and his front bumper was dented."

An Explorer with a broken headlight and dented fender. Coincidence? "Did he give the color of his Explorer?"

"No, and I didn't ask. As I said, I was really busy while you were gone." She turned back toward the young man. "I'll need your birth certificate or a passport."

Katherine knew she needed to know the vehicle's color. "When Mrs. Morgan comes out, have her wait in the interview room. I'm going to go call this guy."

Gordon was still back in their work area, glaring at his keyboard as he used his index finger to type. He stopped the moment she came into the area, and turned toward her. "Anything new?"

"I'm not sure." She carefully showed Gordon the note the kid delivered. "First off, the kid who delivered this told Alice a man wearing a bear mask gave it to him."

"Interesting. So maybe you and Cora did see someone wearing a mask."

"That's what I'm thinking, but I have no idea what the note means, or why the boy was supposed to deliver it to me at exactly five o'clock."

Gordon frowned. "Do you think this might be connected to

our missing teenager . . . or Phil?"

Katherine shook her head. "Why would Phil send something like this?" She placed the note the boy delivered in an evidence bag. "He knows how I feel about anyone calling me Kat, and he's got to know we're looking for him. As for the girl, I don't think she was kidnapped. Seems someone who works for the girl's father called the Canadians this morning and faxed them a picture of Misty. They were warned to keep an eye out for her, and to stop her if she tried to cross the border."

Gordon frowned. "You're saying the border agents were contacted, but not us?"

"Seems so."

"Damn." He leaned back in his chair. "Anything else I should be aware of?"

"Maybe. Alice took a call about an Explorer that sustained damage while its owner was hiking. I think it might be the same vehicle I saw parked near my house."

"Same color?"

"That's what I want to know." She moved over to her desk and picked up her phone.

Two tries produced busy signals. Grumbling, she was about to try again, when Gordon stopped her. "I've been working on these stupid reports ever since Jim went off duty. I need a break. I'm going to grab something to eat; then I'll drive over to Dyea and take a report on this damaged Explorer."

"Get a picture. I want to see if it's the same one."

"Should I dust for bear paw prints on the steering wheel?"

"Very funny." She rolled her eyes at him.

After Gordon left, Katherine headed back to the front office. Crystal was in the interview room. She'd kicked off her shoes and sat with one leg crossed over the other, her miniskirt hiked up, exposing a lot of evenly tanned thigh. A can of soda and a glass of ice had replaced the ice water of earlier, but both were being ignored. Crystal's attention was focused on the loose end of a wire sticking out from the spool on the table. Like a child with a toy, she kept twisting the wire into abstract shapes.

Hair that had looked windblown and unkempt before she went into the bathroom now haloed Crystal's face in an orderly fashion. Even her lipstick had been freshened, the delicate pink almost identical to the color of her sweater.

That Crystal Morgan had taken time to fuss with her hair and makeup didn't surprise Katherine. Her mother would have done the same. No matter what the crisis, her mother always wanted to look her best. Husband loses his job? Buy a new dress. House repossessed? Change the color of your hair.

Katherine had a different mindset. Although department policy required a clean, neat appearance, she didn't wear any makeup and her Kevlar vest hid any curves a man might find attractive. No long, flowing hair, plunging necklines or high-heeled shoes like the women police officers on TV wore. Practical was Katherine's mode of dress. Pants rather than a skirt, comfortable shoes, and hair short and straight. A quick shampoo, a blow dry, and in ten minutes she was ready to go to work. So what if Jim and Doug called her Butch behind her back. They didn't know her past, and that was fine with her.

"Have you heard from your husband?" Katherine asked.

Crystal stopped fussing with the wire and looked up. "Not yet. What about you?"

Katherine carefully pulled the note she'd received out of the evidence bag and showed it to Crystal. "I received this while we were gone. Does it mean anything to you?"

"It looks like a clock."

"Did you receive anything like this?"

"No." Crystal looked confused. "Why? What's supposed to happen at five?"

"I don't know. I was hoping you might have some idea."

"Do you think it's a ransom note?"

"I don't think there's going to be a ransom note." Katherine slipped the clock note back in the bag and set it aside. "We have now learned that your stepdaughter's picture was faxed to the Canadian customs agents this morning."

"This morning?" The blonde straightened in her chair. "You're kidding."

"Your husband's friend, Mr. Nanini, contacted them."

"How in the hell did Vince know Misty was missing?" Crystal Morgan paused, a frown creasing the makeup on her brow. "I mean, I thought he was out of town."

"How can I get in touch with Mr. Nanini?"

"I, ah . . . He . . ." Crystal looked baffled. "I guess you could call his office. How early did he call?"

"I don't know." That was one thing Katherine wanted to ask the man.

"Tom must have gotten a ransom note and called Vince."

"Actually, it sounds more like Mr. Nanini considers her a runaway."

Crystal Morgan frowned. "Why would she run away?"

"Are you sure you and the girl didn't have an argument? Some sort of disagreement?"

"No . . . I mean, yeah. Sure, I got after her for that skinny-dipping fiasco last night, but—" The phone rang out in the office area, and Crystal looked in that direction. "Maybe that's Tom. I gave them the station's number, not the pay phone's."

Alice answered the call. A second later, she held the phone toward the interview room. "It's for you, Mrs. Morgan."

Crystal rose slowly and without bothering to put on her shoes, sauntered over to take the phone from Alice. Katherine stayed where she was. Although she could hear only one side of the conversation, she could tell as much from Crystal's body language as from her words. Before she even said hello, Crystal struck a seductive pose, one hip balanced on the edge of Alice's desk, shoulders back and chest thrust forward.

That position changed quickly; Crystal's pose becoming defensive. "Hey, don't blame me for what's happened. You know how she's been with me."

The tone of her voice expressed her irritation, and Katherine knew the woman had minimized the friction between her and her stepdaughter. Not that it meant anything. Mothers and daughters—especially teenaged daughters—didn't always get along.

"What do you mean I should have gone after her?" Crystal snapped. "I was in the shower. I didn't have a stitch of clothes on. We were supposed to meet for lunch."

Crystal paused, listened to her husband's response. All pretenses of congeniality were gone, her expression defiant. "Yes, I know I waited a long time before calling you. I hoped I'd find her, and—"

Another pause; another change of expression. More than irritation? Katherine wondered. Perhaps hatred?

"Yes. No. So I've heard."

Katherine watched Crystal take a deep breath, and knew the man on the other end of the line was lucky he was in China. If looks could kill, he'd be dead. "Well, nice of you to let me know. How did Vince find out?"

Katherine left the interview room, wrote a question mark on a piece of paper, and slipped it in front of Crystal. Crystal glanced at the mark, then said to her husband, "Just a minute. I need to tell a police officer something."

Holding the phone to the side, she answered Katherine's question. "Tom says after Misty called him yesterday, he not only called me, he called Vince. This morning Vince went to our house and checked Misty's computer. Seems my sweet little stepdaughter agreed to go with me on this cruise simply so she could meet up with some guy here in Skagway."

Crystal turned back to the phone. "No wonder she was so agreeable. So, where was she going with this guy?"

Katherine had a feeling she already knew the answer and wasn't surprised when Crystal said, "Canada?"

Whatever Tom Morgan said next really irritated his wife. "Well, it would have been nice if you'd shared your thoughts," she grumbled. "If you'd said something when you called me yesterday, maybe I could have stopped her."

Katherine wasn't sure what Crystal's husband said to that, but Crystal's reaction was clear. "No, you didn't. You asked me if everything was all right. Well, as far as I knew, everything was all right." She smiled. "So does your invincible Vince have her now?"

A sequence of Crystal listening, and then responding, followed.

"Dammit, Tom, don't you go blaming me. I didn't know you'd called this morning. I didn't get your messages until I went on the ship just a while ago . . .

"No, I didn't turn off my cell. My frickin' phone is dead. Your daughter was supposed to plug it in last night . . .

"I do, too, care about Misty. Just ask the officer here. I've been frantic."

For a moment Katherine thought Crystal was going to hand the phone to her so she could confirm that statement, but then Crystal continued. "You're the one who's always too busy for your daughter. And just because she hasn't crossed the border doesn't mean everything's fine. She—"

Whatever he said to cut her off made Crystal frown. "Well, if he's already in Skagway, tell him to come to the police station. No sense in them checking places Vince has already been to."

She listened for a bit longer, a smile having replaced her earlier frown. A smile that didn't reach her eyes. Finally, Crystal

Morgan nodded. "Oh, I do understand, dear. You'd just better hope Vince or the police find her soon."

Crystal cooed, "Love you, dear," before hanging up, but the tense lines of her body belied the words, and Katherine knew all was not well in the Morgan household. But that was their problem. She was more interested in the Skagway police department's involvement in this mess.

"Tom says Misty's run off with some college kid," Crystal said. "He figures Vince will find her in no time."

"This Vince is here in Skagway, looking for your stepdaughter?"

"Tom said he was flying up and should be here by now." She shrugged and began rubbing the back of her neck. "It will be interesting to see if he finds her."

"You don't think he will?" The woman's attitude surprised Katherine.

Crystal stopped rubbing her neck and smiled at Katherine. "I was kinda hoping you'd find her. Be nice to see a woman succeed where Tom's invincible Vince failed."

"I would think simply finding your stepdaughter would be your priority."

"Oh, believe me, it is."

Crystal's look of sincerity might have fooled Katherine earlier, but having watched the woman as she talked to her husband, Katherine wondered how much was an act. What the blonde couldn't do, however, was keep the pleasure out of her voice when she spoke. "Seems neither Vince nor his partner were around when Tom called them last night. That didn't sit well with my husband. As far as he's concerned, everybody should be at his beck and call, twenty-four-seven."

Including you, Katherine thought, almost feeling sorry for the woman.

Almost.

"Earlier you said this Vince and his partner were computer gurus. Are they also your husband's bodyguards?"

"Bodyguards?" Crystal shook her head. "No. Vince could be one, I guess, if he wanted to. From what Tom has told me, Vince was a terror in the Marines, and, when he went to work for the FBI, he went through their training at Quantico. But, Bob, on the other hand, is your typical computer geek. He's a wimp."

"Bob . . . ?"

"Bob Lilly. The other half of VR Protection Services. Their ad says they stop spies from stealing industrial secrets." She chuckled. "I guess it's a good thing their ad doesn't say they can stop teenagers from running away." Again she smiled. "Anyway, they have other clients besides Tomoro Industries, but Tom's company is a big part of their business, so when he says jump, they jump."

"Did your husband mention the name of the man your stepdaughter was running off with?" With a name, they should be able to find the two, especially if the guy was a local.

"Tom said it's Brian. Brian Payne . . . or something like that." Crystal snorted. "You'll have to ask Vince. He's the know-it-all."

"And you think this Vince guy is here in Skagway?"

"Should be." She smiled. "He's easy to spot. He looks like Vin Diesel. You know. Bald. Muscular. Kinda good-looking." She sighed and glanced at her diamond-studded watch. "The ship's going to leave soon. I guess I'd better go back, pick up a few things, and arrange for the rest of our clothes to be shipped home. Once we find Misty, Vince can fly us back to Seattle. Damn, I hope he brought one of Tom's planes, not that Wright Brothers reject he owns."

CHAPTER THIRTEEN

6:00 P.M.

Jake Mathews watched an unfamiliar turbojet expertly touch down on the asphalt runway. Although there was no control tower at the Skagway Airport, he'd been listening to the radio chatter on the common frequency monitored by all pilots. When the King Air broadcast his intention to land, one of the Wings of Alaska pilots relayed the necessary information regarding the runway, best approach, and the danger of pedestrians and uncontrolled vehicular traffic.

"No moose today," the pilot had said. "At least not so far."

"Moose?" the other pilot had responded, then chuckled. "Roger."

No moose and no bears, which always pleased Jake. It was getting late, and the tourists returning from helicopter flights to the Chilkat, Ferebee, and Meade glaciers didn't need any wildlife on the runways causing havoc.

In the summer, aircraft were constantly taking off and landing at the state-owned airport. Most were planes and helicopters transporting tourists, but around ten percent were transients. An unfamiliar plane was not a unique event, and once it was down, Jake went back to his job of keeping the Wings of Alaska planes fueled and in good repair.

He was working on an engine when a voice behind him disturbed his concentration.

"I hear you're the man to talk to about fuel."

Jake straightened, turned, and found himself facing a man who could have easily been a cover model for a muscle magazine. The guy was clean shaven—from the top of his head to his chin—and casually dressed in a white T-shirt, khakis, and sneakers. Jake put the guy's age around forty, give or take a few years.

"You heard right," Jake said and grabbed a rag to wipe the oil from his hands.

"I'll need a fill-up," the man said and nodded toward the King Air now tied down near the other private planes. "I assume you take credit cards."

"Any of the big three. You need anything else done?"

"Nope. She's good." The pilot glanced toward the small terminal building. "But I do need to find a car to rent. I just checked, and the ones here are booked solid."

"There are a couple of independents in town." Jake motioned toward the downtown area with his hand. "About a half-mile from here."

"And how far is the police station?"

Jake raised his eyebrows, but he didn't ask why the pilot wanted to know the location of the police station. He simply gave directions.

CHAPTER FOURTEEN

Before Crystal left, she hinted that a ride back to the cruise ship would be nice. Katherine ignored the hint. Enough pampering the tourists. If the woman wanted to wear three-inch heels, so be it, but she needed to understand there were consequences. At her own desk, Katherine suffered the consequences of a teenaged-runaway. Once they found the girl, there would be a report to write. No need to wait until then to start. She could list what they'd done up to this point.

She was typing the names of tour agencies she'd asked Alice to contact when Gordon called in. He'd connected with the owner of the Explorer. It was red, and had obviously been in an accident. Besides the broken front light, there were scrapes of green paint on the dented bumper. "Do we have any accident reports involving a green vehicle?" he asked.

"I haven't taken any, but I'll check with Alice."

"You know how I kidded you about the paw prints on the steering wheel," Gordon said. "Well, I didn't find any—didn't even look for any—but there was a tuft of brown fur on the seat. Not real fur," he quickly added. "That fake stuff they use for coats and stuffed animals . . . or on a costume."

Or part of a costume. "I'll call the visitor's center," Katherine said. "See if they had someone wearing a bear mask today."

"If so, the guy's got a lot of explaining to do."

Katherine agreed, starting with why he was parked across the street from her grandfather's house that afternoon and what the

66

note meant.

"I'll finish this accident report and come back to the station," Gordon said. "Anything new with the missing teenager?"

"We have the name of the kid she ran off with." Katherine quickly summarized all that had transpired.

"I don't know of any Brian Payne in Skagway, but it could be one of the seasonal employees," Gordon said, echoing her thoughts. "You're sure they didn't cross into Canada?"

"I'll give Canadian customs a call and see if there's anything new," Katherine said, almost hoping the constables on duty would say Misty and her boyfriend had found a way across the border. Once in Canada, the girl would be their problem. Less paperwork for her to deal with.

As soon as she ended her call with Gordon, Katherine dialed the number for the Canadian customs' station on the Klondike Highway. Constable Howard Wiffle answered the phone. "Now you've brightened my day," he said the moment she identified herself. "Did you change your mind about going out to dinner with me?"

She'd forgotten the last time they'd talked he'd asked if she'd like to go out to dinner. She'd thought her refusal would have quelled that idea. Obviously the man was persistent, and, on the off chance he'd written the note she'd received, she asked, "Did you send me a note? Something about getting together at five tomorrow?"

"No, but I can pick you up at five, if that's what you'd like."

"I'm pretty sure I'll be working at five." Especially if Phil didn't show up. "And this call isn't about going out to dinner. We have a missing teenager, and—"

Howie stopped her before she finished. "Come on, Katherine. We're doing our job. As I told Alice and that Nanini guy, your teenager hasn't gone through here. We've even checked the video from the security cameras."

"What about Brian Payne, the guy she's supposed to be with?" If they found him, he might be able to tell them where Misty was. "Has he been through there today?"

"Payne? Mr. Nanini said the guy's name was Bane. Brian Bane. And, no, we haven't seen him, either. You might want to check with U.S. customs. From what I understand, Bane is Canadian. If he entered Alaska, they'll have a record."

Brian Bane, not Payne. Katherine didn't recognize that name either, and it seemed Misty Morgan was still the Skagway police department's problem. "Well, as long as you're sure she hasn't crossed, we'll keep looking for her around here."

"Trust me," Howie said. "I would have noticed if a pretty blonde went through here today." The moment the words were out, Howie backtracked. "Noticed, but only . . . I mean . . . I, ah . . . I prefer brunettes. So, when are we going out, Officer Ward?"

"I thought I explained," Katherine started, then stopped at the sound of a *psst*. She glanced behind her and saw Alice back by the coffee machine, pointing toward the front office.

"I've got to go," she told Howie. "I'll talk to you later."

The moment Katherine hung up, she turned toward Alice. "What?"

"He's here," Alice said, her voice barely above a whisper. "And wait 'til you see him." She fanned herself, and grinned. "He wants to talk to the officer in charge. At the moment, that's you."

Katherine supposed with Gordon out of the building that was true. She also assumed this smoking hot "he" was the guy Crystal Morgan's husband had sent.

She took a moment to straighten her uniform, then followed Alice back to the office area. Her first impression was that Crystal had been right; Vince Nanini did look like he could be a bodyguard. He certainly didn't fit the computer geek stereotype.

He had the bald head and swarthy complexion like Vin Diesel, but he was bigger than the actor. Not just in height, but in the width of his shoulders and the size of his biceps.

His white T-shirt stretched over a solid chest and flat abdomen, then disappeared beneath the waistline of a pair of tan khakis. Nikes covered his feet. He wore no jewelry, no heavy chains, rings, or earrings. Nothing custom made or terribly expensive, except, perhaps, for the watch on his right wrist. Katherine had a feeling it cost a small fortune. Definitely more than her trusty Timex.

"Mr. Nanini?" she said, holding out her hand.

He didn't offer his.

"*You're* the officer in charge?" The scowl he gave her was accompanied by a quick up-and-down look.

From behind the counter, Alice answered for her. "This is Officer Katherine Ward. Our chief is in the hospital, and Sergeant Landros is out of the office at the moment."

"I *am* the officer handling this case," Katherine added, letting her hand drop back to her side. She knew some men still held chauvinistic views about women police officers. She'd learned the best way to correct that was to take control. "May I see some identification?"

He pulled out a passport and a business card and handed her the two. "My partner and I specialize in computer security," he said. "Tomoro Industries is one of our clients. Thomas Morgan, the president and owner of that business, is also a personal friend, which is why I'm here. It appears Mr. Morgan's teenage daughter has run off with a guy she met through the Internet."

"So I've heard." Katherine looked at his business card—which identified him as Vincent Nanini, President of VR Protection Services—and then at his passport. Actually, his full name was Vincent Dominic Nanini, age thirty-eight, height six feet two and weight one-ninety. Those pounds were all muscle, from what she could see. His address was in Seattle, Washington.

She handed back his passport but kept the business card. "Crystal said you worked for the FBI. May I also see your badge?"

"I'm not an agent," he said. "I did work for the bureau for a while as a consultant."

"Are you presently with any law enforcement agency?"

"No, we—"

She waved off his explanation. "Then I'll be asking the questions."

CHAPTER FIFTEEN

Bitch, Vince thought, but kept his features neutral. He saw no sense in getting angry. Some women had to prove they were as good as a man, especially short women. He doubted Officer Ward topped five feet four.

Her haughty attitude, lack of makeup, and short haircut made him think, if anything, she was trying to hide her femininity. Not that she was completely succeeding. There was something very feminine about her, a sparkle in her eyes and a beguiling softness about her mouth. Even her police uniform couldn't hide a nice figure.

She didn't look more than twenty-five. Probably new to the force.

Too damn young for you, he told himself, not quite sure where that thought had come from. Even worse, he realized he'd glanced at her left hand.

She wasn't wearing a ring.

If she noticed the direction of his gaze, she said nothing, but got right to the point. "Why do you think Misty Morgan has run off with a man?"

"Because this morning I discovered those were her plans."

"She told you?"

"Indirectly. Look, how I found out isn't important. What I need from you is assistance in finding her."

Vince knew he'd said that wrong the moment the words were out of his mouth, and he saw Officer Ward's jaw tighten and her chin rise. Dammit all, he hated dealing with law enforcement. He'd seen how haughty the FBI agents could get when working with the public. It was one reason he'd walked away from that job.

"The only way you're going to receive any assistance," Officer Katherine Ward said, each word tightly enunciated, "is if you answer my questions. Now, how did you learn that Mr. Morgan's daughter planned on running off with a man?"

If she wanted details, he would give her details. "I went to the Morgan house this morning and logged onto Misty's computer. Tom has had us occasionally check their home computers for viruses and spyware, but our job doesn't involve monitoring his daughter's on-line activities. Tom felt that would infringe on Misty's privacy."

"By 'we' you mean you and . . . ?"

"My partner, Bob Lilly."

"So this morning you go on her computer and immediately see something that tells you she's planning on running off with this Bane guy?"

"It wasn't quite that easy, but yes."

"Crystal Morgan said her husband suspected something was wrong yesterday. Why did it take you until this morning to check the girl's computer?"

"Because yesterday, I was in Washington, D.C., on business. As lucrative as our contract is with Tomoro Industries, we do have other clients."

Of course, Tom hadn't seen it that way. As far as he was concerned, when he called, either Vince or Bob should have been sitting in their offices ready to act.

"I was in D.C., and my partner was in L.A. I took a red-eye back to Seattle, but I still didn't get to the Morgan house until after eight this morning."

"All right then, why didn't Mr. Morgan call his wife last

night and have *her* stop the girl from running off? Or call the cruise line? They could have stopped her from disembarking."

"I can't answer for Tom, but I'd guess he didn't do any of that because yesterday he only suspected something was wrong. It wasn't until I actually found the plans for the rendezvous that any of us truly knew what Misty was up to. Also, according to Tom, when he talked to his wife yesterday, she said not to worry; Misty was fine."

"So, where's the girl now?"

"I have no idea." And having to explain things to this woman wasn't getting him any closer to finding Misty.

"Why contact the Canadians and not us?"

"Because, according to the plans Misty and this Bane guy made, that's where they were headed. Straight for the border. I called them because I'd hoped to stop her there."

"But, you didn't," another voice responded from behind him, one Vince recognized immediately.

He turned and faced Crystal Morgan. "No, I didn't because she never made it there."

"And, of course, neither you nor Tom called me this morning to let me know what was going on."

"Tom said he'd get in touch with you himself."

"Misty's been acting like a brat."

"You're the one who wanted to take this trip with her."

"I wanted to bond with her, but all she's interested in are boys. You're the security guy. You should have known this would happen."

What he should have known was Crystal would try to shift the blame onto him. Well, he wasn't about to let her off the hook.

"Tom hired us to keep hackers from getting into his company's computers. Our contract doesn't include watching over wives and children. Besides, I told you to hire a bodyguard."

"For a man who doesn't want to watch over wives and children, you certain have been spending a lot of time with Misty." Crystal faced Officer Ward and the dispatcher behind the desk. "He doesn't know it, but I've seen him groping Misty."

Vince tensed. "What the hell are you talking about?"

All three women looked at him.

"When you've come over and taken her downstairs. I've seen you hugging her. Grabbing her."

"I was giving her self-defense lessons."

"Sure you were."

"I'm her godfather. I was trying to show her ways to protect herself."

Except, lately, she'd treated him like the enemy.

Crystal gave him a smug grin, then looked at the two other women. "Wouldn't you think a computer whiz would warn a teenager about the dangers of the Internet?"

"I did." He didn't like the way this conversation was going, especially the way Officer Ward was looking at him. "I told Misty to be careful, that you never know exactly who you're texting. She told me to stop bird-dogging her."

"And, now she's gone," Crystal said, her gaze returning to him. "Hmm. Guess you're not so great after all."

CHAPTER SIXTEEN

Katherine had had enough of their bickering. "I need answers, not accusations," she said. "Mr. Nanini, what do you know about this man the girl has allegedly run off with?"

Vince Nanini looked away from Crystal and back at Katherine. "His name is Brian Bane, he lives in Alberta, Canada, and he's twenty-one."

"Was he on the boat with us?" Crystal asked.

Nanini glanced back at her. "No, they set it up to meet here in Skagway."

Crystal snorted. "The little sneak."

"Do you have a picture of this Brian Bane?" Katherine asked, wanting to keep them on track.

"Yes." Nanini pulled two glossy four-by-six photos from the briefcase he'd brought with him. "I printed his off the Internet, along with the one Misty posted. Our young lady was passing herself off as an eighteen-year-old college student, and, as you can see, in this picture, she does look that old."

Katherine took the two pictures. Mr. Brian Bane looked like a nice, clean-cut college boy; however, pictures posted on the Internet weren't always the true images of the person posting the messages. More than one pedophile had been snared by officers posing as young children.

"I checked the guy out," Nanini said. "He is who he says he is. In the last message between them, Bane told Misty he'd meet her in front of the city visitors' center at seven this morning, that he'd be driving a rusted, green and silver Chevy Blazer. I've got the license number."

He pulled out his wallet, found a slip of paper, and handed it to Katherine.

A green SUV. The color wasn't uncommon, but it was the second time the color green had been mentioned in less than an hour. She wondered if this Blazer might also have some dents, with perhaps traces of red.

"We'll get this license plate number out to all of our officers," Katherine said. "I assume Canada customs also has this information."

"They do."

"So, Mr. Nanini," Crystal said, a self-satisfied arrogance in her tone. "Any idea where my darling stepdaughter might be?"

Katherine had Alice call the hotels, lodges, and bed-and-breakfast places in Skagway along with the Chilkoot Trail outpost in Dyea. With each, she had Alice ask the same question. "Do you have a blonde female in her late teens or a brown-haired male in his early twenties registered, either together or separate?"

The answer was always the same. "No."

Alice also checked with each establishment to see if they had any rooms available. Crystal had already said, with the cruise ship gone, she would need some place to stay. Vince Nanini had indicated, if necessary, he could sleep on the plane he'd flown into Skagway.

For a while it looked like Crystal Morgan might have to sleep in one of the station's two cells, but finally Alice smiled. "The Bonanza has a last-minute cancellation."

Gordon returned from Dyea, clipboard in hand, and Katherine introduced him to Vince Nanini. She wasn't surprised when the man started talking to Gordon as if she wasn't there. As

Nanini summarized what he knew about Misty Morgan, his attitude clearly indicated he now expected Gordon to take over the search for the girl. Gordon's response, however, didn't please Katherine any more than it obviously did Nanini. "Officer Ward is in charge of that investigation," Gordon said. "I'm sure she'll keep me up to date on her progress."

He then started for the back of the station, and, for a moment, Katherine didn't know what to say. If this had been a kidnapping, she would have willingly endured a chauvinistic ass like Nanini. But Misty Morgan hadn't been kidnapped. She was simply a rich kid who'd run off with a boyfriend.

"I'll be right back," she said, motioning for Vince Nanini and Crystal Morgan to stay where they were.

Gordon had grabbed a bottle of water from the refrigerator and was about to settle into his chair when Katherine caught up with him. "I think you should handle this case," she said, keeping her voice low.

He glanced past her, at the hallway that connected their offices to the front office. The layout of the station gave a more open feel to the building's limited space, but it also allowed voices to carry. In a way that was good, especially if there was a disturbance in the front area. Anyone on duty could react immediately. But there were disadvantages as well.

Gordon also kept his voice low. "What's a matter, Katherine? You gonna let that guy scare you off?"

"That guy," she said, "can stick his attitude where the sun don't shine. He's not the problem."

"Then what is?"

She wasn't sure how to explain without revealing too much. "Gordon, we're dealing with some nationally known rich guy's spoiled brat. How long do you think it will be before the media catches on that she's missing? How long before reporters show up in Skagway?"

"So?"

"Be honest. Do you really think I'm the best person to deal with reporters?" She hoped her past behavior would convince him she wasn't.

"Katherine, if this goes national, whether you're in charge of the case or not isn't going to matter. We're all going to be dealing with the media."

Not what she wanted to hear.

"So, find the girl before it does go national."

"But—"

"No buts. Find that girl."

Resigned to the inevitable, Katherine turned to walk back to the front office, but before she'd taken two steps, Gordon asked, "Don't you want to know about that Explorer over in Dyea?"

She stopped where she was. "What'd you find?"

Gordon placed the bottle of water and clipboard he'd been carrying on his desk and pulled out a small digital camera. "Take a look." He clicked on the camera and brought up an image. She came closer, and he handed her the camera. "This the same Explorer you saw parked in front of your place?"

He'd taken several pictures of the vehicle, some from a distance and some close up. Katherine scanned through all of them, going back to the one that showed roughly the same angle she'd seen when leaving her house. "Looks the same," she said.

"I dusted for fingerprints, but didn't find any. Not even those belonging to the vehicle's owner."

That in itself was unusual. "Someone wiped it down?"

"Must have." Gordon removed an evidence bag he'd attached to his clipboard, and opened it. "Here's your bear."

Katherine took the bag and looked inside. She could see a tuft of dark brown, almost black, synthetic hair. "Vehicle's owner said he didn't know where that came from. He's not happy about this. Said he'll be at the campground tonight, but he's heading for Whitehorse tomorrow. He'll get the headlight fixed there."

"And you're sure he wasn't driving when the accident occurred?"

"His buddies vowed they'd all been on the trail for the last three days, and the way they looked and smelled, I believed them."

"How'd someone just drive off with his SUV? Did he leave his keys in the ignition?"

"Almost as bad," Gordon said, shaking his head. "The kid left a sign on the windshield that they'd be gone until late today. He said he did that so if they didn't make it back, someone would come looking for them. Oh, and he also used one of those magnetic hide-a-key gadgets. Had the key under the front fender. Our bear-man must have seen the sign, found the key, and gone for a joy ride."

"So why was bear-man parked on my street?" she asked and handed the bag back.

"Coincidence?"

The way he said it, Katherine knew Gordon didn't believe that any more than she did.

"I'm going to download these pictures and make some prints. Maybe someone in town will remember seeing the truck today. Still no word from Phil?" Gordon asked.

"Not a peep."

"I think we'd better alert the park rangers. Only reason I can think of why he hasn't called in is he's hurt."

She'd been thinking the same thing. "I'll have Alice call them before she goes home."

"Good." He picked up his bottle of water. "Let me know if you do hear from him . . . or if you find the girl. And get rid of those two. The guy may work for the girl's father, but he has no authority on this case."

"You want me to tell him to get lost?" Katherine smiled. "Oh, he's going to love that."

CHAPTER SEVENTEEN

The Bonanza was a restored, two-story Victorian that a couple of newcomers had recently opened as a bed-and-breakfast. Like so many of the buildings in Skagway, the house looked much the same as it had when Skagway was the boomtown gateway to the Trail of '98 and the Klondike gold fields. The differences between what the lodging would have been like back then and nowadays were running water, indoor plumbing, TVs, radios, telephones, and maybe even the Internet.

Katherine took Vince Nanini along when she drove Crystal over. He hadn't argued when she'd told him there was nothing more he could accomplish at the station, and he hadn't said one word about wanting Gordon in charge of the case. Katherine figured she'd drop Crystal off at the bed-and-breakfast, and then take Nanini to the airport.

Crystal frowned when Katherine pulled up in front of the Bonanza. "I guess it will do," she said. "At least it will give me a chance to rest. Freshen up."

Nanini unloaded Crystal's luggage from the back of the Tahoe. "If we find Misty before it gets too late," he told the blonde, "I'll come by and pick you up, then fly both of you back to Seattle."

"In what?" Crystal asked as she retrieved her carry-on bag. "That puddle jumper you think is so great?"

"The King Air is a good plane."

The blonde rolled her eyes, and then looked at Katherine.

"My husband has a fleet of planes, some of them absolutely fantastic to fly in, but what does this guy fly? A stripped down, crappy turbojet you practically have to crawl into."

"Then stay here after we find her," Nanini said and started to get back into the patrol unit.

"Hey," Crystal yelled. "My bag."

For a moment Katherine thought he would ignore the order. Finally, he gave an exasperated sigh and grabbed the suitcase Crystal had taken off the ship.

Katherine smiled and walked back around to the driver's side. It was good to see a chauvinist kowtow to another woman. Something about that man had irked her from the moment she met him. His attitude, she supposed. Body language often spoke louder than words. Both Crystal Morgan and Vince Nanini thought they'd stepped into a small-town, backward police department with an officer who wouldn't be able to find the nose on her face, much less Thomas Morgan's daughter. Well, she'd show the two of them.

She'd just clicked her seatbelt into place and slipped her key in the ignition when the passenger door opened and Nanini, absent bags and Crystal, slid into the Tahoe. "I think we should check the campgrounds," he said before even closing his door.

She shook her head. "There is no 'we.' I'm taking you to the airport."

"That will only waste time. I don't need anything from my plane and the sooner we find Misty, the sooner I can get back to my real job."

"You're not going with me." This wasn't something she was going to argue about. "If we learn anything, I'll let you know."

"If you think I'm going to sit around, waiting to hear from you, you're mistaken. Either we do this together or we waste time duplicating efforts." He clicked his own seatbelt into place.

"You get in the way of our investigation, and I'll arrest you."

"I'm not going to get in your way. I know what Misty looks like. I've memorized that Bronco's license. You drive, I'll look."

She wasn't buying his argument. "Why this passionate interest in finding this girl?"

"I told you; I'm her godfather. I've watched this kid grow up." He cleared his throat. "I don't want Tom losing his daughter, too."

"What do you mean?"

"I lost my own daughter when she was just four."

She heard the change in his voice. A slight catch, and it made her curious. "What do you mean, 'lost your daughter'?"

"She died of cancer. Now, are we going to sit here and discuss my life story or are we going to look for Misty?"

CHAPTER EIGHTEEN

Vince held his breath, unsure what the woman seated next to him would do next. She obviously didn't want him around. She'd even inched away when he slid onto the front seat, almost as if she were afraid of him.

"I promise I won't get in the way," he said. "I think the sooner we find Misty the better. I'm sure she's doing this to get back at her father. Ever since he married Crystal, Misty has been upset with him. I'm sure this is just her way to gain his attention, but I don't think she's really thought this all the way through."

"She thought it through well enough that we haven't been able to find her," Officer Ward said.

He'd concede that. "Since they haven't tried to cross into Canada and aren't staying in a room, they've got to be in one of the RV campgrounds. I mean, from what Misty posted on-line, Bane has to have arrived expecting to have sex with her. I'm guessing he either brought a tent or his Blazer's been rocking all day."

"Or, he has a friend who has a place here."

"Bane never mentioned a friend in Skagway."

"I'm sure our dispatcher has already called the campgrounds."

"And, that's it? You're going to depend on a phone call?"

He saw her bristle. "After I drop you off, I plan on personally checking each of them."

"There's what, three in town, one out in Dyea? We drive through, either you or I spot a green Blazer, case closed."

"And, then what?"

"We pick up Crystal, I fly the two of them back to Seattle, and Daddy grounds his little girl for life."

"It wouldn't be quite that simple."

He didn't think it would.

"She's under-age."

"She duped the poor guy."

"Doesn't matter."

"So, you go by the book."

"It's the only way to survive."

Nanini shook his head. "Life should be more than simply surviving."

She scoffed, but he noticed a slight smile as she reached for her radio. "I need to let our dispatcher know where I'm going."

While still in Seattle, waiting for his plane to be gassed and prepped for the flight, Vince had studied several tourist brochures about Skagway. He knew the Pullen Creek RV Park was located on the waterfront just off Congress Way, close to the railroad depot and downtown Skagway. According to what he'd read, its proximity to an array of shops, bars, eating places, and historical sites made it a popular destination in the summer.

Officer Katherine Ward drove slowly through the park, both of them looking for the Blazer in front of, beside, and behind the RVs and tents. She stopped the Tahoe often, showing Misty's and Brian's pictures to the campers walking or sitting out in the open. One woman said she'd seen a blonde, teenaged girl and a young man who might have been twenty. They'd had their backs to her, so she couldn't be certain they were the two in the pictures.

It turned out to be a false lead. The brother and sister were traveling with their parents. And, no, they hadn't seen anyone who fit Misty's or Brian's description.

After Pullen Creek, Officer Ward drove them to the Garden City RV Park, and they repeated the procedure. Then on to Skagway's Mountain View RV Park. In each location, they showed anyone they met Brian's and Misty's pictures and described the green and silver Blazer. No matter how many times they repeated the routine, the answer was always the same. No one had seen either of the two.

Vince could tell Officer Ward was disappointed with their efforts. Through all three parks, she'd said little—asked no questions of him, made no comments, and generated no small talk. Before exiting the last RV park, she pulled her cruiser to the side, leaned back against the vehicle's seat, and gave a frustrated sigh.

"On to Dyea?" he asked, hoping she wasn't about to give up the search.

She glanced his way, nodded, and again straightened in her seat. "I guess so. But before we drive over there, I need to check on my grandfather."

"Is he ill?" He wanted her concentrating on a missing teenager, not an ailing grandparent.

"No, he's fine. He just forgets things sometimes."

"How old is he?"

"Almost ninety."

"Alzheimer's?"

"Probably." She glanced his way. "I don't want to talk about it."

"It's nothing to be ashamed of. One out of every five people over the age of eighty has it."

"Fine. I still don't want to talk about it."

Vince had a feeling there were a lot of things this woman didn't want to talk about. Nevertheless, he wanted to know where they were headed. "Is he in a nursing home?"

"No." She gave a slight shake of her head. "We don't have any of those in Skagway. I've asked a neighbor girl to help him in the evenings. Tonight's her first night. This won't take long. I just want to make sure everything is working out all right."

"Okay." He didn't know what else to say. Although finding Misty was his first priority, he figured saving the girl's virginity was a lost cause. If he'd known what was up in time to stop this harebrained idea of hers, maybe he could have convinced her that jumping into bed with some guy she'd met on-line was no way to gain her father's attention. As it was, too many hours had passed since her planned rendezvous. Plenty of time for a randy male to talk a horny teenager into doing the deed.

Vince couldn't see anything wrong when they neared the small, yellow cottage with the green trim, but he could tell Officer Katherine Ward did. Her "Hmm," was accompanied by a frown, and the moment she'd parked her Tahoe in the driveway, she released her seatbelt and opened her door.

Vince followed her to the side of the house. An old man stood back by a row of rose bushes, the hoe in his gnarled hands barely digging into the soil at the base of one of the bushes. "Poppa," Katherine said as she neared him. "I thought you'd be inside, watching the ball game."

Her grandfather looked at her, a slight frown touching his brow. "Is it that late?"

"Yes, it's that late."

The old man's gaze turned to Vince, the wrinkles across his forehead deepening. "Do I know you?"

"Poppa, this is Vince Nanini," Katherine said. "He's helping me look for a girl. Did Sarah fix your dinner?"

"Sarah?"

"Sarah Wilson. The Wilsons' oldest daughter. Remember? She was supposed to come over and fix your dinner tonight."

He shook his head. "I don't think I've had any dinner."

"I'm going to check inside," Officer Ward told Vince. "I'll only be a minute. I'm sure he's had dinner. He just forgets."

"Go ahead." Vince didn't see any way to stop her, and it felt good to stretch his legs. He stepped closer to the old man. "So, you grow roses."

CHAPTER NINETEEN

To Katherine's dismay, she didn't see any dishes or silverware in the drain, and when she checked the refrigerator, the food she'd left for Sarah to prepare was still sitting there, untouched. As far as Katherine could tell, her grandfather had been right. He hadn't had any dinner.

It took her less than a minute to find the phone number for the Wilsons. Sarah's mother answered on the second ring. "I'm glad you called," Mattie Wilson said. "Could Sarah come home for a short while? I forgot something at the store and I need to go get it, but I don't want to leave Austin and Susan alone."

"Sarah's not here," Katherine said. "That's why I called. As far as I can tell, she hasn't been here at all tonight."

"But she has to be." A note of panic entered Mattie Wilson's voice. "I mean, where else would she be?"

"I'll take a look through the house, but she didn't fix my grandfather's dinner, and . . . Hold on, just let me look." Katherine put the phone down on the counter and made a quick tour of the house. The television in the living room was off, there was no fourteen-year-old sprawled out on the couch, and Katherine's bedroom and her grandfather's were empty. When Katherine again picked up the phone, she was worried. "Mattie, she isn't here. I don't think she's been here at all today."

"But she has to be. She was all excited about this job and left early. I think she wanted to talk to you before you left for work."

"I left early today," Katherine said, confused by what Sarah's mother was saying. "Maybe it wasn't me your daughter wanted to see. Maybe by leaving early she figured she had enough time to visit with one of her friends. Do you think she might be over at one of their houses? That she forgot she was supposed to be here?"

"Sarah? No, not Sarah. Austin, yes. He gets with his friends, and he forgets everything. I never know where he'll end up. But, with Sarah, if she says she's going to do something, she does it. She—" Mattie stopped, and Katherine heard her take in a shaky breath before she asked, "Where could she be?"

CHAPTER TWENTY

Doris Goldstein had grown accustomed to the rhythmic clack of the train's wheels on the track, along with the to-and-fro sway of the car. She couldn't say the same about the view out the windows. The brochure used the words "breathtaking" and "spectacular" to describe the White Pass & Yukon Route, and she would admit it was amazing that anyone could lay a hundred and ten miles of track on a cliff that climbed from sea level to almost three thousand feet in twenty miles. But it was exactly that climb, the tight curves, and the idea that at any moment the train might go crashing down the side of the mountain that had her closing her eyes for a good part of the ride. She might live on the twenty-third floor of a New York high rise, but she didn't walk along the outside of the building on a space barely wider than a hallway. Even the tunnels scared her.

"Such a lot of trees," her husband, Ira, said. "Open your eyes, Doris. You're missing the view."

"What I'm about to miss is my lunch," Doris said, but she opened her eyes. At least they were heading back to Skagway. Soon this ordeal would be over. "How can you see?" She dared a look out the window. Although the sky was still light, the river valley between the mountains was bathed in shadows.

"I can see." Ira held the binoculars toward her. "Look across the valley. There's a tour bus on the road over there. With these glasses, it looks like it's only a few feet away."

"I know, I know. Such a good deal you made buying those.

You've been telling me that every day since you bought them."

In spite of her grumbling, she took the binoculars and looked across the pass at the bus traveling down the Klondike Highway. Once she'd adjusted the focus, the bus did seem as close as her hand. She could even see a break in the guardrail the bus was passing.

"They should take care of that," she said.

"Take care of what?"

"That broken guardrail. Guardrails are there for a purpose." Using the binoculars, she looked farther down the side of the mountain. "Do you think someone went over the side?"

"How should I know?"

Spruce and fir trees were interspersed with rocks and boulders. How shrubs and trees managed to grow on such a rugged surface was beyond her. The valley looked as if a giant had chiseled his way through the granite mountain, making a colossal wedge.

As deeply shadowed as the valley had become, she could see fairly well. A touch of silver amid the green caught her eye, and she grunted.

"What?" her husband asked.

Doris lowered the binoculars. "There's something down there."

"You saw something?"

"That's what I said." She handed the binoculars back to him. "A truck. Or a car . . . Something."

Ira raised the glasses to his eyes and stared out the window. "I don't see anything."

"Halfway down." She tried to find the spot without the binoculars. They were rapidly moving away from the area, and she couldn't be sure exactly where she had seen what looked like the back end of a vehicle.

"I see nothing," Ira repeated.

"It was there." She sat back in her seat. "We're too far away now."

"Maybe. Or maybe you saw a rock that looked like a car. I'm hungry. I hope we get back to the station soon."

"You're always hungry," Doris said. "And it was no rock. I think that's why the guardrail is broken. Someone drove over the side."

"So, I'm sure somebody's reported it by now."

"Maybe. Maybe not. We need to tell someone."

"So, who you gonna tell?" He put the binoculars back in their case and snapped it shut.

"Someone," Doris said, looking around the train. *Where was a conductor when you needed one?*

CHAPTER TWENTY-ONE

Vince knew something was wrong the moment Officer Ward stepped out of the house. For a moment she simply stood on the doorstep, staring ahead. He had a feeling she wasn't even aware of his presence.

He saw her shudder, saw the quiver of her chin and the tightness of her mouth. Leaving her grandfather's side, Vince walked over to her. "What's the matter?"

Her head jerked, and she looked at him. Even so, it took a moment more before he knew she saw him. Her voice was shaky when she spoke. "We've got another teenager missing."

"Another runaway?" It seemed too much a coincidence.

"No. I don't think so." She took a deep breath. "I mean, I don't think she's run away. Maybe she's just with friends. Maybe . . ."

She didn't finish, and once again she was staring off into space. "So, what are you going to do?"

"Do?" She looked at him, and then abruptly turned back toward the house. "I need to call Sergeant Landros."

Vince glanced at her grandfather. The old man was once again hoeing around his flowers, his actions robotic and producing little results. He seemed totally unaware of his grand-daughter's distress. Vince followed her through the side door into the house.

He stepped into a small room, hooks on the side walls holding a variety of coats and jackets, while boots and shoes were scattered about on the floor. Another door—open—led to a spacious kitchen. Officer Ward stood by the counter, phone up to her ear. Vince leaned against the kitchen doorway and listened.

Tension radiated from every inch of the officer's body, her breathing shallow, and her words stilted. "You're sure?" she said. "I mean . . ." She paused. "No, I understand."

She placed the phone back in its cradle and stared out the window above the sink. Vince cleared his throat, and she turned and looked at him. "Is everything all right, Officer?" he asked.

"I don't know." She sighed, and then forced a smile. "Probably. Probably just a case of a forgetful teenager."

She looked at the refrigerator against the opposite wall. "Gordon told me to go ahead and fix my grandfather some dinner, and to get something to eat myself. He said, while I'm doing that, he'll check around town. He thinks the girl who was supposed to come here probably got sidetracked and is with friends."

"And what do you think?"

"I don't know."

Concern laced her words, making him worry. "How old is the girl?"

"Fourteen."

He saw her frown, and then shake her head, as if brushing away another bad thought. Her smile was tight. "As long as I'm making sandwiches, do you want one?" Again, she shook her head. "No, of course you don't."

"A sandwich sounds great."

"No, no." She waved a hand in the air. "You'll get a better meal in town. The Corner Café isn't far from here."

"I'd rather have a sandwich." Actually anything sounded good. It had been a long time since he'd eaten. "Anything I can do to help, Officer Ward?"

"Maybe set the table." For a moment she stared at him, then

she managed a smile. "And I guess if we're going to have dinner together, you can call me Katherine."

"And you can call me Vince."

He found where they kept the flatware, dishes, and napkins. She made turkey sandwiches and heated a can of tomato soup. Her breathing remained shallow and her mind seemed to be elsewhere. Finally, he asked, "Are you close to this girl?"

She jerked around and looked at him, and he knew she'd forgotten he was even in the kitchen. "Close?"

"You seem very upset."

"I . . . No. I mean, yes. Around here, we all know each other, but . . ." She shook her head. "I'm . . . I'm just worried."

She walked to the door and called to her grandfather. Vince waited out of the way until the old man came inside, washed his hands, and sat down at the table. Katherine set food in front of her grandfather and then went to the refrigerator for a bottle of milk.

Vince stood by the table, waiting for her to sit. Her grandfather started to eat, stopped, and looked up. "Well, are you going to stand there all day? Sit down. Katherine, bring your boyfriend some food."

"Coming right up." Katherine motioned for Vince to sit in the chair to the right of her grandfather. "He's not my boyfriend, Poppa. Mr. Nanini's helping me with a case."

The old man merely grunted and started slurping his soup. She poured his milk, then looked at Vince. "Milk okay for you?"

"Milk's fine," he said, though he would have preferred a stiff drink.

The sandwich and soup weren't anything special, but they were better than the granola bar and coffee he'd had that morning or the overcooked hamburger he'd gotten the night before while waiting for his flight out of Washington's Reagan National.

Initially he hadn't been overly worried when he received Tom's phone call; he really thought Tom was overreacting. He'd thought Bob would be in Seattle and could go to the Morgan house and check Misty's emails. It was only when Vince learned that Bob was also out of town that Vince decided—for the sake of friendship, and maybe the fear of losing the Tomoro contract—he would take a red-eye back to Seattle. Now he was glad he had.

His food gone, Vince noticed Katherine had barely touched hers. One bite, maybe two, of her sandwich and a spoonful or two of the soup. She might be an officer who went by the book, but she obviously cared about the people she served. Knowing what had happened to Misty had eased some of his fears, but he wouldn't feel relieved until they'd found her. Damn, headstrong kid.

As soon as they finished eating, Katherine stacked their dishes in the sink and gave her grandfather a kiss on his forehead. "I've got to go, Poppa," she said. "I'm going to go look for Sarah. She's missing."

Vince also stood. "Nice talking to you, Mr. Ward."

"Nice talking to you." The old man pushed himself away from the table and started looking around. "Did we get a bill, Katherine?"

"We're at home, Poppa. You don't have to pay for dinner."

"Oh." He smiled up at Vince and sat back down. "That's good, isn't it?"

"Very good." Vince shook the old man's hand. "Take care."

"I'll be back in a while," Katherine started for the coat cloak room. "If Sarah shows up, tell her to call her mother."

"Sarah?" The old man frowned. "You mean the little Wilson girl?"

"Yes, but she's almost grown up now. She's a teenager, Poppa." Katherine paused at the door. "You coming, Nanini?"

"My granddaughter went missing when she was a teenager," Russell Ward said, and sighed. "She was gone for a long time."

"Your granddaughter?" Vince looked at Katherine. "Is he talking about you?"

Katherine had a hand on the knob, but she didn't open the door. Like a deer caught in the headlights, she stood frozen in place.

"I think I'll go watch some TV," the old man said and slowly stood and moved away from the table.

"You coming or not?" Katherine asked, a throaty rasp to her words.

"I'm coming," Vince said, hurrying to follow Katherine out of the house and to the Chevy Tahoe. "Did you run away?" he asked before she had the vehicle's door open.

"What I did as a teenager is none of your business," she said and slid into the cruiser.

She was on her radio-phone by the time he made it to the passenger side and climbed in. Vince said nothing until she signed off. "News about Sarah?"

"Maybe." Katherine started the motor. "Gordon thinks she might be in Dyea, at a rafting party. From what he's learned, a lot of kids were going there." She slipped the Tahoe into gear and backed out of the drive.

"If there's a party, maybe Misty's there."

"I'll look for her."

"I thought I was going with you."

"No." She glanced his way. "Buckle up. I think it would be better if I dropped you off at the airport."

CHAPTER TWENTY-TWO

This time Katherine ignored his protests. She wanted Vince Nanini out of her cruiser and out of her life. The man asked too many questions, and her grandfather had said way too much. Why did that particular memory have to come back while Vince was in the house? She and her grandparents had vowed never to talk about her past, not to anyone in Skagway. Why couldn't her grandfather have remembered that?

She made the drive from her grandfather's house to the airport in less than three minutes. Not that she had to drive fast. Skagway's one-runway, no-control tower, public airport was located only three blocks from her grandfather's house. "I should go with you," Vince argued as she pulled into the parking area.

"No need. I've got their pictures." Katherine motioned toward the two photos they'd been showing in the RV parks. "If they're at the party, or if any of the kids at the party have seen them, I'll let you know right away."

"If I'm with you, I'll *know* right away," he said, not moving out of the cruiser.

"This is not open for debate, I—"

The call that came over her radio stopped her. For a moment she didn't move, didn't breathe . . . and she had a feeling Vince Nanini didn't either. And then he groaned. "Did he say a green Chevy Blazer?"

That was what she'd heard.

"Where did it go off the road?" he demanded. "Where are they talking about?"

"The Klondike Highway," she said and again put the Tahoe into gear. She knew she shouldn't take him with her. She also knew he'd get there, one way or another.

"Damn." He sank back against the seat. "How long ago did it go over the edge? Are they dead?"

"Vince, hush." She'd turned on her siren, but she needed to concentrate as she made her way toward the highway. "You're hearing as much as I am."

CHAPTER TWENTY-THREE

8:30 P.M.

Charles Bell heard the chatter on the radio and smiled. The police were on their way.

Finally.

He'd known he would need a police radio. Getting one had been easy. A few questions asked, and he'd picked his target. A police officer who liked to fish. Unmarried. A friend of Russell Ward.

In Skagway, the police were friendly, accustomed to tourists' questions. "Do you know a good fishing spot?" he'd asked, and Officer Friendly was hooked.

The poor guy never saw it coming. Just like the Graysons never did.

The first calls that had come through the radio that morning had been inquiries about Phil Carpenter's whereabouts, along with reminders that he was on the schedule to work today. Then came the warnings that he was late. As time progressed, the voices became more demanding, concerned. "Phil, where are you? Are you all right? Check in . . . please."

Was he all right?

Evidently they hadn't found Officer Carpenter or they would know the answer to that question. Maybe they would never find him. It had certainly taken them long enough to find the Blazer.

Bell glanced at the clock on the wall. Talk about inefficiency. Over twelve hours had passed since he'd watched the kid's SUV

101

go off the road and over the edge. He'd almost resorted to making an anonymous call, but now he could hear what was going on, could imagine their reactions.

The buzz on the radio excited him. They were swarming to the site like bees to the sweet nectar of new blossoms. The image aroused him, and he licked his lips.

For the last few hours, he'd forced himself to ignore the pressure in his jeans. He was in Skagway to do a job, and until he knew the father would get the message, he'd put aside his own needs. But now—at last—*she* would understand what was happening. She alone would realize it wasn't just the money he was after.

Revenge was going to be sweet, as sweet as the taste of honey.

Smiling, The Beekeeper left the kitchen and walked toward the bedroom.

CHAPTER TWENTY-FOUR

A caravan of emergency vehicles joined Katherine's Tahoe as she sped up the Klondike Highway. Skagway's search and rescue team had responded the moment the call went out. Sirens blaring, they arrived one after another at the section of damaged guardrail. Even so, Gordon's cruiser was already parked by the side of the road. It took Katherine a moment to spot him.

"Stay here," she told Vince and left her vehicle.

Gordon nodded as she approached. "Doesn't look good," he said.

She moved closer to the edge of the road and glanced at the valley below. She could see a man working his way down the steep and rugged mountainside toward an outcropping of rocks and brush. Barely visible was the rear end of an SUV. "Who reported it?"

"One of the passengers on the train," Gordon said. "She told the conductor. At first, he thought she was talking about that truck that went off the road last April."

"That was pulled out in May."

"I know. Thank goodness he decided to give us a call. When I heard the woman saw what she thought was a green truck, I—"

"Is it a green truck or a green and silver Blazer?"

Katherine turned at the sound of Vince Nanini's voice. He hadn't stayed in the Tahoe as she'd requested, but with the rescue workers talking and moving around, she hadn't heard him come up behind her.

Nanini looked directly at Gordon and repeated his question. "The woman on the train . . . Did she see a green and silver Blazer?"

Gordon hesitated, a slight frown crossing his brow as he looked at Nanini, then he shrugged. "She said she saw what looked like the rear end of a vehicle. She had no idea what make or model it might be. As I was telling Officer Ward, the conductor thought it was a truck that went through here last April. Driver was killed in that accident, and we didn't remove the truck until a few weeks ago."

"And you mean to tell me the guardrail still hasn't been fixed?"

Katherine could tell from the look Gordon gave her that he didn't like the tone of Nanini's voice. Repairs to the Klondike Highway weren't the police department's responsibility. The highway didn't even fall under the jurisdiction of Skagway's road commission.

She answered for Gordon. "I believe it's on the schedule for next month. As for the color . . ." Again she looked over the edge. "It looks green to me. We'll know the make and model in a minute. Who's down there, Gordon?"

"Sam Sutherland. He started down just before you arrived." Gordon moved closer to the edge of the roadway, but not as close as Katherine stood.

It was well known that Sergeant Gordon Landros was afraid of heights. Even flying was an ordeal for him, especially in a small, single-engine plane or a helicopter.

"Is Sam down there yet?"

Katherine recognized Terry Biscaro's voice even before she turned and saw him coming up beside her. He'd been a volunteer search and rescue worker for years and had helped Katherine in the past with a couple of accident calls. Middle-aged and his hair turning gray, he'd competed in more than a dozen Iditarod Sled Dog Races, retracing the eleven-hundred-mile route from Anchorage to Nome in March of each year.

"I think he's getting close," she said, afraid to move any nearer to the edge. One more step would take her into thin air.

From his position behind her, Gordon spoke into his radio. "Sam, can you tell what it is?"

A helicopter came up the valley from Skagway, the thump of its blades drowning out Sam's answer. Terry held his radio up close to his ear, then yelled to Gordon, "It's a Blazer."

Katherine glanced back at Vince. The taut line of his mouth indicated his tension, and he came closer to Terry and Katherine. "Have them check the license plate number," he said and pulled the slip of paper with the license number out of his wallet and handed it to Terry.

The three of them waited, saying nothing as Terry relayed the letters and numbers through the radio. Katherine saw Vince close his eyes when the answer came back.

"That's it." He moved closer to Terry, practically yelling in the man's ear. "Can he see anyone in it? A girl? A teenaged girl?"

The helicopter was directly above them now, the pilot talking to Gordon. Katherine had a choice: stay where she was and hear what Sam said to Terry, or step back and find out what the helicopter pilot was telling Gordon. She stayed near Terry.

"No girl," Sam answered over the radio. "Only one occupant. Male. Early twenties. Window's open. I'm feeling for a pulse."

A moment of silence. Two. Three. Behind them cars passed or parked along the shoulder wherever possible. Passersby gawked while members of the fire and rescue departments congregated in small groups, waiting for orders. Gordon continued talking to the helicopter pilot, his words only occasionally distinguishable over the other noises. Katherine knew she was holding her breath. Finally Sam's voice came through

Terry's handheld radio.

"No pulse. In fact, the guy's in full rigor."

Since the entire muscle contracting process of rigor mortis took from eight to twelve hours, and could last another eighteen hours, the condition of the body meant if Misty Morgan did meet her on-line boyfriend at seven, as planned, they couldn't have had much time together.

"Uh oh," Sam Sutherland said from his location below.

"What?" Terry asked.

"This guy didn't die from a car accident."

Terry glanced at Katherine as he spoke into his radio. "How can you tell?"

"Because I'm looking at a bullet wound," Sam answered. "Terry, this guy's been shot. Tell Gordon he's got a murder to investigate."

Katherine heard Nanini catch his breath. The news had surprised her, too. An SUV going off the side of the road was bad enough, but a shooting?

"There should be a girl with that guy," Nanini said, his voice tight. "The driver of that Blazer was meeting a girl in Skagway this morning."

"Sam, are you sure there's no girl in the vehicle?" Terry Biscaro asked. "Maybe outside of the vehicle?"

"I don't see one."

"Have him look around," Nanini said. "Maybe she crawled away."

Maybe she's still alive, Katherine heard in Nanini's plea, but she knew there could be another answer. The girl's body could have been thrown out of the Blazer as it tumbled down the side of the mountain.

"I'm looking," came Sam's response. "Doesn't really look like it. Passenger door's jammed against a tree. Windows up. No way anyone got out that way and no sign anyone climbed across the body. Wait. Here's something . . ."

Sam paused, the silence coming from the two-way radio nerve-wracking. Finally Terry asked the question going through Katherine's head. "What is it, Sam?"

"It's a note . . . pinned to the guy's shirt."

"Can you read it without disturbing the crime scene?"

"I don't think so. Maybe. Give me a sec."

For Katherine, it seemed more like an eternity before Sam spoke again. "I read it, and it doesn't look good."

"What's it say?" Katherine and Vince asked almost in unison.

"It says," Sam answered, " 'Honey is sweet, money is sweeter. One hundred million, if you want to see her.' And then, below that, it says 'Hi Kit Kat' and there's a bloody fingerprint with two small smudges coming off of it. Don't know what that's supposed to be."

"A bee," whispered Katherine, the fear gripping her chest nearly taking her breath away.

CHAPTER TWENTY-FIVE

Vince felt as though someone had punched him in the stomach. *One hundred million if you want to see her.* It *was* a kidnapping. Both Bob and he had warned Tom that all the media attention he'd been receiving was putting him and his family in danger. He'd told Tom he needed to beef up his security, had urged both Crystal and Misty to take a bodyguard along on this cruise. He would have gone himself, if necessary. He could have put off his work in D.C. for a week or so.

But, no, Crystal had turned them down; had pooh-poohed the idea that either Misty or she might be in danger. And, for once, Misty had agreed with her stepmother.

He turned toward Katherine. Her face had lost its color, and she kept glancing around, as if looking for someone . . . or something.

"Kit Kat?" Vince said, watching how she reacted.

She visibly tensed.

"Is that note referring to you? Do you know who did this? Who has Misty?"

"I . . ." She looked down at the ground and shook her head. "No. It's just the . . ."

"You all right, Katherine?" Gordon asked, coming closer.

She faced him and nodded. "Yeah. Just a flashback to an old case."

"A case you were involved in?" Vince asked. "Kat *is* a nickname for Katherine."

Gordon answered for her. "Maybe so, but Officer Ward doesn't use a nickname."

"Still—"

Gordon cut him off. "The note was meant for the girl's father. Is there someone he knows, maybe someone who works for him, who's called Kat?"

"No one I can think of," Vince said. No one, at least, that Tom had ever mentioned to him.

The sergeant glanced up at the sky. "Even though we have this note, I'm having the helicopter look for the girl. She may have gotten away."

Vince didn't hold much hope. Nor did he believe the note had nothing to do with Officer Katherine Ward. Not after seeing her reaction.

As Gordon keyed in to talk to the helicopter pilot, Vince took the opportunity to question Katherine. "You said something when that note was read. What did you say?"

"Nothing important. I'm probably wrong."

"Wrong about what?"

For a moment, he didn't think she would answer. When she did, she led Vince a short distance away from Gordon and the others. "There's a man," she said in a hushed tone. "His name is Charles Bell. He used to keep bees in his backyard, so the media called him The Beekeeper."

"The Beekeeper?" Vince repeated, something familiar about the name.

Katherine nodded. "After he was arrested, he started making little drawings using a fingerprint with smudges to represent a bee. There were photos of them in the papers. Anyone could have seen them . . . anyone could be imitating him."

"Why was he arrested?"

Katherine looked at him, then away. "He murdered people. Kidnapped a teenager."

Vince didn't like hearing that. "So you think he's here?"

"He can't be." Her attitude became more positive, and she faced him again. "He's in a mental hospital in Michigan. A hospital for the criminally insane."

"Which makes this person a copycat." It happened, especially if the papers ran enough information about a criminal.

"It's got to be. This is probably some creep who remembered that kidnapping, heard your boss's daughter would be here, and . . ." She looked back toward Skagway.

"And what?" Vince asked.

"There's an Explorer in Dyea . . . I saw it this morning." She turned away from Vince and raised her voice. "Terry, have Sam check the Blazer. See if there are any signs of red paint on it. Maybe on the back bumper or the side of the vehicle."

They waited as the SAR volunteer relayed the message. Vince didn't understand the significance of the paint, but when the answer came back that there was red paint on the bumper, Gordon seemed to know what that meant. "I'll contact Jim," he told Katherine. "Have him bring the guy and the Explorer in."

"What about the note?" Vince asked. "Can they bring up the note?" He wanted to see it for himself.

Gordon hesitated, and then nodded. "I'll get someone down there to photograph the scene. As soon as we have that, I'll have them bring up the note."

A wrecker arrived, and Gordon went over to talk to the driver. Vince glanced at his watch. It was nearly nine o'clock. With the time changes he'd experienced in the last twenty-four hours, his internal clock was off kilter, and Alaska's long hours of daylight this time of the year weren't helping.

Yesterday, if he'd been in Seattle, not Washington, D.C., when Tom called, he could have gone straight to Tom's house, would have discovered Misty's plans last night, and would have been here before the cruise ship docked and Misty disembarked.

Then none of this would have happened.

Had someone known both Bob and he would be out of town when something could have been done to stop this tragedy? Or, was it all a coincidence? A terrible coincidence.

The thrum of helicopter blades made Vince look up. This was the second time the copter had passed over the area since they'd arrived. *Looking for the other body that was supposed to be in the Blazer. Looking for Misty.*

A waste of time, if that note was for real.

"Where are you, Misty?" he whispered.

CHAPTER TWENTY-SIX

The bed stopped creaking. No more moaning, grunts, or heavy breathing. Misty lay very still, kept her eyes closed, and forced her breathing to remain slow and regular. *Please think I'm asleep,* she prayed. *Please don't do that to me.*

She had no idea if it was day or night or how many hours a drug-induced sleep had held her captive. Like a cork bobbing along in a stream, her thoughts continually disappeared, then resurfaced. Each time she became aware of her surroundings, she fought to hold on to that clarity, afraid if she didn't, she might succumb and never awake.

Maybe that would have been better, she realized. *Total oblivion.*

At first Misty hadn't understood what was happening on the other bed. She'd thought she was dreaming when she heard a man's voice, so soft and seductive. She'd thought she was with Brian, that everything had been a terrible dream.

And then she shifted position.

Just slightly.

Just enough to feel the strips of cloth wrapped around her wrists and ankles tighten.

It was then that the girl on the next bed started pleading. Her "No, please no," had a panicky sound, and Misty had opened her eyes and looked in that direction, but only for a moment.

Only long enough to see that the bedroom door was open, allowing a diffused amount of light into the room. Long enough to see the ornately shaped metal bedposts above her head and below her feet, the nightstand in the space between her bed and the other bed, and the lamp on the stand. Long enough to see a girl lying naked on the other bed, her arms tied to the bedposts above her head, and a man crouched over the girl.

He didn't heed the girl's pleas, and in spite of his assertion that a flower needed pollination to survive, Misty wasn't sure if the girl would survive. Not the way she screamed when he drove his hips into hers.

Misty closed her eyes at that point, blocking out the sight, but she couldn't block out the sounds: the girl's moans and gasps, the sucking sound . . . his heavy breathing.

It seemed as if he would never stop.

Misty shivered with fear. Here she'd been afraid that Vince would stop her, that he would be the one who ruined her plans. She did everything she could think of to keep him away. Now she'd give anything for his protection.

Who was this monster who killed and raped?

Hot tears gathered under her lids, a tightening in her chest choking off her breath. This was not what she'd planned.

The other girl was crying now, soft, gulping sobs. Misty heard the creak of bed springs and realized he was climbing off the other bed. Her senses on alert, she held her breath and listened.

Even with her eyes closed, she knew he was standing beside her, staring at her. Could he tell she was awake? Did he know she'd heard him? Heard them?

Misty had no idea who the other girl was, where they were, or why. The girl's voice had sounded young. Scared.

Sex was supposed to be fun, something to be enjoyed. At least that's what Misty's friends had told her . . . what she was supposed to discover with Brian. The way the girl had begged this man to stop, Misty knew she wasn't having fun.

A virgin. The girl had to have been a virgin. Misty's friends had said it hurt the first time, but only for a while and then it got better. It hadn't sounded like it got better, not to Misty.

Well, when her turn came, she wouldn't cry or scream. She wouldn't give the asshole that pleasure.

How long did it take before a man wanted to do it again? she wondered. How long before he climbed onto her bed.

Misty knew he'd come. The heavy breathing had turned rough and ragged, and then there was the smell.

She knew that smell. Crystal sometimes carried it on her nightgown when she came out of the bedroom early in the morning. At least, she used to. For some time now Misty hadn't noticed the smell, hadn't seen her father look at Crystal with that stupid, hungry look he'd had the first few months after the wedding.

A hand touched her arm, and Misty gave an involuntary gasp and opened her eyes.

"It's okay," the man said, his voice once again as seductive as it had been earlier. "I'm not going to touch you."

"You're already touching me," she said, and jerked her arm as far back as the binding on her wrist allowed. "Do you know who my father is?"

"Of course I know who your father is." He chuckled. "Why else do you think you're here? Your father is a man who'd better be willing to pay a hundred million dollars for your safe return."

A hundred million dollars? Misty groaned. Would her dad pay that much for her? Did he have that much money?

How many times had Vince told her she had to be careful, that someone might see her as a way to get to her father's money? How many times had she laughed at him and told him to stop being so paranoid?

"Vince will get you," she said, for once wanting Vince Nanini to poke his nose in her business.

"Vince?" The man's voice was calm, his hand once again

making contact with her arm. "Oh, I don't think so. And if he should show up, I'll take care of him just like I did that kid you were with. Do you need to go to the bathroom?"

She almost said yes, then stopped herself.

"She's already been," he said, when she hesitated. "You were still asleep when I took her, and I didn't want to wake you."

By "she" he meant the other girl. The one he'd just raped. The one Misty couldn't really see—not clearly—but could hear crying. "Is that how you do it?" Misty asked. "Take the girl to the bathroom first so she won't pee on you when you rape her?"

"I told you, I'm not going to touch you." Again, he chuckled. "I have one for the money, and one for the honey."

"You're a sicko," Misty said, then wished she'd kept her mouth shut. Nothing like stating the obvious to a man who had her tied to a bed—a man who'd already killed one person that she knew of.

Instead of getting angry, he laughed. "Oh, no, I'm cured. That's what the doctors said. So, do you need to go?"

Chapter Twenty-Seven

Katherine tried to keep the terror racing through her under control. Over and over, she told herself it couldn't be *him*, not here in Alaska. It was a copycat, just a coincidence that some creep had kidnapped a girl in Skagway . . . had signed a ransom note with her nickname and a bee symbol.

Except, she didn't believe in coincidences.

As far as she knew, the only people still alive in Skagway who knew about her past were her grandfather and the chief. She'd had to tell him when she interviewed for the job. Gordon didn't know, nor did Alice, nor Phil, nor any of the other officers and staff. And up until this evening, her grandfather hadn't mentioned the incident to anyone. At least, she didn't think he had.

So who would know?

Katherine forced her mind back to the months after her release. The media had hounded her, which was why her grandparents had decided to make Skagway their permanent home rather than a summer residence. Once the trial ended, they'd officially changed her name and gone into seclusion. Even when she returned to Michigan, something she felt she had to do, no one called her Kit Kat. All through college, the police academy, and her three years as a public safety officer, she was known as Katherine Ward. Katherine, not Kathy, or Kate, or Kat, or Kit Kat.

So, who around here would know her connection to The Beekeeper?

She hoped the note would provide an answer to that question. Every nerve on edge, she waited with the others for Sam Sutherland to climb back up from the Blazer.

"It's in here," Sam said, and handed an evidence bag to Gordon. "It was pinned to the victim's shirt, right over the guy's heart. I used gloves to remove it, so any fingerprints you find should be the killer's."

Gordon also slipped on latex gloves before touching the note, and Katherine edged close to his side so she could look over his shoulder. Nanini, on the other hand, seemed more interested in questioning the rescue worker. "There are definitely no signs of a girl?"

"None that I could see, but there are other volunteers down there now, looking for her. I'm going for a cup of coffee." Sam raised his voice so Gordon and Katherine would hear him. "If you need me, I'll be over there."

He motioned toward a blue pickup parked a ways from where the guardrail was broken. The pickup's driver had let down the tailgate and set out a pump pot of coffee, along with Styrofoam cups, and a box of doughnuts. Several of the volunteers were already gathered around the area, and Sam soon joined them.

Gordon studied the note for what seemed an eternity, keeping it close to his body so she couldn't get a clear view. Finally, he showed it to her.

The note was written on brown paper, approximately three inches wide and five inches long. It looked like a torn section of a grocery bag, the edges ragged. A pen had been used to write the short message, but the mark below the written words was obviously a bloody fingerprint, the center of the print clear, but the sides smeared, making it look like a bug . . . or a bee.

Katherine couldn't stop the shudder of fear that coursed through her body, her stomach twisting into a knot that drove bile into her throat. She wanted to crumple the paper, get into her Tahoe and drive as far from the area as she could possibly go. She wanted to scream.

This had to be a bad dream—like so many she'd had over the years. It couldn't be real; couldn't be him. Yet, she knew the note was real, and that she couldn't cut and run. She had a grandfather to take care of, a job to do.

"Is that the same kind of mark as that bee guy you told me about made, or do you think it's a copy?" Nanini asked, his nearness surprising her. Caught up in the grip of fear, she'd forgotten he was around.

Years of police training kicked in, along with the hours she'd spent in therapy, learning how to control the fear, and Katherine answered with as little emotion as she could muster.

"I can't tell for sure."

"You said this Beekeeper guy was in a mental hospital."

"He was." She'd been there for the sentencing, had heard the judge. But she knew about criminals and life sentences. Fifteen years and they were back on the street, back committing crimes. Killing people. Raping young girls.

Katherine shuddered and squeezed her eyes tight. "Sarah."

"What about Sarah?" Gordon asked.

"She's missing, too."

"She might be at that party over in Dyea."

Katherine hoped so.

"How much did this Beekeeper guy ask for when he kidnapped the teenager?" Vince asked.

He asked for my body and soul, Katherine thought. "Nothing," she answered. "At least no money."

"It was a girl he kidnapped?"

"Yes," she answered, trying to keep all emotion out of her voice. "He broke into her house during the night, abducted her, and kept her his prisoner for just under nine months . . . until someone recognized her and reported it to the police."

"Are you talking about Elizabeth Smart?" Vince asked.

"No." Though Katherine had studied the Smart case, looking, she supposed, for some connection between that girl's abductor and Charles Bell. She hadn't found many similarities. "Bell wasn't as kind to his victims as Elizabeth Smart's abductor," Katherine said, knowing what she was about to tell him was all public record. "He wasn't even as nice as Michael Devlin, who kidnapped those boys in St. Louis. Or Ariel Castro, who held those three girls for a decade. As the prosecutor pointed out during the trial, Charles Bell not only kidnapped the girl, he purposefully eliminated her family."

"I remember that case," Gordon said. "Didn't he kill the parents and a younger brother?"

Katherine nodded, a lump in her throat stopping her from saying more. She stepped away from the two men, closer to the edge of the road, and stared down at the valley. She hoped they would think she was following what was happening below, and that neither man would see the tears forming in her eyes as she tried to push back the memories. *You can't change the past.* That's what her therapist had said, over and over during their sessions. *You can't change the past, so focus on the future.*

"You used to live in Michigan," Gordon said behind her. "Any idea what hospital this guy's supposed to be in?"

She nodded and wiped the tears from her eyes.

"Then we need to call," he said. "See if he's still there. If he is, then we know we're dealing with a copycat."

"Use my phone," Nanini insisted, already in the process of unclipping his from his belt. "It's satellite. It should work up here."

CHAPTER TWENTY-EIGHT

Vince expected the sergeant to make the call. Instead Katherine took the phone. She didn't call information for the hospital's number; simply started punching numbers as she walked over to the side of the Tahoe. Curious, he waited until she turned her back to him, then followed her, stopping close enough to hear her say, "I need to talk to Dr. Bremner . . . Or Dr. Redmond. Whichever one's on duty tonight."

That she knew the names of the doctors told him this wasn't the first time she'd called, and, as she waited for a response, she reminded Vince of a taut spring—motionless energy. Her voice had an edge that relayed an internal turmoil.

"I don't care if it's after hours," she groused. "Tell him Katherine Ann McMann is on the phone."

Vince frowned. She'd said "Katherine Ann McMann," not Katherine Ward. Dammit all, he did remember the case. Not from when it happened but from what he heard later.

He'd been overseas when Katherine Ann McMann was kidnapped. Out of touch with the media. Fighting terrorists, not following home-grown abductions. By the time he was stateside, another kidnapping was making headlines.

Katherine Ann McMann.

Yes, the details were coming back.

While working for the FBI, he'd assisted on some kidnapping cases, especially if they involved the Internet. His job was to track the predators and relay the information to the agents.

They sometimes mentioned other cases . . . other victims.

McMann.

The bits and pieces he recalled weren't good.

There'd been questions about the girl's complicity in the crime. She'd been cleared, classified as a victim, but some of the agents weren't convinced. Was it rape or consensual sex? Word was she actually tried to protect her kidnapper when the police arrived.

The Beekeeper.

Had he missed that name this morning when checking Misty's posts? Did she make arrangements to meet someone besides Brian Bane? Sixteen-year-olds could be so smart and so naïve.

Not that the adults in Misty's life had helped the situation.

Her father was way too involved with his business. Her mother had died. Her stepmother was too self-centered to care about a teenager. More than once Vince had told Tom he should spend more time with Misty. Building a successful business wasn't as important as a child. Vince knew that from personal experience. He'd been focused on his career when his little girl was diagnosed with cancer. He barely had a chance to know her.

Vince had tried to offer Misty some of the attention she was missing from Tom and Crystal, but Misty had rebelled. She didn't want his advice, acted bored when he tried to show her self-defense moves, and told him she didn't need a "birddog."

Birddog? What she needed was a keeper.

He'd been angry when he discovered Misty's plan to run away with the Bane kid. Running away no longer sounded all that bad.

Katherine glanced over her shoulder, looking directly at him, frowned, and opened her mouth as if to say something. Then immediately she switched her attention back to the phone.

"Good," she said. "Yes, get him."

Soon we'll know, Vince thought, and wondered if Misty had remembered any of the self-defense moves he'd taught her. If only she'd taken him seriously, taken the danger she might be in seriously. But, no. She'd flirted with him when he tried to teach her ways to defend herself. To please her father, she went through the motions, but she never truly made an effort to learn how to maim or escape.

"Come on," Misty had said. "Get real. You want me to ram my fingers into a man's eyes? That would be like . . . I don't know . . . yucky sick."

He was the one who felt "yucky sick" now. If only he'd gotten here earlier. If only he'd been there to stop her. She would have been angry and frustrated, but she would be physically all right . . . And that kid in the Blazer wouldn't have a bullet in him.

"Dr. Redmond," Vince heard Katherine say, and he stopped thinking of what might have been and concentrated on what Katherine was saying.

"I'm calling about Charles Bell." Her voice sounded strained. "How is he doing?"

Vince moved closer. He could read the tension in her body, saw her take in a deep breath as she listened to the doctor's response. She seemed to pale, and he doubted she was even aware that she was shaking her head. Her body language told him she was distressed; nevertheless, he was surprised when she started shouting, her voice going shrill.

"God damn you. How could you? You were to call me. Tell me if this ever happened."

The outburst over, she turned quiet and listened. Vince watched her chew on her lower lip, close her eyes, and take in a deep breath. By the time she hung up, she had her cop face on. Posture rigid, she turned toward him and said, "He's out."

"So he's here?"

"Seems so."

She handed back his phone and started toward her sergeant. Vince grabbed her wrist, pulling her back. "Before you talk to him, I want the full story."

A twist of her arm, and she was loose, facing him. "What do you mean?"

"You know what I mean. McMann. I remember that name. You were the girl."

She looked away. "I need to tell Gordon what's up."

"And I need to know what your involvement is in this."

"My involvement?" She looked back at him, glaring. "I am not involved."

"What about that note?"

"I didn't know they'd released him."

"Where would he take Misty?"

"I don't know." She looked up the highway, then back at him. "We checked if a blonde teenager crossed the border, but Charles could have put a wig on her, could have done something to disguise her looks. I need to go to the Canadian customs station at Fraser, talk to them."

She pointed toward Gordon. "Tell him I'll be right back."

Vince had no intention of staying where he was. Before she had a chance to drive off, he slid in on the passenger side of the Tahoe. "Get out," Katherine ordered. "This is police business."

"This is my best friend's daughter," he said. "And we're wasting time. Let's go."

She hesitated, then shifted into drive. "Put on your seatbelt."

As they headed up the highway, toward the Canadian border, Vince pushed for answers. "Tell me what this man, this Beekeeper, is like."

She glanced his way, her solemn expression masking all emotion, then returned her attention to the curving road. "What's there to tell? He's a monster, and they've let him loose."

"Why did he take Misty?"

She shook her head. "I don't know why. Maybe when she got off the ship, she smiled at him. Said hello. With people like Charles, that's sometimes all it takes."

"What caused him to take you?"

Katherine glanced his way. "Oh, that's an easy one to answer."

"So, what's the answer?"

"He took me, he said, because I looked like his daughter."

CHAPTER TWENTY-NINE

Katherine refused to say anything more. For nearly seventeen years she'd kept her past a secret. She wasn't about to tell all, especially not to a civilian. Besides, Vince wouldn't understand. There were times when even she didn't understand what had happened or why.

At the Canadian customs station, Katherine pulled a yellowed, folded, newspaper clipping out of her wallet and showed it to the two constables on duty. "That was taken sixteen years ago," she said. "He's aged since then. When I saw him five years ago, at an evaluation hearing, he'd gained weight, had some gray in his hair, and wrinkles near his mouth and eyes."

Charles Bell had been in his early thirties and oh so good looking the first time she saw him standing by his mailbox. Her mother had warned her about talking to strangers, but this was a neighbor, not a stranger, and the reason they'd moved to this neighborhood—according to her parents—was it was safer than the one they'd left.

Safer. Now that was a joke. And she'd been so foolish. Foolish and angry.

Maybe her parents were happy with the new house, but she wasn't. She'd had to leave her friends, was in a new school, and her mother refused to let her paint her bedroom purple. When Charles asked how she liked her new home, she'd been more than willing to tell him. And, unlike her busy parents, he took the time and listened.

125

In some ways the media was right. She did have a crush on him. But it was one thing to be fourteen and have a crush on a good-looking neighbor and quite another to go through what she went through.

They called him The Beekeeper, but he was more like a spider, slowly drawing her into his web. He wasn't outside every day when she came home from school, but, looking back, she realized he was out there more than any other neighbor. Always smiling. Always asking her questions.

Was school getting any better? Did both of her parents work? Did she have a boyfriend?

When she saw him unloading insulation from his van, she asked him what he was building, never imagining it was for the cell he created in his basement—her home for eight months and twenty days. She thought it was wonderful when he told her he was a contractor. She thought it would please her mother that she'd found someone who could do the renovations her parents had been talking about.

Naïvely she brought him into their house, showed him where her parents slept, where her brother slept, and where she slept. Their house's floor plan was just like his, he said. Even the security system was the same.

He told her he could do the work; but her mother hired someone else. For almost nine months that poor man was the prime suspect in the slaying of her family and her abduction. His fingerprints were all through the house. Charles Bell wore gloves.

Charles wasn't dumb. Not then, not now. He could have changed his appearance since she last saw him. Grown a beard. Dyed his hair.

She gave that information to the Canadian constables. They couldn't be positive, but they didn't think they'd seen anyone who matched Bell's description.

Howie had gone off-duty, but the pictures of Misty that both Vince and Alice had faxed to the station were posted on the wall. Vince asked them to imagine her with different colored hair. No luck there, either.

As Katherine led the way back to the Tahoe, she glanced over the craggy landscape that surrounded them. The gold seekers back in 1896 had had a rough time crossing these mountains; how could a man who'd spent the last fifteen years in a hospital and a sixteen-year-old girl who didn't like to hike handle the terrain?

"He could have found a way to sneak across the border," she said, "but my bet is he's in Skagway."

"Why do you say that?" Vince asked.

"Because he kept me in the basement only four houses away from where I lived."

"And no one knew?"

"No one. The room was soundproof. The one window was covered, and, in the beginning, he rarely turned on the light. For the first two weeks of my captivity, I was in total darkness except when he came to see me."

Just talking about it brought back the memories—and the terror. A tightening in her groin reminded her of how she reacted whenever she heard his footsteps coming down the stairs, while the sickening sensation in her stomach mimicked the effect of his touch.

"Katherine?"

She blinked, shaking off the image of that room and the memories of what he did to her. Vince Nanini was staring at her, a concerned look on his face.

"Are you all right?" he asked.

"I . . . I'm—" She forced herself to take a deep breath and shove the past back into the recesses of her mind. "I'm okay," she finally said and slid behind the steering wheel and started the engine.

She needed to approach this as a police officer, not as a woman terrified of the man who'd changed her life completely. She needed to control her emotions.

"Any houses with basements around Skagway?" Vince asked as he buckled his seatbelt.

"A few. Mostly the newer ones that have been built outside of town."

"I don't see her going quietly," he said, almost to himself. "Not Misty. She's a fighter. If there's half a chance, she'll try to get away."

Katherine understood his hope. She also knew the reality. "He'll threaten her. He killed that kid in front of her as a warning."

"He threatened you?"

She nodded.

"So where's he have Misty?"

She glanced his way. "You think I know?"

"I don't know what I think. But you know Skagway. Where would a man—a stranger to the area—take a teenaged girl? We had enough trouble finding a place for Crystal to stay. Where would he find a hideout?"

A logical question, she decided. "I don't know where he would take her. That's what we have to figure out."

"Do people rent out houses and apartments during the summer season?"

"Some do." She headed the Tahoe back down the Klondike Highway. *Call the landlords,* she told herself. At this hour most would be in bed, but time was of the essence.

She slowed as they once again approached the spot where the Blazer had gone over the edge. Before she stopped, she said, "When a child is taken, the first forty-eight hours are the most

128

important. In my case, Charles broke into our house on a Friday night. No one knew what had happened until Monday morning, when my parents didn't show up for work and my brother and I weren't at school. If Misty and that young man down there met in Skagway this morning and took off right away, we've already lost more than a quarter of that time. We need to get things rolling as quickly as we can."

CHAPTER THIRTY

Gordon watched Katherine's Tahoe slow and come to a stop. "She's here now," he said into the satellite phone he held. "I'll tell her, but she's not going to be happy."

He listened to the response to his statement, all the while watching Katherine and Vince Nanini step out of the patrol unit and start his way. "I understand," he said. "Yes, helluva mess, but I can handle it. You just concentrate on getting better. Goodbye, sir."

Gordon handed the phone back to the SAR volunteer standing next to him and dismissed the man. He didn't want others overhearing what he had to say to Katherine. As it was, she would be upset when he issued the chief's order, but she'd really be angry if he also, inadvertently, revealed her secret.

Learning why Officer Katherine Ward would know so much about The Beekeeper had stunned Gordon, but now that he did know, her behavior around him and others made sense. When she first joined the Skagway police department, he'd thought her reticence to talk about her past was a snub. And he certainly couldn't understand why she wouldn't give Phil the time of day. Gordon knew the officer had the hots for Katherine.

At one point he'd thought she might be a lesbian, but her behavior didn't fit that concept either. In fact, thinking back over the three years he'd known her, he was surprised she functioned as well as she did. He couldn't imagine going through the terror the chief had described: seeing her parents and younger brother killed, being held hostage for nearly nine months. Constantly raped.

Ten years her senior, Gordon was living in Fairbanks, just beginning his career as a police officer, when Katherine's grandparents permanently moved to Skagway, bringing her with them. She had moved back to Michigan by the time Gordon became a part of the Skagway police department. He didn't know anything about Katherine Ward until three years ago when the chief said they were hiring a former resident who was coming to them with three years experience on the Kalamazoo force.

Alice had said she remembered Katherine as an angry and confused teenager and hoped she'd changed. Alice knew everything that went on in Skagway.

Gordon wondered if she knew about Katherine's past. The real story.

And what was the real story today?

Was Katherine involved in this homicide and kidnapping?

The chief had said he didn't think so, but Gordon wasn't so sure. If she'd come right out and told him how and why she knew this Bell guy, maybe he wouldn't have his suspicions. But she hadn't been up-front with him. As usual, she'd skirted the truth.

He had no choice but to take her off the case.

"So where did you go?" Gordon asked the moment Katherine was within hearing distance.

"To talk to Canadian customs. As soon as I heard Bell was no longer being held in Michigan, I wanted to show them his picture."

"Which you just happened to have with you."

He could tell he'd taken her by surprise, that she didn't know how to respond. He answered for her. "One of the EMTs brought up his satellite phone. I talked to the chief. He told me everything."

"Oh." Her posture alone showed her tension, her back so straight she could have passed inspection with flying colors. "I guess I should have said something."

"I guess you should have."

"How's the chief doing?"

"Fine. Getting antsy to get out of there." Gordon could have added that he, personally, wished the chief was out of the hospital and able to come back to Skagway and take on the responsibility of this murder and possible kidnapping. But, since that wasn't going to happen, it was his duty to carry the load.

"The constables we talked to are sure Bell hasn't crossed into Canada," she said. "Vince and I were just talking about where to look, and I thought—"

Gordon stopped her with the lift of his hand. "You're off the case."

Katherine's reaction was immediate. "Gordon, no. I can handle this. I've got to. He's here because of me. I'm sure of that."

"This isn't negotiable," Gordon said. "The chief said to send you home, and I agree."

"You can't do that." She looked at Vince, at the search and rescue volunteers still working near the edge of the road, and then back at him. "You need me. We're shorthanded as it is."

"If you want to do something, find Phil. Then write up a full report about this Bell person."

"You want me off because you're afraid I'll try to help Bell." She was practically in tears.

He didn't say anything.

"I don't care what the papers said. I didn't help him. I was the victim."

"Which is exactly why you're being taken off the case," he said. "You know as well as I do that's procedure if an officer has a personal connection. You wouldn't want a good defense lawyer getting him off because of a technicality, would you?"

"No, of course not, but I can't just sit around and wait for you to find him."

"You're going to have to, Katherine. Now, go. Check on that other girl you think is missing. Find Phil."

"What about sending out Amber alerts? Contacting the state troopers and the National Park Service? Seeing if Haines can help?"

"That's being done as we speak." Not that he thought the small police department in Haines could spare any officers. And, even if they could, logistics simply didn't work.

"I could—"

"No!" he said before she went on. "You're off the case."

CHAPTER THIRTY-ONE

Vince watched Katherine stalk over to her Tahoe and get in. She gunned the engine and spun the tires as she took off. He'd thought about going with her, but if she was off the case, there wasn't much sense in doing so. He'd seen her shocked reaction when she realized what the mark on the note meant, heard her anger when she learned that Charles Bell was no longer in the mental hospital. Either she was a fantastic actress or she wasn't involved with Misty's kidnapping.

He looked back at the area where the Blazer had gone over the side. Crime-scene tape now blocked off a portion of the road and most of the shoulder. The note had indicated this Beekeeper guy had Misty, but it could be a bluff.

Vince turned to Sergeant Landros. "Could you tell if he took her out of the Blazer before it was pushed over the side?"

The sergeant hesitated, and Vince hoped he wouldn't be a tight ass about talking to someone not in law enforcement. Besides, he didn't want details, just assurance that Misty was still alive.

A slight nod was the man's first tell. Then a relaxing of the shoulders and a deep breath. "We're pretty sure she wasn't in the vehicle when it went over," Landros said. He motioned toward the dirt and gravel of the road's shoulder. "We pretty much destroyed any ground evidence when we arrived, but we did find what looks to be a crushed hypodermic needle."

Which meant Misty was drugged, assuming the needle wasn't

simply one that someone tossed out when driving by. "Any idea what Bell may have used on her?" Vince asked.

This time Landros shook his head. "Once we get the pieces to the crime lab in Anchorage, someone should be able to tell us what was in it. But that's going to take a while."

"So you're thinking he shot Bane, tranquilized Misty, transferred her to his vehicle, and then pushed the Blazer over the side."

"Looks like it."

"Damn." Vince shook his head and turned away, looking down the highway toward Skagway.

"I assume you'll let the girl's father and stepmother know what's happened and about the ransom demand," Gordon said.

Vince nodded. "If someone can give me a ride back to Skagway, I'll let Crystal know, and we'll call Tom."

"One of the volunteers can take you down. Once you've informed the family, it would be helpful if you'd stop by the station and give our dispatcher any information about the girl that might help with an Amber alert."

"What about the other girl?" Vince asked. "Katherine seems to think this guy might have her, too."

"Let's hope not," Landros said and waved toward a group of volunteers standing around the coffee dispenser on the tailgate of the blue truck.

Chapter Thirty-Two

The hazy, doped-up feeling Misty had experienced for most of the day—at least what she thought was a day—was finally gone. She was glad, but clarity brought reality, along with fear, anger, and even hunger. She'd pulled on the cloths binding her wrists and ankles until her skin was raw. She'd tried slipping her hands out, tried breaking the metal posts she was tied to, and tried twisting her body so she could gnaw on the cloth. Nothing worked.

Over time, the other girl's sobs had slowly subsided until they'd turned into sniffling and an occasional whimper. Their captor had closed and locked the door when he left, putting the room back into total darkness. How long he would be gone, Misty didn't know.

"Hey," she said softly. "You over there. Are you okay? I mean, kinda?"

"Yeah . . . Kinda," came the quavering response.

The voice sounded young, and Misty wondered if the girl was one of the kids she'd met on the cruise ship. "What's your name?" she asked.

"Sarah. Sarah Wilson."

Misty didn't remember a Sarah. She'd been hanging out with a Heather, a Greg, a Lisa, and a Britany, but there were other kids on the ship. A bunch of younger ones they did their best to ignore. "How old are you?"

"Fourteen."

No one Misty would have paid attention to. "So, were you on the *Holiday Festival?*"

"No." The girl hiccupped, and then sniffed. "What's your name?"

"Misty. Misty Morgan. Are you still tied up?"

"Yeah. You?"

"Yes." He'd untied her when he took her to the bathroom. She should have tried to escape then, but her legs had been so wobbly, he'd had to help her walk out of the bedroom and down a short hallway to the bathroom. Even then he hadn't completely freed her. All he'd done was undo the knots around the metal posts. He'd left the strips of sheeting around her wrists and ankles.

"Does your blanket smell?" Sarah asked.

"Yeah. Smells old. Yucky. Like the blankets at my grand-mother's house. Have you tried to get loose?"

"A little, but every time I do, the cloth around my wrists just seems to get tighter."

"Same here. If I could get one near my mouth, maybe I could chew it off."

"I don't have any clothes on. Do you?"

"No." Not that Misty would let that stop her from escaping.

The girl sniffed again. "I shouldn't have stopped and talked to him. I should have just walked by, pretended I didn't even hear him."

Misty heard the guilt in the girl's words. "What did he say?"

"He asked if I lived on the block, and if I knew which house the policewoman lived in. My mother's always telling me to be careful, not to talk to strangers. So why did I?"

"I keep wondering why I didn't run when I had the chance," Misty said. "Or fight. I've had a guy—an ex-Marine—teach me self-defense, but do you think I used anything I knew? No; I just sat there and let him jab me with that needle."

"Was that what it was?" Sarah sniffed. "He showed me a mask . . . said he was in a play about the three bears. He seemed kinda weird, and I started to walk away. All I remember is hearing the car door open, a hand going over my mouth, and something sharp against my neck. I . . ."

Sarah didn't finish, soft sobs replacing words, and Misty closed her eyes. They'd been drugged. But with what? And how long had it been since he'd opened the truck door and jabbed her with that needle?

She had no sense of time. She did recall starting to wake up and hearing him say, "Too soon." After that, he rubbed something cold over her skin, and, once again, she felt something prick her skin. She must have fallen back asleep after that.

Now that she was awake, she wished she were asleep, that this would turn out to be a terrible nightmare.

"Mama. I want my mama," Sarah sobbed.

"Me, too," Misty agreed, though she knew there was no way her mother could come.

Would her father? Would he pay that much money for her? Last time they talked, all he kept telling her was he was busy and didn't have time to talk. He was always too busy for her, never around. A daughter was a burden. You didn't pay millions of dollars for something you didn't want.

"*TSTL. Too stupid to live.*" That's what her dad said about people who did dumb things. She'd been stupid. Would he let her die?

A knot of fear twisted in her gut. The guy said he wouldn't touch her, wouldn't do to her what he'd done to Sarah, but what if her father didn't pay? What then?

"Sex with a guy," Jasmine, her best friend back home, had said, "is like nothing you can do by yourself. Just wait, Misty. You're gonna love it."

Misty had been going to "do it" with Brian. Back in May, when she turned sixteen, she'd decided she didn't want to be a virgin all of her life. She'd already met Brian on-line. He was cute. Older. He thought she was older, too, and he didn't question her age when she suggested spending the summer traveling across Canada. "Sounds like fun," he'd typed.

It would have pissed her dad off royally. Would have pissed Vince off, too. He was always telling her to be careful, to be smart, especially when it came to guys. "They'll promise you anything," he was always saying, "but they only want one thing."

Vince had been a super pest ever since that article about her dad came out. Old Baldy kept telling her, "Be careful who you hang with. Be careful who you talk to. Be careful, be careful . . . be careful." She told him she got the message. He told her if she ever needed help, to give a yell.

"Vince!" she yelled into the darkness.

"Don't!" Sarah begged, the plea almost a sob. "Don't yell. Don't make any noise that will bring him back. It . . . it hurt. It hurt a lot."

Misty was sorry she had yelled. Talk about stupid. And now she'd upset Sarah. "I hear it gets better after the first time," she said, hoping that might comfort the younger girl.

"I don't want it to get better. I don't want it to happen. Never, ever again."

Misty had heard the way he'd panted and grunted. The bed shaking. Sarah crying. It didn't sound sexy, not the way it was described in romance novels or shown in the movies. Where was the high Jasmine had talked about? The thrill? The excitement?

"What if I have a baby?" Sarah said and hiccupped. "I don't want a baby. I have a brother and a sister I have to take care of. Katherine says I should go to college, and—"

"Who's Katherine?" Misty asked.

"She's one of Mama's friends. She was gonna pay me to fix

139

dinner for her grandfather. All I had to do was spend some time with him. She's gonna wonder why I never showed up."

"Think she'll report it to the police?" Misty asked, hoping a call from Sarah's mother's friend would start a search.

"She *is* the police."

For the first time since coming out of her stupor, Misty felt hope. "Won't she come looking for you?"

"I don't know. Maybe. Do you know where we are?"

"In a house." She'd figured that much out when he took her to the bathroom. "But where the house is, I don't know." The bathroom didn't have a window she could look out. "I think he's covered the windows with something to block out the light and sound. I can't hear anything, can you?"

They both stopped talking and listened. It was then that Misty heard a key slip into the lock on the door.

CHAPTER THIRTY-THREE

10:00 P.M.

He's here. In Skagway. Here for me.

Knuckles white, Katherine forced a surge of bile back down her throat as she sped toward her grandfather's house.

Dammit all, I saw him. Looked right at him when I left for work.

The figure she'd spotted in the red Explorer had to have been Charles. She didn't know how long he'd been in Skagway, but he knew where she lived. May have been watching her for days. Weeks.

While watching for her, did Charles see Sarah? Did he have her as well as Misty?

Mattie Wilson couldn't afford to pay a ransom, but Sarah was fourteen. The same age Katherine Ann McMann was when Charles took her. God, she hoped she was wrong, that he didn't have Sarah.

Please be here, Katherine prayed as she parked her cruiser in front of the closed garage door.

"Poppa?" she yelled as she entered the house. "Sarah?"

"What?" she heard from the living room. "That you, Katherine?"

"It's me." She felt some relief as she came up beside her grandfather. He, at least, was all right. But she saw no signs of the teenager. No extra dishes or glasses by the sink, no soda bottle or fast food wrappers in the trash. "Did Sarah ever show up?"

"Sarah?"

Katherine could tell he'd once again forgotten Sarah was supposed to be there. "Never mind." She placed a hand on his shoulder, feeling how thin he'd become in the last few years, the line of his collarbone easy to trace beneath his lightweight flannel shirt. "How's the game going?"

Her grandfather nodded toward the TV, a commercial in progress. "I think it's over."

"You ready for bed?"

"I suppose." He pushed himself up from the chair, groaning as he did. "I think I fell asleep while I was sitting there."

Not an uncommon occurrence lately. His body and mind were shutting down. His loss of memory was the saddest part of the disease. She knew it was foolish to ask; nevertheless, she did. "Poppa, do you remember someone calling about Charles Bell? Someone from a hospital in Michigan?"

He stood next to his chair, frowning. "Bell? Why does that name sound familiar?"

"He's the man who kidnapped me," she said. "Back when I was a teenager." She didn't mention Bell was the man who killed her parents and brother. No need to remind him of that. "He's supposed to be in a mental hospital, but they let him out."

"Bell," her grandfather repeated and shook his head. "I don't think so."

"How about a letter?" Katherine knew her grandfather was even less likely to remember a letter, but just in case. "The doctor said they sent a letter." One informing her of Bell's pending released. "I don't remember seeing it."

The blank look in her grandfather's eyes told her he had no idea what she was talking about.

"Ah, never mind," she said. "It's not important."

Except, it was. If she'd received the letter Redmond said he sent, she would have opened it right away. Would have hoped it announced Bell's death. And, once she learned he was going to be released, she would have voiced her objections; would have given dozens of reasons why he should never, ever be released.

Now it was too late to object. Now Bell was out; was here in Skagway.

She glanced toward the kitchen. "While you get ready, I want to make a phone call. Okay?"

"Sure. I'm fine." He smiled and gave her arm a pat. "I've been putting myself to bed for a long time. I can take care of myself."

She watched him shuffle toward the bedroom, a lump in her throat. For years her grandparents had been the element of stability in her life, there when she needed them. They understood her during the traumatic years after her rescue, encouraged her when she proclaimed she needed to go back to Michigan, needed to face her demons. And, they welcomed her when she returned. Now her grandmother was gone and her grandfather was slowly slipping away, both in mind and body. She didn't want to lose him. He was her last link to the past, her family.

A tear slipped down her cheek, and she quickly wiped it away and headed for the phone.

Katherine tried the Wilson number three times, getting a busy signal each time. Finally she gave up. A quick good-bye to her grandfather, and she headed back to her cruiser.

The Wilson house was a mere block away, and, during the short drive, Katherine hoped more than anything that Sarah would be there . . . or that Mattie Wilson would know where her daughter was. Dealing with an irresponsible teenager would be far better than what Katherine feared.

At least her parents didn't have to endure the agony of

wondering what had happened to their daughter. No dealing with news reporters asking stupid and rude questions. She hated how, at a time when parents needed the support of friends and family, reporters wanted to know everything about their lives, asked stupid questions, and often blamed the parents for the tragedy.

Blamed the victim.

Like vultures the media had buzzed around her after she was found, dropping innuendoes about her relationship with Bell, and accusing her outright of encouraging him. Only after she changed her name and left Michigan did the stories stop.

For years her grandparents had spent a few weeks each summer in the yellow and green cottage on Skagway's Main Street. When they moved in as year-round residents with their teenage granddaughter, people were told her parents and brother had died in a car crash. If anyone knew the truth, they said nothing. And Katherine said nothing. Over time, the terror subsided. Life went on. Occasionally a nightmare brought back the memories; especially whenever she heard of other teenagers being kidnapped and held captive.

She'd silently celebrated their rescue and understood their anguish, but she'd never reached out to any of them, never shared her experience. All she wanted was to forget it had ever happened. But, now she couldn't. Now Bell was here, and a teenager was missing.

Maybe two.

Once again terror clutched her heart and made her hands shake.

In front of the Wilson house, Katherine took in a deep breath, forcing herself to control the fear. Mattie Wilson came out the front door even before Katherine stepped away from her cruiser. From the look on the woman's face, Katherine knew Sarah wasn't home.

Half Tlingit, Mattie had the features of Skagway's "First People"—the broad nose, high cheekbones, and narrow eyes. "Have you found her?" Mattie asked, her voice begging for comfort.

"Not yet." Katherine wasn't about to mention Bell. Not until they were sure he had Sarah. "We're going to put out an Amber alert, so I need information from you. Do you know what she was wearing when she left? And do you have a recent picture?"

"Yes. Yes, of course." Mattie turned and started back into her house. "Come on in," she said over her shoulder. "I'll get a picture."

Katherine followed her into the house. Although she'd known Mattie for years, they weren't close. Katherine blamed herself. Charles had taught her to trust no one. Also, even though Mattie and she were the same age, the months Katherine spent as Charles's prisoner and the months after her rescue, when the legal system wasn't quite sure what to do with her, put her behind in school. Mattie was a high-school senior when Katherine entered Skagway High as a freshman. And, before the year was over, Mattie ran off with a truck driver. Five years later, she returned—no truck driver, no wedding band, and three kids— Sarah, Austin, and Susan.

Twelve-year-old Austin now sat on the carpet, in front of an older-model TV, playing a video game. Eleven-year-old Susan was curled up on a threadbare, tweed couch, the telephone receiver pressed to her ear. Both had inherited their mother's looks and weight problem along with her lack of housekeeping skills. Toys, books, papers, and magazines were strewn around the room, while in the kitchen dirty dishes still sat on the table and counter.

Both of the children looked at her, their eyes widening slightly, probably because the few times she had come over, she hadn't been in uniform, wearing her belt and gun. "You find

145

her?" Austin asked.

"Not yet."

"Oh." He turned back to his video game, and the girl said something into the telephone.

"I've been trying to call you," Katherine said, now understanding why she kept getting a busy signal.

Mattie glared at her daughter. "Susan, I told you not to call anyone. Get off that phone right now."

"I didn't call anyone," Susan argued. "Brenda called me. And we were talking about Sarah."

"Does this Brenda know where Sarah is?" Katherine asked, hoping someone had a clue. "Know anything about her disappearance?"

Susan asked the person on the other end of the call, shook her head, and then hung up. "Is Sarah gonna be all right?"

"I'm sure she'll be fine," Katherine said, as much for Mattie's sake as for the girl.

Nevertheless, Mattie didn't look convinced. "I'll find a picture," she said and headed for one of the bedrooms.

Katherine focused on Susan. "What was your sister wearing when she left to go to my grandfather's house?"

The girl shrugged. "I don't know. Jeans, I guess. A shirt. Sandals."

"What color shirt?" Katherine pulled a small notebook out from her jacket pocket.

"White . . . Maybe. Mom hasn't done wash for a while."

Over at the TV, a high-pitched whistle was followed by the nerve-grating sound of metal crunching against metal and the boom of an explosion. "Woooo hoooo," yelled Austin. "I did it!"

He turned toward his sister. "I made it to level five, smarty pants."

It irritated Katherine that the boy wasn't more concerned about his sister. "You—" she said, pointing at him. "Anything you can tell me?"

He frowned. "You mean about Sarah?" He shrugged. "She's a pain in the butt, that's what she is. Always giving me orders."

For a moment Katherine was pulled back into her past. Her younger brother used to say the same thing about her. He was always complaining that she was too bossy, grumbling that he wished he was the older sibling.

She wished he were still alive.

With a shake of her head, Katherine pushed the memory back and focused on the two children in front of her. "Look," she said, trying not to make it sound too much like an order, "Your mother is having a hard time. She needs help. How about you two take care of those dirty dishes?"

"That's Sarah's job," Austin grumbled.

"And Sarah's not here," Katherine said.

For a minute he simply looked at her, then he nodded and pushed himself up from the carpet. "Okay, but, Susan, you've gotta help, too."

"Whatever," Susan said and slowly rose from the couch.

The two had just made their way past Katherine and into the kitchen when Mattie came out of the bedroom. Her eyes glistened with unshed tears and her cheeks were moist. In her right hand she held two pictures. "These are last year's school pictures. Now that her hair's longer she usually wears it in a ponytail."

She handed the pictures to Katherine. "I wasn't sure which one was the best, so take both."

Katherine did. What she noticed right away was how different Sarah looked from her sister and brother. The girl obviously took after her father, whoever that might have been. More important, Katherine noticed how much the pictures in her hand resembled the ones she had given her mother when she was fourteen.

Same straight, brown hair.

Same brown eyes.

Same look of innocence.

Katherine stared at the pictures and knew exactly why Charles had taken the girl and what would happen to her.

"Damn you," she muttered.

"What?" Mattie asked.

Katherine hadn't even realized she'd spoken aloud. Gordon was right; she was too close to this. What he didn't understand was being close would give her an advantage.

Ignoring Mattie's question, Katherine focused on the details that would help. "I need to know what Sarah was wearing when she left here today. Does she have any distinguishing birthmarks? Anything that would help others recognize her?"

As soon as Katherine had the essential data, she said goodbye and headed for the door. Mattie went with her, and it was only as Katherine was about to step outside that Mattie took her hand. "Find my baby, okay? And, when you do, if some outsider has raped her, don't just file this away, not like they did with me."

"You were raped?" Katherine had never heard this story.

"Not here. Not in *Shgagwéi*," she said, using the Tlingit word for the town. "It happened after I left. Everyone thinks Sarah is the truck driver's child, but she isn't. We were just friends. I wanted out of here, and he took me. I don't even know who Sarah's father is. I was attacked on my way home from work. I reported it to the police, but they didn't care. If a Tlingit raped a white woman, it would be front-page news. But a white man rape a Tlingit . . ." She shook her head. "Nothing."

"Well, *I* care," Katherine said, realizing she and Mattie had more in common than she'd ever realized. "We'll find Sarah, and we'll find whoever took her."

But, Katherine knew the girl they brought back wouldn't be the same innocent child who had left the Wilson house only a few hours earlier.

CHAPTER THIRTY-FOUR

10:30 P.M., Thursday

Vince didn't stay long with Sergeant Landros and the rescue workers, only long enough to question several of the volunteers about possible locations a kidnapper might choose to take a teenager. He also asked questions about Officer Katherine Ward. He learned little about her private life, other than she didn't date, didn't attend many social events, and the ones she did attend were either associated with her job or because she'd brought her grandfather.

After making sure Landros didn't have anything new to report—and Vince wasn't sure the guy would tell him if he did—Vince hitched a ride back to Skagway with one of the volunteers heading home.

When the man dropped Vince off at the Bonanza, the woman who let him in to the bed-and-breakfast wasn't sure she should bother Mrs. Morgan, not until Vince convinced her that this was an emergency. Five minutes later, Crystal Morgan descended the stairs wearing a robe with a ship's logo.

She'd removed her makeup, and her hair was mussed, but Vince saw no signs of tears. "This better be important," she complained the moment she saw him. "I'd just gotten to sleep."

"They found a vehicle over the side of the mountain. The driver's dead."

Crystal frowned. "I don't understand."

"It's the guy Misty was running off with."

"Oh, shit." Crystal sagged into the leather-upholstered chair in the parlor. "What about Misty? Is she dead?"

"Missing, and there was a ransom note pinned to the guy's shirt."

"So she *has* been kidnapped."

"Yes. The police think the kidnapper is someone they call The Beekeeper, a man named Charles Bell."

Crystal nodded, her eyes focused on the floor, not him.

"Have you heard of him?" Vince asked.

She nodded again, and then looked up. "That is, if he's the same one who kidnapped some girl years ago."

"They think it is. And, here's the irony. It seems that girl he kidnapped years ago is Officer Ward."

"You're kidding."

"No; she admitted it. And, it gets even worse. They think he may have taken another girl."

"Another girl?" Crystal leaned back in her chair, her carefully plucked eyebrows furrowing.

"A local," Vince said. "She was supposed to be working at Officer Ward's house tonight, but she never showed up."

"So is Officer Ward now out looking for this Beekeeper guy?"

"No. They took her off the case."

"Took her off the case? Why?"

"That's procedure. An officer doesn't work a case where there's personal involvement."

"Yeah, but I'll bet she is," Crystal said. "Involved, that is. If I remember right, the papers said it might not have been a kidnapping; that the girl had a crush on Bell and talked him into killing her family so she could have their money. She's probably doing the same thing here—getting him to take Misty so she can have Tom's money. How much are they asking for?"

"One hundred million."

He expected her to react to the large amount, but she merely nodded and said, "Even splitting it with Bell, that's a hell of a lot of money. Have you told Tom?"

"Not yet. I wanted to tell you first and have you with me when I called him."

"Good idea." She stood and glanced around the room. "We need a phone. Need to call him right away. If that bitch hadn't kept sending me back to the ship, hadn't kept denying this was a kidnapping, Tom could already be setting things up so the money could be wired wherever they wanted it to go."

"We can use my phone," he said, "but I'm not sure Office Ward is involved. She seemed truly surprised when she heard about the mark on the note, and really tense and angry when she learned Charles Bell was no longer under lock and key."

"Oh, come on." Crystal shook her head at him. "She could have been faking, putting on an act. You men are so easily fooled."

Vince supposed she was right. Although he prided himself on being able to read people, he had been fooled before.

"Give me the phone," Crystal said, motioning toward the holder on his belt. "The sooner Tom knows what's up, the sooner he can get the money together. Then Misty will be released, and all of this will be over."

Vince wished he felt as confident as Crystal sounded.

CHAPTER THIRTY-FIVE

"If you want to help, find Phil," Gordon had said.

"Damn you, Phil, where are you?" Katherine grumbled as she drove the short distance between Mattie Wilson's house and Phil's.

His was a two-story clapboard, its pink shutters a garish contrast to its peeling, blue exterior. Whereas most of the houses in Skagway were surrounded by lawns and flower gardens, Phil's hosted weeds and bare dirt.

Unlike her grandfather, who loved tending his roses almost as much as he loved fishing, Phil's obsession with fishing was all consuming. However, he'd never missed a day of work because of a fishing trip. Something had to have happened to him.

Many of the lakes he fished involved long hikes up steep mountainsides. He could have fallen. But wouldn't his fishing buddy have reported an accident? Gone for help?

Or did both of them fall?

Did they run into a bear?

Bear attacks were not common, but they did occur. Especially if the bear had cubs.

Katherine tried to shake off a feeling of dread as she parked in front of Phil's house. Weeds poked through the gravel of his empty driveway. She could see the note Gordon had said he'd left taped to the front door; nevertheless, she went up to the door and rang the bell.

No answer.

153

She tried the doorknob.

Locked.

She stepped back and stared at the house. Drapes and shades blocked her view inside, the house silent. She considered simply driving off, then decided to go around to the back. Years before, when she first returned to Skagway, she'd heard Phil tell her grandfather where he hid an extra key. Maybe, if he hadn't moved it, it would still be there.

And it was.

"Phil," she called out as she entered through his back door.

The only response was the hum of the refrigerator.

She'd been in the house twice to retrieve her grandfather when he forgot the time. Phil had offered to give her a tour of the place, but she had refused. Nevertheless, she had a general idea of its layout: kitchen, dining area, living room, Phil's bedroom, and a bathroom on the first floor. Additional bedrooms upstairs.

She started with the kitchen.

On the counter, a loaf of bread had been left open, several slices missing. Next to it was an empty lunch-meat container. Crusted egg stuck to a dish and a fry pan that had been piled in the sink. Beside the pan were a dirty knife and fork . . . and two empty coffee cups.

An array of delicately tied fishing flies lay on the table, along with the materials needed and the equipment to tie them. Katherine did see an unassembled graphite rod on the floor, but she knew that meant nothing. Phil owned dozens of rods. What she didn't see were his waders, fishing vest, or the box that held his favorite flies, extra line, and tools for repairs.

"So you did go fishing," she murmured, not surprised by the evidence. "But, where?"

In the living room, Katherine stepped over the TV remote on the floor and checked the date on the *Anchorage Daily News* spread out on the couch—two days old.

An empty beer can lay on its side, and she found a T-shirt tossed in a corner near the bathroom, but nothing was broken. No signs of a struggle. No indication that anything dire had happened to Phil, yet Katherine couldn't shake off an uneasy feeling.

Again she called out his name.

Still no answer.

In the bathroom, clothing littered the floor, the toilet seat was up, and a soap-ring lined the tub. Again, no signs of a struggle.

She only meant to give a quick peek into his bedroom. At the already open doorway, she let her gaze slide over the unmade bed and the open issue of *Playboy* that lay on the floor. She chuckled. *So you do think of something other than fishing.*

Her amusement ended the moment she saw the framed picture on the night stand.

Within the confines of a plain wooden frame was a picture of her, standing by a picnic table, wearing shorts and a halter top. The backyard was hers. It had to be. She never went out in public wearing shorts and a halter top. She even remembered when her grandfather took the picture last summer. He'd teased her and said he was going to submit it to *Playboy.*

Evidently he'd given a copy to Phil.

That he had the photo framed and kept it by his bed bothered her. She knew Phil liked her. Even though she'd done everything in her power to discourage him, he'd come on to her once when he'd had too many beers. She'd told him to forget it, that she didn't date coworkers. When he kept asking, she threatened to slap him with a sexual harassment suit.

That, she thought, had ended his infatuation. Evidently she'd been wrong. Maybe she did need to file a complaint.

Katherine checked the upstairs bedrooms. As far as she could tell, they were only used for storage. Finally, as she started down the stairs, she keyed up her radio and called Gordon. "Still no sign of Phil," she said when he responded. "I'm inside his house. Looks like he hasn't been here for two days."

"And your boyfriend's not coming back."

It took Katherine a moment to realize the seductive voice wasn't Gordon's. "Who is this?" she demanded, nearly dropping the radio.

"Oh, come on now, Kat," the voice purred. "Don't tell me you don't remember me?"

Her stomach twisted into a knot, and Katherine sucked in a breath. She did remember. She remembered the sound of that silky smooth voice, the touch of his hands, and what he did to her. Those memories had haunted her dreams for years. "Charles?"

"What?" Gordon demanded from his radio. "Who's on here, Katherine?"

"A good friend," Charles responded. "Isn't that right, honey. Have you missed me?"

"No," Katherine gasped, as much a denial of his presence as a response. Legs shaking, she sank down on the bottom step. "Go away," she moaned.

"Oh, no, not yet."

"Katherine," Gordon shouted into the radio. "You're at Phil's?"

"Yes," she said feebly.

"Is Bell there?"

"No." She looked around. "I don't think so."

"Get out of there," Gordon ordered.

"Run," said Charles, his tone mocking. "Run for your life, little girl."

Katherine drew her semi-automatic. Every nerve ending on alert, she rose to her feet and stepped away from the stairs, expecting at any moment to see the man who'd destroyed her family and her innocence.

"Did you get my note?" Charles asked, barely above a whisper. "Did you get it at five o'clock?"

She didn't answer. Every step she took, she checked ahead and behind her, half expecting Charles to appear.

"Did you appreciate the significance of the time?" he asked. "Five o'clock. The exact time you betrayed me."

"I didn't betray you," she argued.

"Did they give you thirty pieces of silver, Kit Kat? Was it worth it?"

She remembered the moment the police had come to the front door, her fear and relief. The media said she tried to protect him. Her therapist said she probably stepped in front of Charles out of surprise. All Katherine knew was one thing: "I didn't turn you in, Charles."

"Say what you like; you betrayed me," he repeated.

At the back door, she expected him to be outside, waiting for her. Cautiously, gun held at the ready, she stepped out of the house.

No one.

"You sat in that courtroom," Charles continued, "pointing a finger at me. At least Judas gave a kiss."

Katherine edged her way around the corner of the house. "I am not a Judas."

"Says you. But it doesn't matter. I've found me a couple of new blossoms."

Katherine stopped. She felt as if she'd been socked in the stomach. "Where, Charles? Where do you have them?"

"That's for me to know, and you to find out. Right, girls?"

She heard two voices in the background. Pleading voices. High pitched. Scared.

"Let them go, Charles," Katherine begged. "Don't . . . Don't do anything to them."

"Too late," he said with a snicker. "At least for one. Money might save the other one. Lots of money."

"If I come to you, will you let Sarah and Misty go?"

"Oh, you'll come to me. But first I want you to tell the father what will happen to his beautiful blossom if he doesn't pay. Tell him he's got until five o'clock tomorrow night. After that . . ."

Gordon's voice came through the radio. "You touch those girls, and I'll see you hang."

"Ah, the big, brave sergeant is making threats." Charles chuckled. "Careful, Mr. Policeman; I'm crazy, you know. I might just go after you, too."

"You're not going to get away with this," Katherine said, tears streaming down her cheeks. "Not this time."

"Right," Charles said, his tone mocking. "Meanwhile, you tell Misty Morgan's father if he doesn't have the money in my account by five p.m. tomorrow night, I'm going to pollinate his beautiful blossom. And, after that, if I don't have the money, both of these blossoms are going to die."

"Charles, don't." Katherine squeezed her eyes shut. "Please."

The crackle of the radio was her only response.

"Charles," she cried. "Are you there? Speak to me."

He didn't respond, and finally she said, "Gordon?"

Her cell phone rang, startling her. For a moment she stood where she was, her semi-automatic aimed straight ahead, her gaze darting from one spot to another. Finally she took in a shaky breath and reached for the phone.

"Yes?"

"It's me."

As soon as she heard Gordon's voice, Katherine's entire body began to tremble. "He was on a police radio, Gordon," she said, a tremor to her voice. "He said Phil's not coming back."

"You think he's using Phil's radio, that Phil's dead?"

Katherine nodded, even though she knew Gordon couldn't

see her. "He's a sociopath, Gordon. He uses people and then he kills them."

"He didn't kill you," Gordon reminded her.

"Sometimes I wish he had."

"We need to find those girls."

CHAPTER THIRTY-SIX

Five o'clock tomorrow. Misty had heard him give the time line. She understood what he'd meant about pollinating the beautiful blossom. That was her. And if her father didn't pay the ransom, not only would she be raped, this man was going to kill her. Kill both of them.

She shivered at the thought.

"Cold?" he asked, and touched her arm. "Oh, my, yes. Now, what kind of a beekeeper am I? I haven't kept a consistent temperature in my hive. Let me get you another blanket, then I'll turn up the heat."

"You're no beekeeper," Misty said, wishing she could smash him like a bee. "You're a monster."

"Tish tish, now," he said calmly and walked away. "It's not nice to call people names."

"Mother fucker. Sicko. Bastard." Misty threw out one insult after another.

In the dim lighting afforded by the open bedroom door, she saw him pause and thought she saw him smile. "Feisty little thing, aren't you," he said. "Afraid Daddy won't pay?"

"He'll pay," Misty said, unwilling to admit her doubts. "And, then he'll see to it that you rot in jail for the rest of your life."

"That's if they ever find me."

"They'll find you. My father is friends with the president. He'll get the FBI after you."

"Oh, I'm so scared." The Beekeeper chuckled, and then slid

open a closet door. For a moment, he flicked on a light, the brightness making Misty blink. Then the light went off, and he slid the door closed and turned back toward the beds, carrying something in his arms. "You cold, too?" he asked Sarah.

The girl's "Uh-huh" was tentative, her shallow breathing a clear indication of her fear.

"This will help."

Misty could tell he was covering the girl with another blanket, but with his back to her, she couldn't tell what else he was doing. Sarah's whimper, however, indicated she didn't like it.

"Can't you leave her alone for a minute?" Misty said, knowing the girl was petrified.

"Jealous?" he asked, and turned toward her.

She could see the smirk on his face. When he'd taken her to the bathroom, she'd made a mental list of his features. During one of Vince's "Be Prepared" lectures, he'd told her, "If you're ever attacked or think you might be in danger, pay attention to what the person looks like. Later, your description will help the police find this person."

For the last hour or more, Misty had mentally gone over what she would tell the police when she was rescued. His eyes were brown, and so was his hair. He had some gray hairs, especially near his ears, and it was cut short so it looked sort of spiky. There were wrinkles around his eyes and mouth. He was sort of tall, but not real tall. Lean. He didn't have one of those big stomachs, like most older men had, but he was old—probably as old as her father—and he smelled like beer . . . and sweat and sex.

"We don't want you feeling neglected," he said and dropped the blanket he was holding to the floor.

"Just go away," Misty said, wishing she'd kept her mouth shut.

"Oh, but you said you were cold. Maybe what I need to do is

warm you up first." He lifted the wool blanket that already covered her, and Misty sucked in a breath.

She could tell her nipples were hard. The rough texture of the wool had been enough to stimulate them. Now exposed to the air, she could feel them pointing up at the ceiling like proud sentinels. "I'm fine," she lied.

"How about down here?" He brushed his fingertips along the sensitive skin of her inner thigh, moving his hand closer and closer to the mound of blonde hair between her legs.

Tingling sensations raced through her body, and Misty knew she had to do something, say something quickly. "I've got to pee," she blurted out. "Bad."

His fingers stopped moving, and he looked at her face, a frown replacing his lecherous smile. "You want to go to the bathroom? Again?"

"Yes. Bad. Really, really bad."

For a moment she thought he would ignore her plea, but then he lifted his hand. "Smart and feisty. But I did promise I wouldn't touch you."

She swallowed hard. "Yeah, you did."

"And a promise is a promise." He untied the strips of sheet binding her ankles first. Once her feet were free, he released her arms by untying the ends of the strips from the bed's metal posts. He left the cloth around her wrists, using the material like a leash. A quick jerk got her to move.

"Don't try anything," he warned, and she carefully slid off the bed, her bare feet touching the plush carpeting that covered the floor.

Her first few steps were hesitant and unsteady, but stronger than the last time he'd taken her to the bathroom. "Don't go away, now," he said to Sarah with a chuckle. He then pushed the bedroom door open wider. A shove between her shoulder blades moved Misty forward, and she stumbled into the hallway.

The entire house was encased in a shroud of semi-darkness, drapes drawn and no lights on; nevertheless, she could see well enough to figure out the layout. Across the hall from the bedroom where he was keeping her was another doorway. It was closed, but she'd bet it opened to another bedroom. Just a short distance farther down the hallway, and on her left, was the bathroom he'd taken her to earlier. Across the hall from that room was another closed door, probably to another bedroom. And just past those rooms, at the end of the hallway, she could see what looked like a front door and living room furniture—a couch and an easy chair.

As she regained her balance, Misty focused on the front door and remembered what Vince had told her while showing her self-defense moves. *You're a woman; you're small and you don't have the strength of a man, so you have to be smarter than your attacker. Use the element of surprise. Get him off balance.*

Making a lunge toward the bathroom at the end of the hallway, as if she were in a hurry to get there, Misty jerked her arms forward, tightening the strips of sheet connecting her to her captor. Then, before he had a chance to react, she took a step back and spun around so she was facing him.

She saw the look of surprise on his face when she drove her right knee up into his groin, heard him suck in his breath as her knee made contact with the soft area of his crotch. The moment he started to double over, she changed directions. Stepping back, she swung her arms behind her, once again tightening the tension on the sheets. Caught off guard, he opened his hands, releasing the cloth bindings. Free, Misty spun back around and raced for the front door.

She had her hand on the doorknob when he caught her. "Bitch," he swore and shoved her to the floor.

The heavy boot of his foot pushed into her back, pinning her to the carpet. She could hear him sucking air through his teeth and knew he was still in pain. The pressure of his foot smashed her breasts into the carpeting, pinching her nipples between the fibers, and she clenched her teeth so she wouldn't cry out.

After a few moments, he sucked in one deep breath and released it, long and slow. "God damn bitch."

Tears slid from her eyes, wetting the aged carpeting beneath her cheek. She'd thought kneeing him would stop him from following her. She'd thought she would get away. But, all she'd done was made him angry.

Now what would he do to them?

CHAPTER THIRTY-SEVEN

11:30 P.M., Thursday

An hour after hearing Charles Bell break in on the police radio, Gordon stared at the site where the Blazer had left the Klondike Highway. It was still light enough to see clearly, but his shift should have ended hours ago, and he was way past exhaustion. Most of the search and rescue workers had gone home, but he and a handful of volunteers would be there until the state troopers or someone from the D.A.'s office arrived and took over. He had no other choice.

In all the years he'd been in law enforcement, he'd never faced a situation like this. Two girls kidnapped, a civilian dead, and one of their officers possibly—no, probably—dead. Gordon had felt betrayed—angry—when the chief told him about Katherine's past. He was still angry. For the last three years he'd worked with Katherine, shared office space with her . . . thought he knew her. Officially he was her superior. The chief should have told him about her past; should have confided in him.

If he had known, he never would have assigned Katherine to a possible kidnapping. Hell, for all he knew, she might be helping Bell.

Gordon stopped himself the moment that thought entered his head. Maybe he didn't know everything about Katherine Ward, but seeing her reaction when she saw the ransom note was proof enough for him that she wasn't helping the man.

Also, the way she'd talked to Bell on the radio didn't indicate complicity. That along with Bell's threats.

The man had made it clear he blamed Katherine for his arrest, and the way Katherine had sounded on the radio and phone, Gordon knew she wouldn't be any good to anyone. He told Katherine to deliver the information they needed for an Amber alert on Sarah—along with a description of the suspect—and then go home. Directly home. He didn't want Bell luring her out to an isolated location on the pretext of a robbery or locked car.

After reminding Katherine she was in danger, Gordon had called Jim and asked him to go to the station and cover the rest of her shift. Gordon could hear a baby crying in the background, and thought Jim might object, but the young officer had actually sounded relieved. Gordon had never had to deal with a newborn, but he gathered from others that the first few months could be rough, especially if the baby was colicky.

Not as rough, however, as being threatened by a kidnapper and murderer.

Gordon shivered and pulled his jacket closer.

What kind of monster are we dealing with?

If they had the manpower, he'd put Katherine under protective custody.

Manpower.

Gordon snorted at the thought. Their force of six was down to four . . . or three if Phil *was* dead.

Katherine hadn't found a body in Phil's house, but Bell had the officer's radio. He also had two teenagers. *But where?* Skagway wasn't some lower forty-eight metropolis. They'd checked the RV parks and most of the houses and apartments known to have summer renters. The only places left were private homes and the national park.

The park rangers had already been told to be on the lookout

for Misty and Brian Bane. So far Gordon hadn't heard anything from them. Another call wouldn't hurt.

He pulled out his cell phone and scrolled through his contact list until he came to Susan Lange's cell-phone number. Ranger Lange had been deputized a few years back, and the chief often called on her when they needed additional help. Gordon liked working with the woman. She was professional, non-confrontational . . . and safely married.

Susan Lange also knew the lakes, rivers, and trails of the area around Skagway like the back of her hand. Maybe she would have an idea where this Charles Bell might hide out.

She sounded as tired as he felt when she answered the phone. Gordon got right to the point. "Have you found anything? Any hikers report anything unusual? Maybe see a guy with two teenagers?"

"Two?" she said and yawned. "Last I heard, you were looking for a college guy and one teenager."

"Situation's changed. College kid's dead, and we've got a pedophile on the loose and two missing teenage girls."

"Jeez. And you think he's somewhere in the park?"

"We have no idea where he's taken them. That's the problem. We're issuing Amber alerts for the girls and a BOLO for him."

"You have a name for this guy we're supposed to be on the look out for."

"Bell. Charles Bell. He's forty-nine, six-one, weighs around one-ninety, has thinning brown hair, and brown eyes."

"And the girls? We already have what you sent on the Morgan girl, but now you're saying there's another one?"

"He's got a local girl. Sarah Wilson. She—"

Lange sucked in a breath. "Oh. My. God. I know Sarah," she said. "She's done volunteer work at the Visitor's Center; helped me with tours. She's a sweet kid."

Gordon closed his eyes. If Bell had molested the girl—and

he'd made it sound as if he had—Sarah Wilson wasn't going to be the same when they found her . . . if they found her.

Got to find her, he thought. *Got to find all of them.*

"When did he take her?" Lange asked.

"We're not exactly sure. Sometime after three in the afternoon."

"Damn."

His thoughts exactly. "There's something else." He hated to even say it aloud. "You know I called earlier and said we thought Phil Carpenter might have had an accident while fishing—"

"We have rangers looking for him," Susan said.

"That's good, but . . ." Gordon took in a breath, then said it. "We now think this Bell guy got to Phil. We think he's dead."

"Dead?" Silence echoed back at Gordon for several moments before Susan spoke again. "You said, 'think.' You're not sure?"

"We don't have a body, but this Bell guy was using Phil's radio."

"Maybe he just took it from Phil."

As much as Gordon wanted to believe that, he knew it was wishful thinking. "This guy doesn't leave survivors."

"And, you're thinking Phil . . . Phil's body might be in the park?"

"That's what we're thinking."

Susan Lange sighed. "I don't like phone calls like this, Gordon."

"I don't either." Simply talking about the possibility of Phil's death was tearing him apart.

"Who's working with you tonight? I hope it's not Katherine."

Gordon frowned. "Why do you say that?"

"Because of Phil. I don't know how she feels about him, but he sure has a crush on her. He asked me once how he could get her to go out with him. She—"

Gordon interrupted her. "Katherine's off the case. She knows this Bell guy."

"Knows him?"

For Katherine's sake, he didn't want to say anything more. "It's a long story. Just be careful, and tell your people the same. This Bell creep probably has Phil's gun, so proceed with caution. Also, Phil's Tahoe wasn't at his house, so if you find the Tahoe, you may find his . . . him." He wasn't about to say *his body*. "Do you need a picture?"

Lange didn't answer immediately. When she did, it was with a sigh. "Yeah, send one. Most of the rangers know him, but not all of the seasonals do."

"I'll get one your way. Oh, and if you need to contact us, don't use the police radio; use the telephone."

Chapter Thirty-Eight

Katherine stood at the kitchen sink, staring out the window at the empty street. The house was quiet except for her grandfather's snoring. She knew she should go to bed, try to get some sleep, but she was too wound up to even consider the idea. She couldn't shake the feeling that Charles was watching her.

Was that something moving near the corner of the house across the street?

Her hand automatically went to her holster.

A cat crept out of the shadows and dashed across the street to a neighbor's yard.

Katherine swallowed hard and released a shaky breath.

If Charles was watching her, he was doing a damn good job of hiding himself. "Where are you, you bastard?" she muttered. Where would a man who had been in a mental institution up until a couple of months ago take two teenagers?

Dragging two girls around the forested mountains and glacial valleys that surrounded Skagway and Dyea would be no easy feat. In addition to the rugged terrain, at this time of the year there were hikers, fishermen, and rafters who might see them. And there would be bears.

He had to be holed up in a house. But which house? They'd checked the rentals, the parks, and—

The ring of the telephone interrupted her thoughts. Heart in her throat, she reached for the receiver. "Yes?"

"I called the station. They said you were home."

In spite of a tremor and sniffing, Katherine recognized Mattie Wilson's voice.

"My neighbor called," Mattie's said. "She said there was something on the radio about Sarah. I listened, but I couldn't find nothing."

"Your neighbor must have heard the Amber alert."

"She said they're also looking for a man . . . A man and another girl."

"We think . . . We think we know who took your daughter."

"Who? Who would do such a thing?"

Before Katherine could think of a good way to tell Mattie, the woman went on. "Is it someone who lives here? The Prescott boy? He's been calling her recently. If he—"

"It's not the Prescott boy. It's no one who lives here," Katherine said, hoping rumors involving innocent people wouldn't start spreading . . . as they had in her case.

"Then I don't understand." Mattie hiccupped. "My Sarah knows better than to talk to strangers. I've told her. I've told all of my children to be careful, that not everyone is nice."

She started crying in earnest, and Katherine wondered if the tears were for her daughter or for herself. Not that it mattered. Mattie Wilson was hurting, and the only way to stop that pain was to find Sarah . . . and quickly.

"Mattie, we're doing all we can. You'll be the first to know when we find her."

A few more words of comfort, and Katherine ended the call. Curious, she turned on the TV in the living room, keeping the volume low. A talk show was on, but the Amber alert scrolled across the bottom of the screen, naming the girls and giving their descriptions. Katherine was about to snap the TV off when the program was interrupted and Charles's picture and pictures of each of the girls appeared on the screen. Charles's photo was the one she'd given Jim when he arrived to take over her shift.

The picture she had from years ago.

They needed something current.

She might be off the case, but that didn't mean she couldn't help. Back in the kitchen, Katherine made another call to the state mental hospital in Michigan. An orderly answered, and Katherine identified herself and asked to speak to the administrator in charge.

"Do you know what time it is?" the orderly grumbled.

She hadn't thought about the time difference, and she didn't care. "We need a current picture of Charles Bell."

"People are asleep here."

"People here wish they could get some sleep," she snapped back. "This can't wait. We have two missing teenagers and a police officer who may be dead. We need that picture."

"Yeah, yeah. Call back in the morning."

She doubted slamming down the phone made a good impression on the orderly, but it helped relieve some of the tension twisting through her body. What she needed was a drink. A good, strong drink.

CHAPTER THIRTY-NINE

2:15 A.M., Friday

It was finally dark by the time Vince left the police station. Sergeant Landros had offered to drive him to the airport, but Vince declined. The sergeant had enough to deal with, and Vince hoped the walk would help clarify his thoughts.

His footsteps echoed on the wooden sidewalks, downtown Skagway virtually empty. The temperature had dropped considerably, and he didn't waste any time browsing in store windows. He had a good memory for directions, making it easy for him to pick a route toward the airport that would also take him past Katherine's house. Not that he expected her to be up at this hour.

As he neared the yellow and green cottage, he saw a light on in the kitchen, then the shadowy motion of someone passing by the window. From the distance, he couldn't tell if it was Katherine or her grandfather, but someone was obviously up.

Vince headed for the side entrance. As he neared, he could see Katherine through the door's window. She was still wearing her full uniform, and was now standing by the sink, looking out the window facing the street. In her hand, she held a glass half full of an amber liquid.

He knocked.

She spun toward him, dropping the glass, her hand going to her sidearm. In an instant the Glock was pointed directly at him. "It's me!" he yelled, not caring if he disturbed the neighbors. "Vince."

She stared in his direction, her arm wobbling slightly. He stepped closer to the door's window area, hoping the light from the kitchen would illuminate his face. He could see her clearly— her hair mussed, her brow furrowed, and her eyes narrowing to a squint. She looked unsteady on her feet, the gun in her hand wobbling, as if too heavy to hold in one place.

For what seemed an eternity she didn't move and neither did he, and then she dropped her arm to her side and took a step toward the door. He watched as she made her way through the mud room, her progress slow and cautious. Heard her turn the deadbolt and release the lock. The moment she opened the door, he caught the odor of whiskey.

"Whadaya want?" she asked, weaving slightly on her feet.

She still held the gun in her right hand, down by her side. Vince glanced at it, then back at her face. "I just came from the police station."

"Did they find 'em?"

"No, not yet."

For a second, Katherine's expression had relaxed, but once again he saw the tension return. "They won't find 'em," she said, shaking her head. "Not until it's too late."

She turned away and wove her way back toward the kitchen. Vince hesitated a moment, then followed, closing the outside door behind him and locking it. In the kitchen, a puddle of liquid surrounded the broken glass on the floor. Katherine stopped and stared at the mess.

"I'm sorry I surprised you," he said. "I'll clean that up."

She turned and looked at him, her eyes reflecting her confusion. "I sink I've had too mush to drink."

"Could be," he said, knowing there was no doubt about it.

"He's coming after me."

"That's what I heard."

"I'll kill him," she said, her voice firmer than before. "The moment I see him, that man is dead."

"But, before you kill him, we need to find the girls."

Her head wobbled in a nod. "Yeah. Gotta find the girls."

Katherine took a step to the side, and Vince heard the crunch of glass. Again she looked down at the floor, and then she bent forward. For a moment he thought she was going to fall flat on her face, right over the broken glass and liquid, but, before she completely collapsed, she put her hands out, breaking her fall. Her gun made a thump as it hit the tile, her right hand covering it.

"Ouch," she yelped, then swore and started giggling.

The way she was bent over and wobbling, he was afraid she would still end up lying on the glass. He quickly moved closer and grabbed the back of her service belt, stabilizing her. A thin line of blood emerged near the palm of her left hand. "I think you cut yourself."

"I sink you're right." Again she giggled, not bothering to straighten up, and started singing. "I had a little drink about an hour ago, and it went straight to my head."

No doubt about it. She was drunk. "Let me help you," he said and eased her back up to a standing position.

"I need to clean up dis mess," she enunciated carefully, looking down at the floor. "And my weapon." She bent over again, picking up the Glock. "Gotta have a clean weapon."

She managed to stand upright again, but swayed back against him as she held the pistol up in front of her face. He could see droplets of whiskey on the barrel of the Glock and knew she was right, but she was in no condition to clean anything at the moment.

"You cut your hand," he said, touching the back of her left arm so she looked at that palm. "Let's get that taken care of first."

175

She held that hand up near her face, her palm almost touching her nose. "I cut myself," she said, sounding surprised.

"Yes, you did."

"Huh." She lowered her right hand, rubbing the barrel of the Glock against her pant leg, and then holstered it.

"Let me look at the cut," Vince said softly and gently turned her so she was facing him. "Let me see if there's any glass in it."

"I cut myself," she repeated and stared at him, her eyes unfocused.

"Yes, you did." He backed up, easing her away from the broken glass and over to the sink. A quick check and he decided the cut was clean, no fragments of glass or dirt imbedded in her skin. He grabbed a sheet of paper towel and pressed it against the wound. "Do you have any bandages?"

"In da bathroom. Why you here?"

"To talk to you."

" 'Bout what?"

He wasn't sure how to answer that. "I guess I need more information. More about this Charles Bell. About why he took you. Why he's taken Misty."

"Don't know why he took Missy. Me?" She snorted. "He took me 'cause I was stupid. A stupid idjit." She laughed. "Can you believe dis. I thought the worse thing in life was having to move to a new school."

She looked up at him, tears forming in her eyes, and then she gave a moan and leaned forward, her forehead hitting his chest. "He killed 'em," she mumbled against his shirt. "Killed 'em all. My mother and father . . . my little brother. My sweet little brother." A tremor coursed through her. "And now he's gonna kill Sarah . . . just because she looks like me . . . like I did at her age. Poor Sarah . . . Poor, poor Sarah."

Her entire body shook as her words turned into tears, and Vince wrapped his arms around her and drew her close. He remembered the snarly, bitchy policewoman he'd met only a few hours earlier. The woman he now held in his embrace was soft and pliable, a vulnerable female who'd been abused as a child, both physically and mentally. A victim. "It's not your fault," he said softly into her hair. "It's not your fault."

He wasn't sure she even heard him, her tears wetting his shirt, and he knew he shouldn't be responding to her physically, but he couldn't stop the surge of desire that pulsed through him. At that moment, he wanted her. Wanted to console her, protect her . . . and make love to her.

He had a feeling she felt his arousal. Suddenly she stopped crying. Eyes wide, she drew back and looked up at him. "Whaz going on? Why . . . ?" She shook her head, as if trying to clear her thoughts. "Why you here?"

"I need some answers." And as far as he could tell, she was the only one who could provide them. "I want to know why Bell is here, in Skagway."

"Why?" She frowned, slightly swaying in his arms. "Because I'm here. He wants revenge. Wants to get back at me."

That didn't make sense. "For what? From what I've heard, you tried to protect him when the police arrived."

"Protect him?" She snorted. "Him? I was scared. Scared of what he'd do to me. Do to them. Only afterwards, during the trial, did I have the nerve to tell them what he did to me. I told them everything."

She smiled at that. A lopsided grin. Vince didn't ask what Bell did to her. He didn't want to know what the monster could be doing to Misty or the other girl.

"I've got to find him," Katherine said and pulled completely free of his embrace. "Find and kill the bastard."

She started for the side door, then stopped, weaving slightly on her feet. She turned back toward him, her face drained of color. "I . . . I think I'm going to be sick," she said and changed direction, heading for the sink.

Vince had to look away as she emptied her stomach. Only when she moaned did he manage to control his own involuntary reaction enough so he could go to her side. She had a dish towel pressed against her mouth, and he focused on that rather than what lay in the sink. "Come with me," he said, moving her away from the counter.

He guided her out of the kitchen and through the living room toward the short hallway he supposed led to a bathroom. Once he found it, he snapped on the light and eased her into the room. "How are you feeling?" he asked, unsure if he should lower the toilet seat lid or not.

"Hmm," was all she said, then groaned, "Ooh," as she looked at herself in the mirror.

She flipped the lid down herself, sat, and leaned forward, her left cheek touching the edge of the wash basin. "I'm sorry," she muttered, lowering the towel only slightly.

"Don't be. You've had a rough day."

Vince ran water from the faucet until it was warm before he wet a wash rag and used it to wipe her face and then her hands. "I don't usually drink," she said as he opened the medicine cabinet, looking for something to cover the cut on her hand. "I learned a long time ago that I can't handle it."

He said nothing, simply opened the box of bandages he found and removed one.

"I should be out looking for Sarah."

"And Misty?" He paused before placing the bandage over her cut. That she hadn't mentioned Misty bothered him.

"And Misty," she said with a sigh.

"If he's here for revenge, why did he take Misty? Why ask for so much money?"

"I don't know."

"And how did he know to contact me?" That was what

178

bothered him.

"You?" She shook her head, as if struggling to comprehend what he was saying. "He called you?"

"He didn't call; he sent a fax. To my office." Feelings of desire were replaced by suspicion as Vince remembered why he'd wanted to talk to her. "A few hours ago I got a call from my partner. Bob had stopped by the office when he got back from L.A. He said there was a fax in the machine, one that evidently arrived after our secretary left. It had specific instructions on how one hundred million dollars was to be transferred from Tom's bank account to an off-shore account."

"Charles contacted you?" she repeated, sitting straighter.

"The fax was sent to VR Protection Services." Vince studied every nuance of her expression. "Signed, The Beekeeper. He didn't even have the guts to use his own name."

"But, why contact you?" she asked, which was exactly what he wanted to know.

"Good question," he said. "You tell me why. Tell me how a guy in Skagway got our fax number. How he would know Bob and I could contact Tom; know we would have the ability to set up a money transfer. Explain how he knew any of this . . . unless you told him."

"Me?" She stared at him for a moment, and then she struggled to her feet so she was standing, facing him. "Dammit all," she grumbled. "I haven't told Charles anything. Up until I saw that mark on that note, I thought Charles was still in a mental hospital in Michigan. I had no idea he was here, or that your boss's daughter would be here, or that any of this would happen. I don't even know your fax number."

She tried to force her way past him, out of the bathroom, but he blocked her escape with his body. He wanted answers. "You could have gotten my fax number off the business card I gave you. And, I'm sure Crystal told you about my friendship with Tom."

"Your business card is on my desk . . . at the station. And, I certainly didn't memorize your fax number. As for your friendship with Misty's father, you yourself have made that clear, but that doesn't mean I know anything about your ability to transfer money."

Anger—and probably the act of emptying her stomach—had countered the effects of the alcohol she'd consumed. No more slurring of her words, no more wobbling on her feet. Her expression was defiant as she glared up at him.

"Then how—?"

"I don't know how."

Vince shook his head. He didn't know what to think. If Bell didn't get the information from her, how did he know?

"Can I have that band-aid?" she asked, glancing at the one in his hand.

"Sure." He handed it to her and watched her place it over the cut on her palm.

Once the band-aid was in place, she looked up at him. "And, now, will you please let me out of here?"

He stepped aside, but followed her back into the living room. She might think the discussion was over, but he still had questions. "How did Bell know Misty would be here today?" Except it was no longer the day Misty had arrived. "Yesterday," he corrected. "How did he know she'd be meeting with that Bane kid yesterday morning?"

Katherine stopped next to her grandfather's recliner. "How should I know?" With a sigh, she turned and faced him. "Maybe he figured it out from that article in the paper, the one that mentioned this trip."

"You saw the article?"

"No, I didn't see the article. Mrs. Morgan told me about it.

How many times do I have to tell you? I did not know your boss's daughter would be here. I did not tell Charles she would be here. I . . ." She sank onto the recliner. "Oh, what's the use. You're never going to believe me."

"I don't know what to believe," he admitted.

"Neither do I." Her shoulders drooped, and she leaned forward, resting her elbows on her knees and cradling her head in her hands. "Will her father pay?"

"I don't know." And that bothered Vince. "Your sergeant said you talked to Bell."

"He was on the police radio. Phil's radio."

"Your missing officer?" He knew that from what Sergeant Landros had said.

Katherine gave a slight nod. "I think Phil's dead. I think Charles killed him because of me."

"What did you do?"

"Nothing." She looked at him, but Vince had a feeling she wasn't really seeing him, that her mind was somewhere else. "Phil had a picture of me," she said. "In his bedroom. He'd asked me out, but I always refused. I thought he was friends with my grandfather because they both liked to fish, but Alice said . . ." Katherine paused, and Vince saw the sadness in her eyes. "I guess he liked me."

"And, that's why Bell killed him?"

"Probably." She leaned back in the chair and closed her eyes. "God, I'm tired."

She looked small in the overstuffed recliner. Small and defeated. He sat on the couch and watched her, multiple questions racing through his head. *Was she as innocent as she proclaimed? If she didn't give Bell the fax number, how did he get it? And how did a man who'd been in a mental hospital know how and where to find Misty? Or Katherine, for that matter?*

Vince knew he'd gone too many hours without sleep to be

thinking clearly. His gut feeling was to believe Katherine, but did he dare trust that feeling?

A soft, rumbling sound drew him out of his thoughts, and he smiled. Obviously he wasn't the only one who needed sleep. Officer Katherine Ward was snoring.

CHAPTER FORTY

Misty lay on the bed, the strips of sheeting that bound her wrists and ankles once again securely tied to the metal posts. Two scratchy, wool blankets now covered her nakedness, but she felt cold. A shivering, deep down inside, shaking, cold.

That he hadn't raped her after her botched attempt at an escape had surprised Misty. As he'd pressed her breasts into the carpeting, scrunching her nipples until electrifying jolts of pain radiated down her sides, he'd said she would pay. And she'd believed him.

She could tell when the damage she'd inflicted on his body subsided, and her nakedness aroused him. He didn't remove his clothing, but, for what seemed an eternity, he rubbed his hips against hers, and she could feel his erection against her buttocks and spine. Her body tense, tears continuing to slide down her cheeks, she tried to force her mind to another level, one where nothing he did to her would truly touch her.

She still expected him to rape her when he pulled her back on her feet and shoved her down the hallway to the bedroom they'd recently left. "Your roommate tried to get away," he told the girl named Sarah as he jerked Misty back onto the empty bed. "Tried to hurt me."

"Did hurt you," Misty said, proud of that much.

"Bitch!"

His fist hitting the side of her face stunned her. Her knees went weak, but, before she could fall, he pushed her onto the empty bed. She wanted to reach up and touch her cheek, but he tightened his hold on the narrow strips of sheet binding her wrists, and had them tied to the bed posts before she could resist.

"Go ahead. Do it!" she cried. "Hit me. Rape me. You bastard."

"Hit you again?" he said, taking one of the strips bound to her ankle and pulling it taut. "Bruise one of my blossoms?"

Misty tried to kick at him with her free leg. "We're not blossoms."

He snatched the attached cloth strip mid-air and jerked her leg down onto the mattress. "Oh, yes you are. Blossoms that I've brought to my hive."

Misty heard him lower his zipper, and she braced herself for what was to come. *It can invade your body but not your soul.* Her mother had said that about the cancer that ate away at her body. Up until the end, her mother had suffered in silence. And, so would she. Misty vowed she wouldn't give this monster the pleasure of hearing her cry.

"You can blame your roommate for this," he said, and Misty didn't understand, not until she heard the creak of the other bed's springs.

"Please don't," Sarah moaned.

"No. Not her," Misty shouted, twisting as far as she could onto her side so she could look at him. "I'm the one who kneed you. I'm the one who got you all hot and horny."

"Hot and horny." He chuckled, and, in the dim lighting, she saw him stroke himself. "Some men call their cocks names. Peter. Or Jack. Me, I call mine The Stinger."

Misty begged, Sarah cried, and their tormentor laughed, but he didn't stop what he'd started, not until he was breathing hard and Sarah's sobs had turned to hiccups. And then he covered both of them with the scratchy, wool blankets and left the room, closing the door and taking away all light.

"I'm sorry," Misty said, wishing there was a way she could reach over and touch the girl on the other bed. "So sorry."

"I—" Sarah started, then stopped.

"I thought I could escape, could get help."

Sarah hiccupped another sob. "He's never going to let us go, is he?"

Misty wouldn't allow herself to think that. "He wants money, my father's money. Once he gets that, he'll let us go."

"No. After he has the money, he'll kill us. That's what they do."

"How do you know?"

"I saw it in a movie."

"Movies are movies. They're not real." Except Misty knew what Sarah had said did happen in real life.

"It might be better to die. I don't want to get pregnant. My mother was raped by a white man, and she got pregnant. And, you know what, they never did anything to the white man."

"Did your mother get an abortion? If you're raped, you can get an abortion."

"No," Sarah said. "She had me."

"Oh." Misty wasn't sure how to respond. "I guess that wasn't so bad, was it?"

"She didn't want me."

"How do you know that?"

"I heard her tell one of her friends."

"Well, you're not gonna get pregnant. And we're gonna make this guy pay. We're not gonna die . . . but maybe he will."

CHAPTER FORTY-ONE

7:30 A.M., Friday

The rich, nutty smell of freshly brewed coffee and the gravelly, quavering sound of her grandfather's voice woke Katherine. "Trail's hard to see," he said from somewhere on the other side of her bedroom door. "And, once you find it, it's no easy climb, but you get to that lake and you'll see more trout than you ever knew existed."

Who is he talking to? she wondered and rolled to her side to look at her bedside clock. The moment she did, a dull, thudding pain in her right temple announced itself, and she remembered the bottle of whiskey she'd nearly emptied. And, then it came back to her in a rush: the glass she dropped, Vince's unexpected arrival, and the mess she made. What she didn't remember was getting into bed.

"You gotta go through Dyea and across the steel bridge," her grandfather continued. "You know where that is?"

"Can't say I do."

Katherine recognized Vince Nanini's deep, resonant voice, and squeezed her eyes closed. She didn't need to look to know she was only wearing her bra and panties. The question was, did she remove her clothing or did he?

Try as she might, she couldn't remember, not for sure. It all seemed like a dream, him helping her into the room, urging her to take off her clothes. The muscles in her stomach tightened. *What else did he do?*

186

"You gotta follow a maze of two-tracks on the other side of Dyea," her grandfather continued. "When the tree limbs are scraping both sides of your truck, that's when you gotta park and go on foot."

"Doesn't sound like a lot of people go there," Vince said.

" 'Course not." Her grandfather gave a snort. "Wouldn't be a pristine lake if they did, now would it?"

"No, I guess not."

Katherine only half listened. The rest of her muddled thoughts focused on her body. She knew from experience what it felt like after intercourse. Charles had given her more than enough proof, and there'd been a short time, while in college, when she'd hated herself—hated all the misery she'd caused—and had turned to booze and sleeping with men as her punishment.

Her head felt the same as back then, but not her body.

So why didn't Vince Nanini make love to her? She knew she'd aroused him when he'd held her. She'd liked the strength of his arms and hardness of his body, had actually been aroused herself. Of course, that was before she threw up, and he started accusing her of helping Charles.

Go away, she silently willed, not wanting to face him again. She'd been stupid to let him in last night. Stupid and drunk.

A knock on her door made her start. "You awake?" her grandfather called. "Your friend needs breakfast."

"Tell him to go away," she called back, the sound of her voice making the band of pressure around her skull tighten. "Tell him—" She stopped, remembering the broken glass on the floor and the mess she'd left in the kitchen sink. Damn, she was going to have to face Vince after all. "Stay out of the kitchen," she ordered. "Both of you. I'll be out in a minute to clean up that mess."

★ ★ ★ ★ ★

Katherine hurried to dress, but with every movement she made, her head threatened to explode. Even the simple act of slipping on a sweatshirt increased the pressure, and after putting on a pair of jeans, she would have skipped shoes and socks if not for the broken glass she'd left on the kitchen floor. She already had a cut on her left hand; she didn't need sliced feet.

What she did need were several aspirins and lots of water or she was going to be sick again.

" 'Morning," she said, keeping her head down, eyes lowered as she entered the kitchen. She ignored her grandfather and Vince standing by the coffee pot, and headed straight for a pair of dark glasses she'd left on the counter by the telephone. Once they were on, it dawned on her that she'd walked right through the area where she'd dropped the glass. Where only a few hours earlier broken shards of glass and a puddle of whiskey had covered the tiles, she saw nothing but the tiles. Sparkling clean tiles.

She lifted her gaze to look at the sink.

That, too, was clean. Spotless, except for one empty water glass.

"I'm sorry, Poppa," she said, guilt adding to her physical misery. "I should have cleaned up before I went to bed last night."

"Cleaned up what?" he asked, glancing around the kitchen.

"The mess out here." She could imagine how gross everything had looked . . . and smelled.

"What mess?" He seemed truly confused.

For a moment she figured he'd simply forgotten he'd had to clean the floor and sink, but then she looked at Vince and knew it wasn't her grandfather who had cleaned up after her. "Oh, God," she groaned and turned away.

"You okay?" her grandfather asked.

"She had a rough night," Vince answered for her.

Katherine refused to look at him. "Why are you still here?"

"Because I need your help."

"I told you last night, I don't know anything."

"But, you want to find them, and so do I."

She sensed him coming closer, but until he nudged her arm, she hoped she wouldn't have to face him.

"Have some coffee," he said and handed her a mug full. "Take some aspirin. I'll fix your grandfather's breakfast. After that, we need to talk."

"Like I said, the lake's not all that big," her grandfather mumbled before using his napkin to wipe the last traces of his scrambled eggs and toast from his mouth. "On one side there's a thick stand of spruce and sheer rock ledges. On the other side you'll find fewer trees and a bunch of boulders you can stand on. Water's crystal clear, and you'll easily see the fish. Problem is catching them."

"Why's it hard to catch them?" Vince glanced her way as she came back into the kitchen. The smile he gave her made her stomach do a flip.

"Don't know. Phil can't figure it out either. You know Phil?"

"Haven't had the pleasure of meeting him," Vince said and stifled a yawn.

Katherine wondered how much sleep he'd gotten. She had no idea when he put her to bed, or how long it took him to clean the kitchen. She didn't want to think of him as kind . . . or attractive. Hadn't he accused her of abetting Charles? Thought she had a part in Sarah and Misty's abduction?

So why did his smile have her pulse racing?

The dark circles under his eyes were more pronounced than the ones she'd noticed under her own eyes when she'd looked in the bathroom mirror. Two cups of coffee and four aspirins, along with a slice of dry toast, had helped both her stomach and her head, at least enough so she could take a shower and put on a clean uniform.

Her grandfather kept talking. "Phil's a good fisherman. Not many nowadays who tie their own flies. Phil's sure he's going to create a fly that will lure those trout into striking."

Or die trying, Katherine thought, the reality of that possibility sending a shiver down her spine. "Poppa," she said, "do you think Phil might have taken that friend of his up to your Paradise Lake?"

"Taken him up to Paradise Lake?" Her grandfather turned to face her. "Phil?"

Now that her head wasn't pounding like a jackhammer, she noticed her grandfather hadn't shaved, a stubble of gristly white hairs covering his cheeks and chin. She hoped he'd cleaned his teeth. If not, poor Vince. Having a conversation with her grandfather when he hadn't soaked his dentures could be torture.

"Yeah. Phil. Do you think he might have taken someone there?"

"I guess he might have." Her grandfather smiled. "You should get him to take you and your friend here up there fishing."

Katherine looked at Vince. "I need to make a phone call."

CHAPTER FORTY-TWO

8:00 A.M., Friday

National Park Service ranger Susan Lange placed the telephone receiver back on its base, and stared at the map of the Klondike Gold Rush National Park tacked to the wall of her home office. Katherine Ward had called asking if they'd checked an area the other side of Dyea. "There's a trail," Katherine said. "My grandfather and Phil call it the 'Trail to Frustration.'"

Susan had an idea where that trail might be and didn't think anyone had gone into that area the previous day. Probably just as well. She didn't really want one of the volunteers finding a body.

As a ranger for the National Park Service, Susan was a federal employee and under the jurisdiction of the Department of the Interior. Over the years, she'd rescued hikers, arrested poachers, and helped fight wildfires. She primarily viewed her role as a protector of the land, but years ago she'd been deputized by the local police and often collaborated with them. Only once, however, had she ever searched for a body, and never for someone she personally knew. She hoped Gordon and Katherine were wrong, that Phil wasn't dead.

After Gordon's phone call, she'd continued searching until darkness made progress not only difficult but dangerous. It was after two A.M. when she took a sleeping pill and crawled into bed next to her husband. Now the aftereffects of that pill had her groggy, and she stared at the map without actually focusing on any particular area.

Not that she needed the map to find the clearing Katherine had described. Just the month before she'd run into Phil there. It had been late in the afternoon, and she'd driven up as he was about to get into his Tahoe. When she saw the fishing rods in his vehicle, she'd asked if he'd caught anything, and he'd grinned and shook his head. He even showed her an empty creel to prove his point.

"I never catch anything up there," he'd said, practically confirming he'd just returned from the lake he'd talked about back in February, when he gave a lecture on fly fishing.

She and her husband had attended that talk, mostly to stave off boredom, not because either one of them was particularly interested in fly fishing. And Phil had made it interesting, using a PowerPoint presentation to illustrate how to tie a fly, which ones he preferred, and why. When a man in the audience asked if Phil always caught fish when he went out, Phil had laughed and told them about Paradise Lake. "First you take the Trail of Frustration," he said, "and climb straight up a mountainside. And when you finally get there, the trout ignore you."

Of course there was no official "Trail of Frustration" in the Klondike Gold Rush National Park, and Phil had admitted the lake wasn't officially called Paradise Lake. "That's just what my fishing buddy, Russell, calls it," Phil had told the audience. "To keep you guys from figuring out where we go."

Susan wasn't surprised. Fishermen often kept their favorite fishing spots secret. She just hoped Katherine was wrong, and Phil's favorite spot hadn't also become his graveyard.

She turned away from the map and slipped on her green ballistic Kevlar vest with its embroidered NPS badge. After making sure she had it buttoned right, and her gray uniform shirt was neatly tucked into her green trousers, she checked her Sig Sauer. If Phil was dead, there was a killer loose.

"Coffee's ready," she told her husband when he came dragging out of the bedroom, rubbing sleep from his eyes and yawning.

He squinted at her. "You're going to work? I thought today was your day off."

"Katherine just called. Probably what woke you. She thinks she might know where we'll find Phil Carpenter."

"So why doesn't she go look for him?" Kevin grumbled as he made his way to the coffee pot and grabbed a mug from the holder beside it. "I was hoping we could go to Whitehorse today."

Susan had also been looking forward to time with her husband, but under the circumstances, she had no choice. "Both Gordon and Katherine think Phil's dead."

Kevin paused before pouring his coffee. His writing often keeping him up late, and it normally took at least two cups of black coffee before he could function in the morning, but now his eyes were wide open. "Dead?"

Susan nodded.

CHAPTER FORTY-THREE

Please let her find him alive, not dead, Katherine silently prayed, but she knew how little regard Charles Bell had for human life. That he hadn't killed her when he had her under his control was a miracle. She never did let him know she was pregnant. She feared—or maybe knew—he wouldn't want her having a baby.

Charles Bell liked innocent, naïve, young girls. He'd told her his wife was barely fifteen when their daughter was born. Katherine had no idea when Charles began molesting his own child, but, according to him, his daughter was thirteen when his wife divorced him and moved to another state, daughter in tow.

He'd been royally pissed.

As far as Katherine knew, she was his next victim. Her therapist had said, if she hadn't been available, he would have found someone else, someone like her.

Someone like Sarah.

One for the honey; one for the money. That's what he'd said over the police radio. Katherine squeezed her eyes shut, trying to block out the image of Charles tasting Sarah's honey.

"Are you okay?" Vince asked, and Katherine blinked her eyes open and gave a feeble nod.

He'd gotten up from the table while she'd been on the phone with Susan, and had washed the few breakfast dishes. Now he stood only a few feet away. His shirt and slacks were wrinkled and there were dark circles under his eyes, but he looked sexy as hell.

She shook off that thought. "We need to talk."

"Drive me to my plane. I need to change and grab a few things."

Her grandfather pushed his chair back from the table and stood. "You wanna see my fly collection?"

"Some other time," Vince answered and walked back to the table to shake her grandfather's thin, gnarled hand. "Right now your granddaughter needs to take me someplace."

Her grandfather looked at Vince, and then at her. Finally, he nodded. "Somethin's going on, isn't it? Something you don't want to tell me. Right?"

How *could* she tell him? she wondered. Her grandfather had never been the outgoing type, and now that he was losing his mental capabilities, he had few social contacts. Phil had been his one consistent male friend. So how did you tell a man who had already lost his wife and only child that his best buddy might also be dead?

She didn't know how, so she said, "We're looking for a missing girl, Poppa. That's all." Which wasn't a lie. Even though Gordon had taken her off the case, she had no intention of spending the day behind her desk or out on the streets talking to tourists.

"Your grandfather's mind seems clearer this morning," Vince said as they left the house and headed for her Tahoe.

She'd noticed that, too. "He's pretty good until around mid-afternoon; then it's like his brain shuts down. The doctor called it the sundown syndrome."

"What are you going to do when he gets so bad he needs twenty-four-hour care?"

"I don't know."

It was a question she didn't want to face. She'd thought having Sarah at the house in the evenings would suffice for a few months, and the chief knew her situation. They'd talked about shifts that would allow her to be with her grandfather when he needed the most help. But, Vince was right. There would come a time when her grandfather would need round-the-clock supervision and help. Could she afford in-home care? Would she put him in a nursing home? There wasn't one in Skagway.

As she unlocked the doors to her Tahoe, she forced those questions from her mind. Right now, two girls needed her help far more than her grandfather. Which gave her an idea. "You said a fax was sent to your office. Did it have the sender's phone number on it?"

"I asked. It didn't." Vince glanced at his Rolex. "Bob was going to call the telephone company this morning, have them trace the number. I'll give him a call once we get to the plane."

"And, if he sent the fax using a computer?"

"It might take a little longer, but we can track it down."

The possibility of Charles using a computer made sense to Katherine. "I've been trying to figure out how Charles would know I was here in Skagway. It had to be through the Internet. It's the only way I can see that he'd know about Misty, know her father was wealthy, and that she'd be coming here. I'm sure that interview her stepmother gave is on-line." Nowadays everything ended up on-line. "A check of the cruise line schedules and Charles would have the exact time when Misty and Crystal would be arriving in Skagway. He might want to punish me for testifying against him, but, once he did that, he'd need money . . . a way to escape."

"So he asks for a hundred million?" She saw Vince shake his head as he got into the Tahoe. "What's he planning on doing— buying his own country?"

Katherine would admit the amount did seem excessive, even

for Charles.

"And, your little scenario still doesn't explain how he knew to fax my company."

Which meant Vince still thought she was responsible for Charles having that knowledge. She glared at him as she settled behind the steering wheel. "I didn't give him your fax number."

"Then who did?"

She considered the question. *Someone who saw Vince's business card on her desk?* Unlikely. No. It had to be someone who knew Vince's connection to Tom Morgan.

"Misty," she said, realizing it made sense.

"You're accusing Misty of being in cahoots with this Bell guy?"

"No, not 'in cahoots.' Terrified." Just thinking about Misty's situation made Katherine remember how she felt those first few hours in Charles's basement. "He makes sure you know what he's capable of doing, reminds you, over and over, that your life is in his hands. He would have made sure Misty saw him kill the guy she was with. It wouldn't take much for him to get her to either willingly or not so willingly tell him about your company and your relationship with her father."

"Which she probably would," Vince admitted. "I told her if she ever got in trouble to call me."

From the look on his face, Katherine could tell it bothered Vince that he hadn't been there for that call. "Thank goodness you did. By giving Charles your fax number, Misty may have given us the clue we need. Have your partner figure out where this computer is located. Do that, and we'll find Misty and Sarah."

CHAPTER FORTY-FOUR

8:45 A.M., Friday

Susan Lange drove the nine miles of dirt road from her house to Dyea through a misty drizzle. She dreaded the next few hours. How would she react if she did find Phil's body?

She considered herself thick-skinned and tough-minded, but she'd been known to cry in sentimental movies, at weddings, and during funerals. What would the two seasonal park rangers who'd volunteered to help with the search think if she got all teary-eyed, or, worse, if she threw up?

They'll think I'm human, Susan told herself and took a deep breath. God, she hoped Katherine and Gordon were wrong and Phil was alive. Possibly hurt, but alive.

She pulled her SUV into the parking area next to the park service campground, and a pint-sized female and a tall, gangly male got out of a rusted Ford truck. Both looked to be in their early twenties and both were wearing the park ranger regulation olive-green jackets with arrowhead shoulder patches, gold badges, and green field caps. Susan had seen the two just a few days before, when she'd stopped by the park visitors center on Broadway. The girl had been handing out maps and brochures and answering questions. The guy had been hovering near the girl, watching her with the look of a lovesick puppy. Susan had had to personally remind him that he was supposed to be giving a tour at that time.

Susan had a feeling these two would have eyes only for each

other, and if she'd had a choice, she wouldn't have chosen them for backup. But she didn't have a choice. The other protection rangers and volunteers were either assigned to different search areas or were taking a break after a long night of searching.

Hand in hand, the two seasonal volunteers sauntered from the Ford toward Susan, and, as they drew closer, she could see a redness on the girl's cheeks that looked a lot like whisker burn. Susan would also bet the hint of red by the side of the guy's mouth came from lipstick. She was pretty sure the two hadn't been discussing search and rescue procedures while awaiting her arrival.

"You're Amy Clark and Martin Liskovic?" Susan asked, even though she was sure the two had to be the ones assigned to her.

"Yes. Ready, willing, and able," the girl said, stopping in front of Susan and saluting.

Martin, Susan noticed, frowned, and she had a feeling he recognized her and remembered the tongue lashing she'd given him. Not that Susan cared. They were there to get a job done, not become buddy buddies.

She didn't return Amy's salute, merely pointed toward her. "You sit in front." Then she pointed at Martin. "You in back."

"We . . ." Martin started, then shrugged and released Amy's hand. "I'll get our things from my truck," he said and started back toward it. Within minutes, with both of her passengers and their equipment in the SUV, Susan pulled out of the parking area.

"I understand we're looking for a missing fisherman," Amy said.

"A missing police officer," Susan corrected. "Who may have gone fishing and hasn't been heard from since."

"He hasn't called in or anything?" Martin asked from the back seat.

"No." That was all Susan wanted to tell them at this point.

"Are we going to West Creek?" Martin asked.

"We're heading that way, but that's not where we'll end up."

She drove over the bridge that crossed the Taiya River and kept going until the narrow road turned into a maze of two-tracks. Katherine had said she wasn't sure the directions her grandfather had provided were exactly right, and Susan wasn't totally sure she remembered exactly where she'd run into Phil, but, when she came to a fork in the road, she choose the middle track—as Katherine had suggested—and prayed Russell Ward's mind was clear this time.

Soon the two-track narrowed until tree limbs were scraping both sides the SUV, the slap of the windshield wipers giving intermittent views of what lay ahead. Only the occasional sight of broken branches and tire impressions in the dirt and grass kept Susan going. A vehicle had been on this trail recently. Whether or not those tracks were from Phil's Tahoe, she couldn't tell.

The trail ended at a small, natural clearing near the mountain's base, and Susan turned off the SUV's engine. This was the spot. She remembered the fallen lodgepole pine she'd parked beside and the nearby European mountain ash bush. Her memory and Katherine's grandfather's directions had been spot on. "Here is where we get out," she told the other two.

"Where's the lake?" Amy asked, looking around.

Susan pointed up the mountainside.

"Up there?" Martin tilted his head back, shielding his eyes from the misting rain.

Susan smiled. *Up there* wasn't a gradual slope. The mountainside went straight up, and, from what Katherine had said, even her grandfather, in his prime, considered it a difficult hike.

"I didn't think we'd be rock climbing," Martin grumbled.

"There should be a trail at the edge of this clearing." Susan pointed toward the rim of the clearing where stands of devils club and alder melded into hemlocks and Sitka spruce. "We'll split up here. Look for a pair of posts. Or any kind of marker; any sign that someone went into the woods."

Susan watched Amy and Martin walk to the edge of the clearing. She wasn't sure if Martin thought she couldn't see when he grabbed Amy's hand, or if he didn't care. Amy glanced over at Susan, indicating her awareness, then said something to Martin and pulled her hand free. As soon as the two reached the wooded area, they did as instructed and started walking in opposite directions. Susan took a moment to call in her location, and then she began searching her portion of the clearing.

Amy was the one who found the posts. "Over here," she yelled, and Susan and Martin quickly joined her.

Just as Katherine's grandfather had said, two posts marked the start of a trail, albeit a faint one. Crushed undergrowth gave proof that the path had been used recently. Susan told her two volunteers to get anything they thought they might need out of the SUV; that they might not be back for some time.

She was wrong, however. They'd barely traveled a quarter of a mile along the trail, Susan leading the way, followed by Martin and Amy, when Susan noticed a dark stain on the ground ahead . . . and a mass of flies. Black flies were common in the summer, but these were blow flies, and the only time Susan had seen them gathered like this was when there was something dead in the area.

She stopped where she was. A line of darkened soil and leaves led from the main path to denser underbrush along the side.

"What?" Martin asked, nearly running into her.

"I hear something," Amy said, coming up behind them.

Susan wondered if she would ever forget that buzzing sound, or the sight of a bare foot, just barely visible through the tangle of underbrush. She took in a deep breath, forcing her rapidly beating heart to slow, and swore.

Martin evidently saw it at the same time. "It's a bare foot," he said.

"A bear?" Amy said behind him, her voice rising and taking on a note of panic.

"No," Martin corrected. "A foot . . . without any shoes or socks. It looks like a man's foot."

Susan only marginally listened to Martin's explanation. In her own mind, she processed what she had to do next. "You two stay here," she ordered, a wave of her hand marking the spot. Subconsciously she may have wanted to shield them from what was ahead, but her primary intention was to keep the area as pristine as possible. Although the foot might belong to someone catching forty winks, the blow flies told her otherwise.

Carefully, she inched her way closer to the foot. The steady, drizzling rain had dampened down the smell, but, as she neared the body, she caught the distinct coppery odor of blood and death. Covered with pine boughs, dried needles, and branches from shrubs, the body was lying face down, and Susan couldn't get a clear view, but she could tell it was a man. Not only was his foot bare, so was the rest of him.

She tried not to step on anything that might be considered evidence, but, with the man's face turned away from her, she couldn't be one hundred percent sure it was Phil Carpenter. Although she knew she shouldn't touch anything, she had to know. One by one, she removed the leaves covering his face.

It was Phil.

She didn't bother feeling for a pulse. The gash on the side of his neck told her there was no hope. Something sharp, probably a knife, had severed the carotid artery. Phil would have died within seconds. He may never have known exactly what happened.

A maggot poked its head up from the edge of the slash, and Susan gulped back the nausea that threatened to erupt from her stomach. She didn't bother trying to stem the tears. This was a colleague, someone she knew. They had a history of living in the area year-round, enduring the long winters, and the annual onslaught of tourists. Police officers didn't get murdered in Skagway. They either stayed until they retired, or they moved on to better paying, more stimulating positions in other cities and other police departments.

She took a step back and pulled out her radio. "You two," she said, looking at Amy and Martin, "go back to the clearing. I'm going to call this in. There's crime scene tape in the back of my SUV. One of you bring it to me. The other stay by the vehicle and, when the police arrive, bring them up here."

"Is he dead?" Amy asked, her voice shaky.

"He's dead," Susan said, hating the finality of those words.

"Is it the fisherman?" Martin asked, his voice only marginally stronger than Amy's.

"Yes," she said and pressed the button to transmit.

CHAPTER FORTY-FIVE

A fine, misty drizzle blurred Vince's view of his plane, the inside of the Tahoe's windshield rapidly fogging up as the warmth of their breaths created a contrast to the chilly outside air. Katherine had asked him to call his office before he went to his plane and see if his partner had discovered the phone number for the fax. Vince figured Bob should have had time to gather that information. What he didn't mention was how Bob would gather it. Katherine might be off Misty's case, but she was still a police officer and letting her know some of the ways they operated wasn't a good idea.

His satellite phone still showed a charge, and Vince tapped the icon for his office number. Edith, their sixty-year-old secretary, answered and put him through to Bob. The first thing Vince asked was, "Have you heard anything more from the kidnapper?"

Bob's response was somber. "We got another fax. This one came through after I left last night. He's given us a routing number . . . and a time limit."

"How long do we have?"

"Until five o'clock this evening. Of course, I don't know if that's five o'clock Skagway time or Seattle time."

"Skagway," Vince said, and glanced at his watch. They had just a little more than eight hours to find the pervert.

"He wrote the time in big letters. I don't like the feel of this."

"Neither do I." Vince glanced over at Katherine. He still had a feeling she wasn't telling him everything, but he would work with what he did know. "You said 'wrote.' Is he hand writing these faxes or sending them through a computer?"

"Unless he's scanning what he's written and then transmitting it through a computer, I'd say he's using a fax machine. Why?"

"Just thinking of ways we could trace these faxes."

"I'm already on that," Bob assured him. "I've got the telephone company tracing where they're coming from, and I'm looking into where the money is to be sent. We'll want to know both."

"I talked to Tom last night," Vince said. "He doesn't want his money sent anywhere, not unless it's an absolute necessity."

"You've got to be kidding." Bob sounded astonished. "This is his daughter we're talking about. The Little Princess."

"Tom feels, even if he pays the ransom, there's no guarantee Bell will let Misty go," Vince said.

"Have you talked to Crystal? What does she say about all this?"

"She asked him what he valued most, his bank account or his daughter? I actually liked her at that moment."

"I don't know why you have such a negative opinion of her."

"She's a user."

"She's beautiful . . . and smart."

"Maybe not so smart, and how much of her beauty is the result of cosmetic surgery?" Again Vince looked at Katherine. "I prefer natural beauty."

She frowned, and Vince had a feeling compliments were not the way to her heart. Not that he was interested in getting to her heart, of course. His physical responses to her were simply a result of too little sleep, nothing more. Nothing stronger.

"Tom liked what he saw," Bob reminded Vince, bringing him back to the subject of Crystal.

"As you said, the lady's smart. She saw how vulnerable Tom was after his wife died, and she played her cards just right. But I think the honeymoon's over."

"Is Tom there yet?" Bob asked.

Using his free hand, Vince wiped the moisturefrom the inside of the vehicle's windshield and stared across the asphalt. "I don't see any of his planes, and I'm sure he'd call me once he arrived."

"Look, you know Tom a hell of a lot better than I do," Bob said. "Let's say we're right down to the deadline. It's almost five o'clock, and you haven't found Misty. How long would it take Tom to come up with that much money?"

"I don't know."

"Jeez, Vince," Bob grumbled. "We can't wait until the last minute to do this. We need to have everything in place . . . You know, just in case you don't find this guy by the deadline."

"You find out where that fax came from, and I'll find Misty," Vince said.

"Vince the invincible." Bob's tone didn't sound flattering. "So, how did you miss that chat room Misty was in?"

Vince knew this wasn't the time for excuses, but he felt the need to explain. "You were there the day Misty whined to Tom that we were all treating her like a baby and that he didn't trust her."

"Yeah, I remember the conversation, but I guess I expected you to keep monitoring her on-line activities."

"I told her I wouldn't." And he didn't go back on a promise.

"And you call Crystal a user." Bob scoffed. "Vince, old buddy, your Little Princess sure duped you."

He hated to admit it, but Bob was right.

"Guess she duped me, too," Bob said. "But, let's be honest. Tom hired us to protect his company. Babysitting a teenager was not part of our contract."

"True." Not that hearing that alleviated Vince's feelings of guilt. And, if he didn't find Misty, they probably wouldn't have a contract.

His gaze drifted back to his plane. No contract, no private plane. No . . .

Once again Vince rubbed his hand across the Tahoe's windshield. "Shit," he said, and wondered why he hadn't noticed it in the first place.

"What?" Bob asked through the phone.

"What?" Katherine asked, clearing a spot on the windshield in front of her.

"Someone slit my tires."

CHAPTER FORTY-SIX

9:00 A.M., Friday

The moment Misty heard the doorknob turn and saw the bedroom door open, her heart started beating faster. She'd barely slept and wasn't sure what time it might be, or when she last ate, but the gnawing sensation now invading her stomach had nothing to do with hunger.

"Good morning, girls," The Beekeeper said, at least giving her some sense of time.

"Please don't," Sarah gasped as he neared her bed.

"Relax, sweetie. I'm here to take care of your needs, not mine."

Once again he'd left the door open, enough light filtering into the room to allow Misty a better view of what was going on. She watched him fold the blankets back from Sarah's naked body, and heard the girl suck in a breath. She wanted to tell him to leave Sarah alone, but she was afraid if she said anything, he'd climb on top of Sarah again . . . Or worse, turn away from Sarah and rape her.

"I imagine you're sore. Need to use the bathroom. Probably feel dirty."

Sarah didn't say anything, the only sound coming from her a small whimper.

"We don't want you all smelly when you get rescued." He moved to the end of the bed, and Misty could tell he was untying the bindings from around Sarah's ankles. She also knew when he looked at her. "They will come to rescue you, won't they?"

"I . . . I hope so," Misty said, not as sure as she'd been the day before.

"Of course they will." He moved to the other end of the bed, releasing the strips of sheeting from around the bars of the headboard, just as he had done whenever he allowed them to get up. "Your father will pay the money, and I'll get what I want."

"What do you want?" Misty asked, afraid his answer might involve her.

"A reunion. Come on, sweetheart," he said, helping Sarah stand. "Time for a little exercise. We don't want you getting bed sores and too weak to walk."

"Please let me go," Sarah whimpered. "My mother needs me. My brother and sister."

"Shh," he soothed. "Soon enough."

Again, Misty could tell he was looking at her. "Don't go away," he said, and pushed Sarah toward the doorway. "You're next."

He didn't close the door behind them, and she could hear their progress down the hallway, could hear the flush of the toilet a few minutes later, then the sound of running water. She wondered if he took the bindings off Sarah's wrists before he put her in the shower. Did he get in with her? Did he do it to her while they were under the water?

The image of them standing under a stream of warm water, him shoving himself into Sarah, made Misty's stomach churn even more. She fought anew against the bindings around her wrists and ankles. She'd pulled and twisted so many times, her wrists throbbed from the effort, and her skin was raw.

Would someone rescue her?

She pulled both arms as far down as she could, her shoulder

muscles aching not only from the strain but from the battering they'd received when she did try to escape. As before, the cloth wrapped around her wrists gave a little, but not enough for her to slip her hand out, not with the material double wrapped around each wrist.

Was her father still in China or was he on his way here?

She'd thought maybe her phone call to him from the ship, her not-so-veiled threat that she might run away, would have caused some sort of reaction. She'd been upset when she thought it was Vince following them on the highway out of Skagway, but at least his presence would have shown her father did care what she did . . . that he did love her.

But, there'd been no Vince; no running off with Brian.

Brian.

Misty closed her eyes, still remembering the sight of him collapsing next to his Blazer.

She never should have suggested the trip across Canada. She never should have agreed to go on a cruise to Alaska. Everything she tried to do turned out badly. If only she hadn't been such a difficult baby, her mother wouldn't have had so much stress, wouldn't have gotten cancer. If her mother were still alive, none of this would have happened. She wouldn't be here, wouldn't be at the mercy of this monster.

Once again, Misty pulled at the restraints on her arms . . . then stopped. Had she heard something tear? Had her right arm moved a little farther than before?

Misty pulled again. Harder this time. Pulled. Jerked. Pulled. Jerked again.

And then she stopped.

She'd heard a tearing sound, had felt a change in the tension around her right wrist.

With renewed vigor, she tugged, twisted, pulled, and jerked. Each movement brought pain to her wrists but also increased the tearing sound and eased the tension on her right arm.

The cloth finally gave with a snap, her right elbow hitting the mattress, a strip of sheeting brushing against her shoulder as her hand moved forward. Her right arm was free.

Quickly, Misty rolled to her side and loosened the binding around her left wrist.

All of her pulling had tightened the knot into a small lump, so she twisted her body until she could suck on the cloth. If she could dampen the material enough, it might give. She broke a fingernail, ignored it, and used the ragged edge to work at the knot.

In the background she heard the water stop running and knew her time was limited. Would he towel Sarah off or bring her back wet? She had to move fast.

Using her teeth, she pried the knot open, unwrapped the cloth, and sat up. The bindings around her ankles weren't as tight, and she'd loosened both by the time she heard his voice.

"Come on; stop shivering," he said. "You can't be that cold."

"Please, I don't want to go back in there," Sarah whimpered. "I don't want you to do it to me again."

"I'm not going to do it; not now," he said gently. "We have your friend to take care of first."

Misty pushed the wool blankets back and swung her legs over the side of the bed. She felt weaker than the last time she'd stood, and her chest ached from being crushed against the floor, but she knew she had to ignore the pain. Without hesitation, she grabbed the lamp on the small table between the two beds. She'd already come to the conclusion that it was the only object in the room that she could use as a weapon. A jerk on the cord freed it from the wall, and, lamp in hand, Misty hurried over to the wall next to the doorway.

In her mind, she rehearsed her moves, just as Vince had taught her. *When attacked, if you know what you're going to do, then you don't have to think about it,* he'd told her. *You just do it.*

In this case, she was going to be the attacker, but she was sure the same rule applied. The Beekeeper—or whatever his name was—would push Sarah through the doorway first, and then he would follow. Misty knew she had to wait until Sarah was clear of the doorway; only then should she bring the lamp down on his head.

Don't give me away, Sarah, Misty prayed, listening to the padding of Sarah's bare feet, along with the muffled sound of his sneakers.

Aim high, she reminded herself, hoping it would be the heaviest part of the lamp that hit his head.

Heart in her throat, she waited, seconds turning into eternities.

Step by step, they came.

She couldn't breathe, the lamp growing heavier, her arms going numb as she held it above her head, ready to strike.

As Misty had expected, Sarah came through the doorway first, the girl's eyes focused on the beds; dark, water-soaked locks of hair hanging down below her shoulders. Misty saw a resigned look on Sarah's face, an acceptance of her fate. The girl moved toward her bed like a zombie, her captor directly behind her.

Sarah didn't look to the side; didn't see Misty at all; just kept walking.

The moment The Beekeeper came through the doorway, Misty slammed the lamp down on his head. She heard a thud and felt a vibration travel through her hands to her arms, and down through her body.

He turned his head slightly toward her, a look of amazement on his face, and then slowly, ever so slowly, he folded before her eyes, his mouth opening, and his knees buckling. She saw his arms stretch forward as he reached for the floor.

Only then did Misty move. "Run!" she screamed at Sarah. "Follow me."

Misty ran for the front door, released the dead bolt, and opened the door before looking back. Sarah was still by the bedroom door, struggling to move forward. For a moment, Misty considered going back to help the girl; then she saw The Beekeeper's arm appear through the doorway, saw the strip of sheeting he still held in his hand. Misty knew then that he had Sarah, and that she couldn't go back, not without help.

A cold, misty rain hit her the moment she stepped outside of the house, reminding her that she didn't have any clothes on. For a second, Misty paused, looking around. A large section of cement in front of the door gave way to a narrow dirt path flanked on each side with patches of shaggy grass that needed cutting. Beyond the path was a dirt driveway that led in two directions, both disappearing into thickly wooded areas.

Which way to go? She wasn't sure. All she knew was she had to get away from the house, away from *him.*

In the distance she heard the sound of a car. It seemed to be coming from her right. Choosing that direction, she ran. And she yelled. At the top of her voice, she screamed, "Help!" Over and over she yelled, hoping someone would hear her.

Gravel tore at the bottoms of her feet, the cloth still tied around her right wrist flapping behind her as she ran. Fine droplets of rain began sliding off her hair and down her face, but she didn't care. She was free. She was going to be rescued.

CHAPTER FORTY-SEVEN

Katherine and Vince examined the King Air's tires. Someone had stabbed at each multiple times. They checked at the terminal, but the Wings of Alaska employee on duty had seen nothing. "One of the problems of a public owned airport with no official attendant on duty twenty-four-seven," Katherine said. "I'll call it in, and we'll write up an official report."

Not that she considered slashed tires a high priority, not with two teenagers in the clutches of a pervert. But she did wonder why Vince's plane had been targeted. Why no other planes had suffered any damage.

"Betsy," she said when her call in was answered by the morning dispatcher. "What's the status on the missing girls?"

"Nothing so far," Betsy responded. "Gordon's not in. You want to talk to Jim?"

She had little choice but to say yes.

"Heard you were off the case," Jim Preto said the moment he answered.

"Officially, yes." Katherine left it at that. "Anything new on Bell or the girls?"

"Not much. A couple of landlords we contacted remembered someone who might have been Charles Bell. Said about a month ago a guy who fit Bell's description asked about places to rent. Seems he never followed up."

"Meaning we're no further ahead than we were yesterday." She thanked him anyway, and then relayed the information about Nanini's slashed tires before she disconnected.

As they walked back to Nanini's plane, he asked, "Is something special happening at five o'clock?"

"Not that I know of."

"Any reason why Bell has picked that time?"

Katherine started to shake her head, then stopped. *Five o'clock.* The exact time Charles had wanted his note delivered to her. The exact time the police had raided his house and freed her, seventeen years ago.

At five o'clock she was no longer under his control . . . now he wanted her back. A shiver ran down her spine, and she forced herself to forget what he'd done to her when he did have her under his control. She wouldn't think about what he might do to her if he once again held her captive. "What did Misty's father say?" she asked, trying to keep her mind on the present. "Can he get his hands on that much money in such a short time?"

"My partner asked the same question. Truth is, I don't know."

"I heard you tell your partner Morgan might not pay."

Nanini nodded. "That's what he said last night, when Crystal and I talked to him."

"I've sometimes wondered what my parents would have done if he hadn't killed them." Having admitted her doubts, she wished she hadn't and looked away.

"It must have been terrible, knowing they were dead and couldn't come to your rescue."

Katherine looked back at him. Would he understand? "There were times, early in my captivity, when I tried to convince myself that my parents weren't dead and that they would find me and rescue me."

"But, nobody came."

The way he said it, she knew he did understand. "Not for a long, long time. Not until I'd given up." And given in.

Katherine flinched when Vince's arm went around her shoulders. "Don't," she said and pulled away, adrenaline shooting through her body.

"Sorry." He raised his hands in supplication. "I didn't mean to scare you."

"You didn't scare me," she lied, her heart beating like a jackhammer. "You took me by surprise. That's all."

"This is bringing it all back, isn't it?"

She forced herself to exhale slowly. Way too much, she thought.

CHAPTER FORTY-EIGHT

Susan Lange was on her radio-phone talking to an Alaska state trooper when Martin Liskovic arrived with the crime-scene tape she'd asked him to get out of her vehicle. Susan motioned for him to cordon off a wide area around the body. While she continued feeding what she knew about the murder to the trooper on the line, Susan watched Martin string the yellow tape from one tree to another. As soon as she'd answered all of the trooper's questions, she signed off. Her next call would be to the Skagway police department.

She knew the chief was still in the hospital, so she asked to talk to Sergeant Gordon Landros.

"He's not in," the receptionist/dispatcher answered.

"Then Katherine," Susan said. "Officer Ward."

"She's not in either," the woman answered.

"Then let me talk to whomever is in charge."

It was Jim Petro who finally took her call. "We found your missing officer," Susan said after identifying herself. "I'm no medical examiner, but I'd say he's been dead for a day or two."

There was a moment of silence before Petro keyed a response. "I'll let Sergeant Landros know. Damn."

"Yeah." Damn pretty much summed it up.

"Cause of death?"

"Sanguination," she said, remembering the path of blood-soaked earth from the trail to the spot where Phil Carpenter's body had been covered with leaves and brush. "Looks like the

killer was behind him, caught him off guard, and cut his throat
before he had a chance to react."

"Damn," Preto repeated, a slight catch in his voice indicating
a stronger emotional response.

"We're cordoning off the area," Susan said, to fill him in.
"And, I've called in the state troopers. They're sending someone."

"Good. Very good."

"I had to move some of the leaves covering his face," she
said, certain the police wouldn't be happy with that. "I needed
to for a positive identification."

"Just a minute," was the officer's response.

She could hear him repeating what she'd said to someone
else. Finally he came back to her. "I guess we already have an
assistant district attorney here for that murder on the Klondike
Highway. Our dispatcher said the two cases are probably related,
and we should be sure the evidence at your site is processed
right. Anyway, until he or the troopers arrive, don't go near the
body. Don't touch Phil's clothing, or—"

She cut him off. "There is no clothing. Your officer is naked.
He's lying on his stomach, just off the trail—which is barely a
trail—and is covered with branches and leaves. There's no sign
of clothing anywhere."

"No clothes?" Officer Preto sounded stunned. "Oh, my God.
Was he . . . that is, do you think he was, ah . . . molested in any
way?"

"Molested?" The possibility surprised Susan, and she glanced
past the spot where Martin was securing the crime-scene tape
to another tree. She could see the soles of Phil Carpenter's feet
and the faint outline of his legs.

When she'd knelt beside him, it was his upper torso she'd
focused on. She'd noted the pale, grayish hue of his skin, the
vacant, unseeing look in his eye, and the blood, already dried,

that rimmed the cut on his neck and trailed to the ground. The manner of death had been quite clear, and she hadn't bothered to check other parts of his body. A medical examiner, during an autopsy, would be able to tell if there were other injuries or if Phil Carpenter had been sodomized.

"Not that I could tell," she said.

"I sure hope not, but, from what everyone's saying, I wouldn't put it past the bastard."

"You know who did this?"

"We think so. So, don't do anything to mess up the evidence."

Considering how young the officer sounded, Susan bet she knew more about preserving evidence than he did. "Just be thankful the bears didn't find him." There wouldn't have been much left of Phil Carpenter if a bear had come across his corpse.

"Amen," she heard the officer say before another voice in the background asked him a question. He relayed it to her. "What about Phil's Tahoe? Have you secured it?"

"There is no vehicle," she said. "And, if there were any tire tracks, I probably messed them up when I pulled in here. This trail is way off the beaten path. If Katherine hadn't suggested we look here, we wouldn't have found him."

"Katherine?" Officer Preto said. "Katherine told you to look there?"

"She called me this morning. Said her grandfather mentioned the lake up the mountainside, and she remembered Phil was still trying to catch trout out of it. She pretty much directed me straight to Phil."

"Katherine," he repeated, and then cleared his throat. "Ranger Lange, you'd better give me the coordinates of where you are."

As she'd already done with the state troopers, Susan gave Preto the global positioning coordinates. That conversation over, she helped Martin finish with the crime-scene tape. As soon as it was up, she told him to go back in her SUV and get in, out of the rain. She'd be down in a minute.

Susan watched Martin disappear down the trail, then she turned back to look at the body sprawled out on the ground. One thing she would never understand was man's inhumanity to man. She'd been raised a Methodist, had listened to various ministers preach about goodness and kindness, had even worn a WWJD bracelet when she was a teenager. What would Jesus do? He'd probably weep, she thought. He'd taught the golden rule: Do unto others as you'd have them do unto you. Well, mankind certainly wasn't following that rule.

Shaking her head, Susan Lange turned and walked back to her SUV.

CHAPTER FORTY-NINE

9:30 A.M., Friday

The parking lot next to the police station was almost full when Katherine pulled in. She recognized some of the vehicles. The three SUVs with red lights on their roofs belonged to members of Skagway's volunteer fire department. A rusted and dented four-wheel-drive Ford truck was owned by Joe Ketterman, a retired park ranger, and the ten-year-old, faded-gold Lexus GX was the pride and joy of Manny Schwartz, a seventy-year-old, retired, San Francisco police officer who spent his summers in Skagway. The black Tahoe with Alaska state government plates had probably arrived from Juneau on the early ferry.

The troops had arrived.

Katherine used the side entrance to the station, and Vince followed her in. As they walked down the short hallway to the booking area, Katherine could hear Gordon's voice. He was up in the front office area, speaking to the owners of the vehicles parked in the lot. Step by step he was relaying what they had learned in the last eighteen hours, giving details about the kidnapped girls and Charles Bell, the "alleged" kidnapper. "The cruise lines have been alerted," he said, "as well as all other means of transportation out of this area. Unless this guy has found a way to walk on water or cross into Canada without going through customs, he's here."

"You've checked lodgings and RV parks?" asked a gravelly male voice that Katherine recognized as belonging to Manny.

"Checked and double checked," Gordon answered. "Now we need the rentals checked."

"But no heroics," another male voice stated. "This has got to be done by the book. We don't want this pervert getting off on a technicality."

Katherine didn't recognize the voice, but she'd bet it was the DA or assistant DA from Juneau. It was up to him to make sure, once they caught Charles, all evidence was admissible in court and no fancy defense lawyer could get him off on a technicality.

"And, be careful," Gordon added, tension lacing his voice. "This bastard has killed two people so far, one of them our own. We don't want him hurting these girls, and we don't want any of you getting hurt."

One of our own. Katherine sucked in a breath, the slice of toast she'd had for breakfast turning into a lump in her stomach. She wanted to go up front and ask Gordon where they'd found Phil, how he'd been killed, and how long he'd been dead, but she didn't want to start crying in front of the others. The creak of a chair brought her attention to her left. In the back office, Jim Preto sat at the break table nursing a cup of coffee and a long face. Although the new baby in Jim's home had been seriously cutting into his sleep time, if she wasn't mistaken, the red rimming his pale-blue eyes was from tears, not a lack of shut-eye.

Jim was lanky as a lodgepole pine, but scrappy as a badger, and this was his second year as a seasonal officer. He was the jokester, always ready with a funny story, always laughing. The look on his face now was anything but amused. He frowned as Katherine and Vince approached, actually glaring at her. "Phil's dead," he said, a spear of accusation in his voice. "Park ranger Susan Lange called it in. She found his body."

"I just heard," Katherine said.

"His throat was cut," Jim said, looking as if he blamed her.

Katherine closed her eyes and fought back the memories of her parents' and brother's bodies, their throats cut and their open eyes staring out at nothing. She remembered the blood. A pool of it under her brother's head. A stream of it flowing down the front of her mother's nightgown. Dark red in the dim lighting. Metallic smelling.

"Oh, God," she groaned and felt her knees buckle.

She would have crumpled to the floor if Vince hadn't grabbed her. His hands locked around her forearms, strong yet gentle, holding her erect and pulling her back to reality. Through her uniform, she could feel the warmth of his fingers, and realized she was leaning against his body.

Don't fall apart, she thought. *Not in front of these two men.*

Reassured that her legs would hold her, she opened her eyes, and took in a deep breath. A step forward released her from Vince's almost-embrace. Jim was watching, still frowning.

"Ranger Lange said Phil was *exactly* where you said he would be."

He'd emphasized "exactly," making Katherine wonder if he believed she was involved in Phil's death. She couldn't have people thinking that. "I told her where I *thought* he might be. That's all."

"Gordon says you know the scumbag who's doing this."

Jim's look was accusing. The same look she'd endured long ago. As if she'd wanted her family killed, wanted to be held captive . . . wanted Phil dead.

"Fuck you," she said and turned to walk away, only to bump into Vince. Unable to contain her anger, she shoved at the wall of his chest. She was not going to stand around and defend herself to an officer who didn't know diddly squat about anything.

"Katherine," Vince said, not moving.

She looked down at the floor, not wanting him to see the tears welling in her eyes.

Another voice repeated her name. "Katherine."

She looked up and around Vince. Gordon stood a few feet ahead of her.

"What's the matter?" he asked.

"Phil's dead."

"I know."

"Jim thinks I had something to do with Phil's death."

Gordon frowned, looking beyond Vince and Katherine and into the office area. She also looked back. Jim had risen to his feet and now stood beside the table.

"You told him I knew Charles," she said, knowing it was inevitable, yet feeling betrayed.

"I just—" Jim started, but a wave of Gordon's hand silenced the officer.

"You—" Gordon demanded and pointed at Vince. "Come with me. The girl's father has arrived. And you—" He pointed at Jim. "Get the list Betsy has ready so these men can get started searching house by house. And you—" His finger pointed at Katherine. "Get on that phone and get us a current picture of Charles Bell. Now!"

CHAPTER FIFTY

The gravel driveway changed as Misty ran forward. What had started as a wide, clearly discernible roadway faded into nothing more than a path. Patches of grass mixed with sharp, little stones and dried pine needles. Each stride she took caused pain, but she didn't dare stop running.

She hadn't heard another car since the first, and, the farther she traveled, the more she knew she was heading in the wrong direction. It didn't surprise her that she'd gone the wrong way. Everything she'd done lately had been wrong.

"Daddy, I'm sorry," she sobbed, the words barely audible.

Her initial burst of adrenaline wearing off, she slowed her pace. Fatigued muscles, unaccustomed to strenuous exercise of any kind, shot internal messages to her brain, begging her to stop. Each breath she took came as a short gasp.

Trees and brush swallowed the path and surrounded her, blocking her view of the house she'd left. In a way, she was glad. Misty knew the foliage was also blocking *his* view of her. She continued on, stumbling over fallen branches and being clawed at by the prickly spines of a sprawling shrub. She'd flaunted her nakedness on the cruise ship, laughing at the shocked expression on the face of the woman who spied her, and putting up a fuss about freedom of expression when the ship's officer made her get out of the pool. Now she felt raw and exposed. Vulnerable.

She'd stopped yelling for help as soon as she realized it was futile. There were no houses around, no knights on white horses riding by who might save her. She couldn't even find the road, much less a car or another person. All she could do was keep going and hope The Beekeeper would give up and go back to the house.

Keep going deeper and deeper into the woods.

A low, drawn-out croak gave her a start, and Misty stopped. She heard it again. Up ahead in the trees. Like laugher, the sound mocked her.

With her eyes, she followed the sound and spotted the source. A large, black bird sat on a lofty pine bough. The raven was watching her.

Like a hypnotist, the bird's gaze held her where she stood. She'd seen several ravens in trees and on buildings when their ship docked in Juneau. They were bigger than the crows she was familiar with, and they'd yelled back and forth at each other, strutting along the rooftops.

They were supposed to be smart. Someone onboard the ship had told her that. She wished she could ask this one which way to the road.

Once again the bird cried out, then it flew away, and Misty felt an aching sense of loneliness. She had no idea where she was, had no clothes to shield her from the scratchy brush, the rain, or the cold. Not even shoes to protect her feet. A tear slid down her cheek, then another. She thought things couldn't get any worse . . . until she heard a branch snap to her right.

With a woof, a bear rose on its hind legs, and looked directly at her. Misty sucked in a breath, staring at the animal. It was so close she could see the twigs and briars that stuck to its pale, almost white fur. Its chest was wider than any man's, each paw as large as a baseball mitt, and its eyes were no more than dark circles in its monstrous head. It opened its mouth, exposing a line of threatening teeth, and gave a huff, the sound deep and guttural.

Misty wanted to scream, but the sound froze in her throat. As if drained of all blood, her legs gave out, and she sank to the ground. Huddled over her knees, she covered her head with her arms, closed her eyes, and waited for the inevitable.

CHAPTER FIFTY-ONE

Vince followed Sergeant Landros along the hallway to the police chief's office. The door was closed, but wood and glass couldn't stop Tom Morgan's voice from carrying into the front area. Although his words were muffled, Tom's strident pitch indicated his anger, and when Vince entered the room, he wasn't surprised to see Crystal cowering in a chair, shoulders slumped and head down. Her husband was glaring at her, a finger pointed her way.

Tom's attention switched from his wife to Vince and Sergeant Landros, but the expression on his face didn't change. Years ago, while serving with Tom in the Marines, Vince had seen his friend's temper erupt. He steeled himself for the explosion he knew would come.

"You!" Tom snapped, transferring his finger-pointing to Vince. "Why didn't you tell me what Misty had planned?"

"Because I didn't know what she had planned."

"You and Bob were checking her computer."

"For viruses. Spyware. That's all. You told us to respect her privacy."

Vince wasn't sure if he should say more. In the service, he'd been in command. He'd given the orders and expected Tom to obey. Since then, Tom had made millions; now had his thick, blond hair trimmed by a stylist; wore a polo shirt, slacks, and loafers that probably cost more than most people made in a month. Tom Morgan was a client, which reversed their former positions, but client or not, Tom needed to hear the truth.

"Maybe you would have known what she had planned if you'd spent more time with her."

"I've been busy. I . . ." Tom started, but then stopped himself. "I called you when I first suspected there was a problem. Where were you?"

"In Washington, D.C. I do have other clients."

"And Bob?"

"Los Angeles."

"How convenient."

Vince didn't like his friend's tone. "What are you suggesting?"

"That one of you . . ." Tom switched his gaze to Crystal, and then back to Vince. "One of you should have known what was going on."

"Maybe that 'one' should have been you," Crystal objected, looking up at her husband for the first time since Vince had stepped into the room.

"Bickering about who was responsible isn't going to help the situation," Sergeant Landros said. "What I want to know is how this Bell guy, this Beekeeper, knew your daughter was going to be here in Skagway."

"Well, I think that answer is easy," Tom said, looking directly at the sergeant. "From what my wife has told me, you have this kidnapper's girlfriend working for you."

"Officer Ward is not and never was Bell's girlfriend," Landros countered, his posture stiffening.

Tom grunted in disbelief, and Vince could understand why. Up until last night, once he'd learned of Katherine's connection to Bell, he'd had the same reaction. Misty's kidnapping, here in Skagway, and Katherine's former relationship with Bell were simply too much of a coincidence. It didn't matter that Katherine had said she was a victim, that she'd thought Bell was in a mental hospital, and that she had nothing to do with Misty's kidnapping. Vince hadn't believed her.

But, last night, when he stopped by her place unexpected and saw her fear, he changed his mind. Her reaction earlier that day, when she realized Bell was involved, had been real. Her anger that the man was again on the loose was real.

"I agree," Vince said, nodding at the sergeant before looking at Tom. "I don't believe the officer is involved. What I want to know is why this Bell guy is sending faxes to my office, not to you."

"Exactly," Tom said. "Why is he? What part do *you* have in this kidnapping?"

"Me?" Vince took a step back. He'd come to help his friend, not to become a suspect.

"You could have stopped her, but, no, you're out of town. Both you and your partner are incommunicado. Nevertheless you manage to get up here after my daughter is kidnapped and just happen to spend the night with my wife."

"I did not spend the night with your wife; I spent it with Katherine."

The moment he spoke, he wished he hadn't.

"Katherine?" both Crystal and Sergeant Landros said. "Officer Katherine Ward?" Landros added, his tone incredulous.

Vince looked at him. "I stopped by her place after I left here last night. I had some questions."

"And, she let you spend the night?" Landros didn't sound convinced.

"We were both tired." Vince wasn't about to tell the sergeant he'd found his officer so drunk that she passed out and had to be helped into bed.

"So you spent the night with Officer Ward." Tom's tone had taken on a hint of suspicion. "And, I'm to believe the two of you aren't involved in my daughter's kidnapping?"

Vince glared at his friend. "I'm going to let that go, Tom,

because you're worried about Misty, but you know me better than that."

"Enough," Crystal said, standing. "Bickering about who might be involved isn't getting Misty back. Tom, we only have a few hours. Pay the money. Once Misty's safe, you can have them all arrested."

Tom shook his head. "What guarantee do we have that he won't kill her . . . that he hasn't already killed her?"

"As of yesterday afternoon, she was still alive," Sergeant Landros said.

Tom looked at the sergeant. "And, you know this how?"

"Yesterday afternoon, when Bell contacted Officer Ward using the police radio, I was listening in, and I heard two girls in the background."

"But, that was yesterday afternoon," Tom said.

"True, and you're right. There are no guarantees that if you give him the money he won't kill your daughter. Which is why we hope to find him before this five o'clock deadline."

"Hope," Crystal said, almost with a sneer, first looking at the sergeant and then at her husband. "So what is it, Tom? Do you 'hope' they find Misty? Is your money more important to you than your daughter's life? Maybe we don't know what he'll do to her once he has the money, but we know what he'll do to her if he doesn't get the money. He'll kill her. Just like he killed that kid she was running off with."

Her outburst surprised Vince. For once it really sounded like she cared what happened to her stepdaughter.

Tom, however, simply shook his head.

With a sigh, Crystal sank back down on the chair and buried her face in her hands. Barely audible, she made one last plea. "Please, Tom, please. Just pay the ransom."

CHAPTER FIFTY-TWO

Misty shivered, the cold cutting deep into her body, her breath coming in short, shallow gasps as she waited for the bear's attack. The snap of a twig, and her muscles tensed.

I'm going to die, she thought, tears slipping out between closed lids.

A memory of her parents standing together, back when her mother was still alive and healthy, came to mind. If only she could go back to that time, back to the happiness they'd shared. Her mother had died slowly, painfully.

Misty heard a grunt and waited, holding her breath. She didn't want to think about how painful this was going to be. *Would she have an out-of-body experience?* She'd heard that happened to some women when they were being raped or near death.

It didn't happen to her mother. Misty had heard her mother beg for morphine, heard her mother crying. Those last few weeks, whenever possible, Misty avoided going home. She stayed late at school, visited friends. She made excuses why she couldn't sit with her mother.

She was a terrible daughter. She deserved to die.

I'm sorry, Mommy, Misty cried, not caring if the bear heard. Let it maul her. Bite her. Claw her. She'd blamed her father for marrying Crystal, for not being faithful to her mother, but she was the one who had let her mother down. She—Misty Morgan—not her father, not the doctors, not even Crystal, who kept saying she wanted the two of them to be friends.

"Do it," she said, and sat back on her haunches, turning slightly to face the bear. She was ready for her punishment.

Ready to die.

Except, the bear was gone.

The spot where it had stood was now merely an open space between two trees. Only the light drizzle of rain remained, and the sound of a car passing in the distance.

A car.

Misty rose to her feet and brushed dirt and pine needles from her legs and hands. The sound had come from her left and slightly ahead. Away from where she'd last seen the bear. She wasn't going to die, and she wasn't far from safety.

She ignored the shivers that continued to spiral through her body and stumbled toward the direction of the car sound. With the swipe of her hand, she brushed wet, clinging hair out of her eyes and behind an ear. Her heart raced, and each breath she took had a slight quiver to it, but she felt energized. Even the stones and pine needles jabbing the bottoms of her feet only brought forth an occasional complaint.

Low-growing brush with sharp barbs cut at her bare legs and snagged the sheeting still attached to her right wrist. She pulled the strip loose from a bramble and started to work on loosening the knot. The sound of another car, this one passing even closer, made her leave the cloth around her wrist. Rescue was only a short ways away.

She'd been climbing from the moment she left the house, but she didn't realize how much altitude she'd gained until she reached the edge of a rocky cliff. By going down on her hands and knees, Misty could see over the edge. Below her the road looked like a wide ribbon, a car going by providing an estimate of the distance. She was too high up to jump, but she might be able to climb down. Large boulders, their faces smoothed by glacier flow, created an uneven wall that led down to the road. If she could reach the first small ledge, she should be able to make it to the next.

Sitting back, she once again began working on the strip of sheet knotted around her right wrist. A bush growing near the edge of the drop off looked sturdy enough to hold her weight. At least she hoped it would. If she tied the strip of sheet around the base of the bush and held on, she should be able to reach that first ledge.

As soon as the cloth was off her wrist, she transferred it to the bush. Twice she checked the knot and pulled on the sheet. It had torn once. She didn't want it to tear now. Satisfied that the material would hold, at least until her toes touched the rocky ledge, she shifted her body to the edge of the cliff. Below her, another car passed. She grabbed hold of the cloth with one hand and took in a deep breath, ready to ease herself over the edge.

Except she didn't move. Couldn't move. The sharp edge of a knife pressed against her throat held her in place, along with the softly spoken, "Gotcha."

CHAPTER FIFTY-THREE

Katherine cradled the receiver against her shoulder, and glared at the clock on the wall above the station's kitchenette. Only fifteen minutes had passed since she'd first dialed the number for the state hospital in Michigan, but it felt as if she'd been on the phone for hours. Getting someone with the authority and the willingness to fax an up-to-date photo of Charles Bell was turning into a battle of wills.

"I know all about patient privileges," Katherine snapped at the woman on the other end of the line. "I'm not asking for his files, just his picture. An up-to-date picture."

Calm down, she told herself. So far, getting angry with the hospital's staff and doctors hadn't helped. Charles had obviously fooled them all. This was the third person she'd talked to who insisted the man the Skagway police department was after couldn't possibly be the same one they'd had in their facility.

The doctor who signed Charles's final release papers upset her the most. "I wouldn't have okayed his release," he'd said, "if I'd thought he was a danger to anyone."

Katherine had erupted at that. "No danger? So far he's killed two people and kidnapped two teenagers."

That was when she was transferred to the woman now on the line.

"Why can't you believe the truth about Charles Bell?" Katherine asked. "The man murdered my parents and brother. Raped and held me hostage for almost nine months. He was crazy then, and he's crazy now."

When Charles's lawyer had presented the insanity plea, Katherine had initially balked. She'd wanted Bell to die for what he'd done to her and her family. Or, at the very least, to be a prisoner, just as she'd been for almost nine months. Only when her lawyer convinced her that Bell would be a prisoner, albeit in a mental hospital, did she allow herself any peace of mind. But, now she was being told he'd been cured, that seventeen years ago his actions were an aberration, his behavior triggered by his wife leaving him.

Katherine knew better. Charles was a cunning, conniving, manipulating controller. He'd controlled her. Controlled his wife until she left him. And controlled his daughter to the degree that she wouldn't even testify against him. Sisi Bell swore her mother was the crazy one, that her father had never done anything to her.

Which was a lie. Charles had told Katherine how he seduced his daughter. He'd been proud of it.

Initially the lawyer assigned to Katherine's case had thought they could overthrow the insanity plea by showing how Charles had planned her abduction, but Charles's lawyer had an excuse or reason for everything Charles did to her. The soundproof room in his basement was so he could play his trumpet and not disturb the neighbors. Katherine had been so upset when he rescued her, he'd had to keep her down there. Of course he had sex with her; he thought she was his wife.

Lies, all lies.

The hospital administrator interrupted Katherine's thoughts. "He started improving dramatically after his daughter came to see him," the woman said.

"His daughter?" Katherine hadn't expected that. "I thought her mother asked the judge to bar Sisi from seeing her father."

"Perhaps when she was underage, but Ms. Bell is a grown

woman now, and, from what she said, her mother has passed on."

Ms. Bell. So Sisi hadn't married. "When did she see him?"

"The first time she came was three years ago."

"She's come more than once?"

"Oh, yes. For a while she was coming every week, and then every few months."

"Why wasn't I told about these visits?"

The woman on the other end of the conversation gave a derisive grunt. "According to our files, you were to be notified if and when Mr. Bell was released. We did that by calling you and sending a letter. I have a note here that says your father took the call."

"Grandfather," she corrected, but she wasn't going to go into why he hadn't told her about the call or why she hadn't received the letter. What was, was.

"So . . ." Katherine carefully phrased her next question. "Where do you think Charles Bell is right now?"

"Living with his daughter, I suppose. She's the one who picked him up the day he was released."

"And, where does his daughter live?"

"Oh, I'm afraid I can't tell you that."

Katherine rolled her eyes. "I'm a sworn police officer. The police are supposed to be notified when a pedophile moves into a neighborhood. You can tell me."

"I'm sure the local police have been notified," the woman said.

"And, which local police would that be?"

Katherine knew she wasn't going to get an answer, not without an official signed and delivered request for that information, but she'd felt it was worth a try. And, after chuckling at Katherine's request, the hospital administrator said, "I do have a picture. Would you like me to mail a copy to you?"

"No, that would take too long. Just scan it and send it to the Skagway police department as an attachment—"

Her request was cut short as the woman began to explain about Michigan's poor economy, the budget cuts that had hurt the mental health facilities, and the outdated equipment they had to work with. Finally, Katherine had had enough. "Fine," she said. "Forget the email. Do you have a fax machine?"

They did.

Katherine gave the woman the fax number for the station, repeated that they needed the picture as soon as possible, and forced herself to say thank-you. After hanging up the phone, Katherine sagged back in her chair and squeezed her eyes closed. *Damn Charles.* She didn't want to be taken back to the past. Her months of captivity had been bad enough, but the trial had made everything worse. Only after her grandparents moved her to Skagway did she begin to feel safe.

It wasn't until she decided to go into law enforcement that she returned to Michigan. There she faced her lingering fears. Her training at the police academy, followed by her years with the Kalamazoo department of public safety, gave her the confidence she'd needed. She had truly thought she'd put Charles and what he did to her and her family behind her.

Except now she knew she hadn't.

Now Charles was here. In Skagway.

But where?

Had Sisi moved here? During the trial, Charles's daughter had told Katherine she would get back at her for what she was doing to her father. Skagway was a small community, but Katherine didn't know everyone. Could Sisi have bought one of the houses on the outskirts of town? Was that where Charles had the girls?

Katherine turned toward her computer. Nowadays people posted their pictures and information about themselves on-line for a variety of reasons, some personal and some for business. Katherine Googled the words "Sisi Bell" and waited as her computer began listing matching sites.

Chapter Fifty-Four

Katherine's Internet search for information about Sisi Bell produced no results. Not even some variations on the name. The hospital, however, did fax the promised picture of Charles Bell. Two, in fact. One, a portrait; the other a full-figure snapshot of him petting a dog. To Katherine, it looked like he'd lost weight since she'd last seen him, and she thought he had more gray in his hair. With the pictures coming through in black and white, not color, she couldn't be sure.

She stared at the man who had murdered her family and made her his prisoner and sex partner. Her therapist had said there would come a time when Katherine would understand she wasn't to blame for what happened. If that was true, the time hadn't arrived. Almost two decades had passed since the night he took her, and, looking at his pictures, she still felt the burden of guilt.

If she just hadn't stopped and talked to him. If she hadn't told him all about her family. If she hadn't walked him through their house. If . . . If . . . If . . .

For years those *if*s had plagued her, and, now he was here, in Skagway, once again killing and kidnapping. She hated to think what he might be doing to Misty and Sarah. No, she knew what he was doing to them, and a chill of fear snaked through her body as she remembered his hands on her. His mouth. His . . .

Katherine shook off that memory and leaned back in her

chair. Charles Bell was in Skagway for revenge. Which meant nothing had changed. She was still the reason terrible things were happening to innocent people.

She stared at the two images lying on her desk. How could a man who looked that kind and innocent—that handsome—be so evil?

Katherine knew good looks had nothing to do with a person's moral character. Ted Bundy was a perfect example of that. He'd used his charm and good looks to meet the young women who became his victims. Thank goodness Bundy was dead. No budget cuts and hospital overcrowding would let him loose.

"Is that him?" Gordon asked from behind her, giving Katherine a start.

She turned to face him. "The hospital faxed them over just a while ago. Copies are being made and handed out to everyone. I thought I'd—"

Gordon stopped her with a raised hand. "You're off the case, remember? Take the day off. Spend some time with your grandfather."

"Take the day off?" She couldn't believe what she was hearing. "You can't take me off the case. You need me. I know what he looks like, what his voice sounds like. These pictures—" She pointed at the two on her desk. "—they show what he looked like when they were taken, but he could have changed his looks since then. Dyed his hair. Grown a beard."

"I'll make sure people are aware of that." Gordon gestured for her to stand up. "I'm sorry, but you know as well as I do if a defense lawyer finds out you were personally involved with Bell prior to this incident, he could have anything you discover thrown out of court."

She smiled. "You're assuming he makes it to court."

Gordon waved a finger at her. "That's exactly what I mean. You're too involved."

"You're shorthanded."

"I'm calling in the FBI."

She scoffed. "And you think *they're* going to find him? They couldn't find me, and I was only four frickin' houses away from where my parents and brother were murdered. Four houses and the—"

Gordon stopped her. "Katherine, go home. You have the day off. Do you understand? Get your things and check out. You are not to go anywhere, talk to anyone, or phone anyone. At least not in connection with this case."

Gordon didn't wait to make sure Katherine left. He knew she wasn't going to follow his orders. He just hoped she didn't do anything foolish, anything that would get her in trouble . . . or killed. On the other hand, she might find Bell. She certainly had the motivation.

"I'm sending Katherine home," Gordon told Alice, who'd come in at ten to relieve Betsy.

Alice nodded. "She's wound as tight as a spring."

The cliché fit. He glanced around. "Where's that Assistant DA from Juneau?"

"In the chief's office."

"They still bickering?"

"Discussing the best way to come up with the ransom money." She scoffed. "So, Gordon, how would you come up with a hundred million?"

"No problem," he said. "I couldn't."

"Me neither." Alice turned back to her computer. "Sure wish the chief were back."

Gordon felt slighted by her remark, but also agreed. He'd give anything to turn this mess over to someone else. "FBI's coming." ASAP he hoped. Bell's five o'clock deadline was getting closer by the minute.

"So where's baldy headed?"

"Baldy?" It took Gordon a moment to figure out what Alice was asking. "You mean Mr. Nanini?"

"Yeah, while you were back with Katherine, he took off like he was on an important mission."

Gordon nodded toward the chief's door. "Must be his boss told him to do something."

The outside door opened and a teenaged boy stepped inside, swiping rain from the mop of hair that hung over his eyes. "Someone took my bike," he said.

"Motorcycle or bicycle?" Alice asked, going to the counter.

"Bike . . . bicycle," the teenager said. "Trek 520. It's a touring bike. Cost a fortune."

He looked close to tears.

"I was visiting with a friend, and when I went out . . ."

Gordon didn't stay to listen to the rest of the boy's tale. Bracing himself for another round of accusations, he opened the door to the chief's office.

CHAPTER FIFTY-FIVE

"Please," Misty begged as The Beekeeper cinched the sheeting strip tighter around the bed post. "Don't . . . don't hurt her."

She blinked back tears and snuffed. Her feet felt raw and dirty. Her legs itched and burned where the thorns had torn her skin. He'd pulled her along by her hair as he forced her back to the house, and she'd tripped and stumbled and wet herself. Her scalp hurt, her body ached, and the smell of her own urine mingled with sweat and fear.

"Don't punish her because of what I did."

She'd thought she could escape. She'd thought she could save them both.

"Do it . . ." She squeezed her eyes shut, her heart beating a staccato. "Do it to me, not her."

"Maybe." She heard him take a step back. "Maybe I will. But not now." He made a snorting noise. "You've put me behind schedule. Almost messed up everything."

She felt something heavy and scratchy cover her body, and she opened her eyes. He'd turned on the light in the room, and she could see him clearly. Eyes narrowed, he glared down at her. "That's a new sheet I used to tie you up with this time," he said. "You're not going to get this one to tear, so don't waste your time trying."

"Why can't you just let us go?" She'd been so close. Another minute or two and she would have been climbing down those rocks, would have reached the road below. Someone would have seen her, would have rescued her.

"And then what? Wait for the police to come get me?" He scoffed. "I had that happen once. I didn't like it."

He took a step toward the door, then stopped and looked back. "Besides, if I let you go, your father won't pay the money, and that's the whole reason you're here, little lady."

He snapped off the light, once again turning the room into a dark prison cell, but, before he pulled the door closed, he spoke to Sarah. "Because you didn't try to run away, I'm not going to punish you. But, while I'm gone, if she tries anything, I will punish both of you. Do you understand?"

Sarah's *yes* was barely audible.

"Good. Now, I'm going to go pick up someone you know. Wish me luck."

"I hope you run into a bear," Misty said as the door closed. "A big, white bear. And I hope he eats you up. And . . . And . . ."

Her rant trailed off, and she took several deep breaths, remembering her fear when she saw the white bear. What was worse? Being attacked and eaten by a bear or being held prisoner by a crazy man who would be coming back in a while to rape her?

"He's going after my sister," Sarah moaned from the next bed. "He's going to bring her here and . . . and . . . Oh, God . . ."

Her voice trailed off into sobs.

"Maybe it's not your sister he's after," Misty said, forgetting her encounter with the bear. "He said, 'Someone you know.' Not 'I'm going to go pick up your sister.' "

"So . . ." Sarah hesitated. "What? He's going to pick up one of my friends?"

"I don't know. But at least he's gone . . . for a while."

"You shouldn't have run off."

"I was trying to get help . . . For both of us. And I almost did," Misty said. "There were just these rocks. And the road was too far below. I couldn't jump."

"He told me he'd kill me if I tried to leave this room," Sarah said. "He didn't tie me up, but he locked me in here, and I didn't know what to do." She paused and sniffed. "Should I have tried to escape?"

Misty remembered seeing two sheets tacked on one of the walls in the room. Both were folded and nailed in the shape of a window. Could Sarah have torn one of those sheets off and gotten out through a window?

"I don't know," she said. "Maybe." She wasn't sure about anything at the moment except the newer strips of sheeting were tighter around her wrists and hurt, and her skin felt itchy and sore, and, even with a wool blanket over her, she was shivering.

"We've seen what he looks like," she said, and suddenly wished she hadn't. "He can't let us live."

"But if your father pays the money . . ."

Misty knew it wouldn't matter.

"I wonder who he's gone after," Sarah said, but Misty wasn't listening. Barely making a sound, she cried.

CHAPTER FIFTY-SIX

Gordon quietly entered the chief's office and closed the door behind him. The assistant DA from Juneau sat behind the chief's desk. He raised a finger up to his lips, indicating the need for silence, and motioned over to where Tom Morgan stood in front of the one window in the office, talking on his cell phone. Crystal remained in the chair she'd occupied earlier. She had her eyes closed, but Gordon didn't think she was sleeping. An occasional quirk of her eyebrows indicated she was listening to her husband's conversation.

"You're sure we can get the money back," Morgan said, then nodded as the person on the phone answered.

"And, you can handle all of this from your end?"

Another nod, and Gordon noticed Crystal seemed to relax. Opening her eyes, she looked Gordon's way and smiled.

"He's supposedly out looking for Misty," Morgan said into the phone, his posture anything but relaxed. "I'm not happy with the two of you. If one or the other of you had been there when I called, this never would have happened."

The tension radiating from Morgan increased as he listened to the other man's response. Gordon could see the outline of a vein on Morgan's temple, and, when the man again spoke, his tone alone indicated his anger. "Dammit, we're talking about my daughter. I don't care if Vince and I have been friends for years or what we went through in the past. If anything happens to Misty, that's over; you guys can cross my name off your client list."

Gordon was glad he wasn't in Nanini's shoes . . . or Nanini's partner's shoes. Not that he expected any words of praise from Morgan if the Skagway police department didn't rescue Misty Morgan. Even though neither of Gordon's marriages had produced any children, he could understand Morgan's anger . . . and probably fear. A missing child was bad enough. To have a child kidnapped, and by a known pedophile, was terrifying.

"Don't make him angry, honey," Crystal said, leaning toward her husband. "We need him to transfer the money."

Morgan looked at her, closed his eyes for a moment, then nodded. The next time he spoke into the phone, his voice was calmer. "Okay, Bob, I'll call my banker and broker. Once they've freed up the money, I'll have them contact you. You'll be in the office?"

The answer must have been positive. Morgan went on. "Don't make the transfer until I give you the word. The police seem to feel they'll find her before the deadline."

When he said that, he looked at Gordon, and Gordon nodded, hoping that was true.

"Thing is," Morgan continued, his gaze never wavering from Gordon's face, "it looks like one of the officers here is involved with this kidnapper."

Gordon shook his head, but he knew Morgan didn't believe him. The assistant DA raised his eyebrows but didn't say anything. Gordon knew he would, later.

"I'm not sure how they did it," Morgan went on, still looking at Gordon. "They must have planned it in advance." He scoffed. "Of course, nobody here is going to admit that."

Gordon didn't bother arguing. He'd met people like Morgan before. The only way to convince this guy that Katherine was innocent was to find and capture Bell. Then they'd all know who was or wasn't involved.

Morgan's attention transferred to his wife. "She's holding up pretty well," he said in response to the person on the other end of the phone connection. "Yes, I guess I am lucky the kidnapper didn't get her, too."

Crystal smiled, but Gordon wondered what the woman really thought about her husband's comment. Gordon didn't trust her, not after the way she'd accused Katherine of being in on the kidnapping.

He felt guilty that he'd originally assigned Katherine to this case. If he'd had an inkling it would turn into a real kidnapping, or that the same man who'd kidnapped her almost two decades ago would be involved, he would have sent her to Anchorage, or Nome, or somewhere far, far away, whether they were shorthanded or not.

The moment Morgan ended the call he focused his attention on Gordon. "How much does that officer of yours know about computers?"

"Katherine?" Gordon shook his head. "I don't know. Enough to get on the Internet and use the programs we have here at the station. Why?"

"The kidnapper—this Beekeeper guy—wants the money transferred electronically to an off-shore account. According to the fax Bob Lilly received, our kidnapper will know when the transfer has occurred." Morgan's gaze switched to the assistant DA, who so far hadn't said a word. "Aren't you curious how someone who's allegedly been locked up in a crazy farm for fifteen years set up an off-shore account? And how did he end up here, exactly where his former girlfriend is a police officer?"

Gordon couldn't let the accusation stand without a response. "From what Katherine . . . Officer Ward has said, Charles Bell is extremely intelligent."

"Intelligent enough to pull this off by himself?" the assistant

DA asked, his eyebrows rising.

"I don't know." That was something Gordon had wondered himself. "But, I'm sure Officer Ward isn't involved."

"Well I'm not convinced," Crystal said, standing and brushing the creases out of her beige slacks. She looked at her husband. "Honey, don't you need to call your banker and broker?"

Morgan looked at her and then shrugged. "I suppose I'd better. God, I hate to do this."

"Tom, this is your daughter we're talking about. She already thinks you value your job and money more than you do her. Don't prove her right."

For a moment, Gordon wondered what Morgan would say. The man stared at his wife, started to open his mouth, then simply nodded and made the next call.

CHAPTER FIFTY-SEVEN

Katherine left the station through the side door and almost ran into Vince Nanini and Cora Tremway. "Something *is* wrong," the elderly woman said, the blue umbrella she held above her head twitching with each word as she pointed a finger at Nanini's chest. "You people don't believe me, but I know I'm right. I can feel it in my bones."

"What do you feel?" Katherine asked, pretty sure anything Cora felt in her bones was due to arthritis and the chilly rain.

The pointing finger switched from Nanini's chest to Katherine's. Faded, blue eyes narrowed slightly and another wrinkle joined the ones creasing the woman's forehead. "That something's happened to them. Something's happened to Martha and John. I've been calling Martha for five days now, and all I get is the answering machine. Same message. They're away from the phone and will call back. But they don't. Call, that is." Cora's gaze switched back to Nanini. "Were you in my history class?"

"No. I'm not from around here." He glanced at Katherine, his look relaying his confusion . . . and perhaps his desire to escape.

"You look like one of the Norris boys." Cora gave him a quick scan, and then said, "She wasn't at Bunco Monday night."

It took Katherine a moment to realize Cora was again talking about Martha Grayson. "Aren't they out of town?" Katherine remembered Gordon telling her that. "They stopped their mail and paper."

Cora shook her head. "Martha didn't say anything about going anywhere. We always play on Mondays. There I was, Monday night, waiting for her to show up . . . and she never did." Again she looked at Nanini. "And, if they're 'out of town,' how come just a while ago I saw John's grey Chevy?"

"You saw John Grayson's Chevy Tahoe?" Katherine repeated. "With John driving it?"

Cora looked away, up the street, her chin slightly raised. "I wasn't close enough to actually see who was driving. But, I know it was John's car."

Katherine tried not to smile. Considering the woman's poor eyesight, chances were it wasn't even a Chevy Tahoe she saw. Just like the white bear Cora said she saw at the Graysons' place was probably a light-colored cinnamon.

"My eyesight may not be the best," Cora said, almost as if reading Katherine's mind. "But, I know that SUV was his. He has one of those pink ribbons on the back, 'cause Martha had cancer a few years ago. And, don't you go smiling. I *did* see a white bear." She said it firmly, then sighed and lowered her gaze. "But I'm not so sure about the bear driving the truck."

Vince Nanini chuckled. "Now that would be something to see."

"Sure looked like one." Cora kept looking at Katherine. "I know you think I'm a crazy old woman, but I'm worried about Martha. Can't you at least go check on her? She could be sick. Maybe hurt. John's a good guy, but he's getting a little addled. I'm not sure what's wrong, but I feel something is."

"I'll go check," Katherine said and touched the old woman's arm. It would at least give her something to do. "Now, did someone bring you into town?" She knew Cora no longer drove.

Cora nodded and again looked up the street. "My granddaughter, Molly, did. She's at the library. She's using one of their printers to get some pictures off a net." Cora shook her head. "We used to catch fish in a net. My father and I would go out early in the morning. We'd put the boat in on the Taiya Inlet, and I would help him set his nets. We—"

Nanini smiled and Katherine chuckled. "This is a different kind of net, Cora. Do you want to wait inside, out of the rain, until Molly's finished getting those pictures printed?" Katherine nodded toward the station's entrance.

"No, I probably better walk back." Cora smiled. "She thinks I'm looking for a book to read. Don't want her worrying about me."

"I can drive you there." Katherine motioned toward the station's parking lot.

"No need. I can still walk. Doctor says it's good for me. You just get along and check on Martha. Okay?"

"I will," Katherine assured her. Not that she thought she'd find anyone at the house, but maybe one of the neighbors would know where the couple went.

Seeming satisfied, Cora nodded, then scowled at Vince Nanini. "You sure you weren't in one of my history classes?"

"Not unless you were teaching in Seattle, Washington."

"No; I did visit there in my younger years, but I did all my teaching right here in Skagway." She kept looking at him. "You should wear a hat. A hat would keep your head warm . . . and dry."

"You're probably right," he agreed, smiling as he wiped droplets of water away from his face.

"Of course I'm right." She glanced at Katherine and winked. "Teacher's always right."

Katherine smiled and watched Cora's slender figure move away from them, umbrella held protectively above the elderly woman's wildly-frizzled, white hair.

"Did *you* have her as a teacher?" Nanini asked, his voice lowered.

"No. I didn't move here until I was a teenager, long after she retired. But a lot of people around here did have her as a teacher. From what I hear, she was pretty sharp in her younger years. Nowadays . . ." Katherine sighed. "She calls us once or twice a month because she thinks she's heard something or believes someone came in and took something. Which isn't easy to tell since she's a hoarder."

"She lives alone?"

Katherine nodded. "In a house that was built after the Gold Rush. From what I've heard, she was born in the house. She moved away when she got married. Came back a few years later, a widow with three children. One daughter and a granddaughter, Molly, still live here. They more or less watch over Cora, take her places." Katherine smiled. "They try to keep her from bothering us, but as long as Cora can remember how to use a telephone or is able to walk a few blocks, I'm sure we'll keep hearing from her."

"So are you going to check on this Martha person, like she asked?"

"I will." Katherine glanced back at the entryway to the station. Gordon might not want her looking for Charles, but he hadn't said anything about a case that might be related to Misty's kidnapping. "There's something I need to do first."

CHAPTER FIFTY-EIGHT

Russell Ward gazed out the window above his kitchen sink. He knew he'd come in here for something, but, for the life of him, he couldn't remember what. It bothered him that he was forgetting things. Not just what he'd come into this room for, or where he put his car keys, or what somebody's name was, but more important things like what the pills were for that Katherine said he had to take. Had he had breakfast that morning? And, what had happened to his wife?

He knew she was gone, but he wasn't sure where she'd gone. To the store? If so, would she be returning soon? He hoped so. He missed hearing her voice, seeing her smile.

Tears filled his eyes, and he blinked rapidly, unsure why he was crying.

A vehicle turned the corner down the street, coming toward the house and drawing Russell's thoughts away from his wife. He knew that car. But why? It wasn't his. He was sure of that, though he couldn't remember if he still had the 4-wheel drive Ram or a Dodge Durango. All he knew was he liked Dodges, and this wasn't a Dodge.

The SUV stopped in front of the house, and Russell leaned forward, over the sink, so he could see better. Now that the car was parked, he could tell it was one of those Chevy Tahoes. Katherine liked them, but the one Katherine drove said *Police* on the side.

At least he thought it did.

He looked at the clock on the microwave. It wasn't even noon yet. Was someone coming over to see him? If so, he didn't remember inviting anyone.

The sound of a car door closing brought his attention back to the window. A man had gotten out of the vehicle. Someone he knew, or at least had met. Russell was sure of that, but he couldn't remember when or where . . . or what the man's name was. Not that that was unusual.

He watched the man walk to the front door. Russell knew then that the guy wasn't a local. Locals never used the front door. They'd come around to the side door and knock, or just walk in with a holler that announced their arrival.

Lean and lanky, the guy kept looking up and down the street, as if expecting someone to come out of a door. Russell watched until he could no longer follow the man's progress, then he stepped back from the sink and waited for what he knew would come next.

The door chimes echoed through the house, and Russell shuffled out of the kitchen and into the living room and entryway. Before he turned the door knob, he glanced down at his clothing, not sure if he'd gotten dressed that morning or was still in his pajamas. To his relief, he saw he had on his favorite brown-and-blue plaid flannel shirt, tan slacks, and brown loafers. A quick check with his tongue assured him he had his teeth in. A hand to his face told him he hadn't shaved that morning. Well, whomever this was would just have to take him the way he was.

"Mornin', Russ," the man said when the door was opened. "How you doing today?"

"Doin' all right," Russell answered, stepping back when the man opened the screen and started into the house. "I, ah . . ." He groped for a name, but nothing came to him. "I'm afraid I don't remember—"

"Chuck," the man answered and held out his hand. "That fisherman buddy of yours introduced us one day. Remember? I was over at his house when you stopped by. You were sort of lost, and we drove you home."

Russell didn't remember, but he shook the man's hand. He did know who Chuck meant by "fisherman buddy." That had to be Phil. Phil Carpenter was crazy about fishing. "How is Phil?" he asked, vaguely remembering Katherine asking him something about her coworker.

"He's been under the weather for the last two days," Chuck said with a grin. "Fact is, he asked me to pick you up and bring you to him."

"Phil wants me to go to his house?" Russell asked. He looked behind him, into the living room. He couldn't remember if his wife was in the other room. If so, he would have to tell her he was going out.

"Do you need to leave a note for Kit Kat?"

"Kit Kat?" That wasn't his wife's name.

"Your granddaughter. Kit Kat. Or whatever you call her nowadays."

"You mean Katherine? No, she . . ." he started to say, then stopped. "Maybe I should."

"If you want, I'll write it for you."

"Yes." Russell nodded, a fog of confusion dulling his reaction. "A note would be good. Katherine's at work, I think. I'm not sure where my wife is. I think she went shopping." He followed Chuck into the kitchen. "She worries if I go out without telling her."

"Well, we'll leave her a note." Chuck rummaged through a couple of drawers, came up with a notepad and pencil and wrote a quick message. "I'm sure Kit Kat will be glad to get this."

Chuck left the note by the telephone, then turned to Russell.

"You mind if we take your Durango? That Chevy is almost out of gas."

So it was a Durango he had. Russell Ward smiled and nodded. He wasn't totally losing his mind.

"Good. You might need this," Chuck said, grabbing a lightweight jacket from a hook in the mudroom area. "The rain has stopped, but it's a little cool out."

Something about the way the guy was taking over and making assumptions bothered Russell. He wasn't sure he wanted to go anywhere with the man. "We can't take my car," he said. "My granddaughter took the keys."

"Now that wasn't nice, was it?" Chuck looked around. "Where do you think she put them?"

"I don't know," Russell said, more truth to that than he liked to admit.

Chuck checked a few drawers in the kitchen, then stepped into the living room and looked down the hallway toward the bedrooms. "Which one is hers?"

"I think you need to leave now," Russell Ward said, wishing Katherine would come home.

"Oh, but we need to go see Phil." Chuck gave a smile, then started down the hallway. "I'm sure I can tell which bedroom is hers."

Russell watched the man go into Katherine's bedroom. "I don't think you should be in there," he said, and shuffled over to the doorway. The man was opening drawers in Katherine's dresser and pawing through her things. "Stop it!" Russell demanded. "That's her room. Her things. I don't go in there, and she knows it."

"Which makes this a good place to hide things." Chuck ignored him and walked over to the closet and slid open the door. "Things like extra ammo." He tossed a box on her bed. "Extra cans of pepper spray." Those also went on the bed. "My gosh, doesn't she wear anything even remotely feminine?" Uniform after uniform was pushed aside, along with hangers of sweatshirts, jeans, bulky sweaters, and jackets. Finally, Chuck reached up on the shelf above the hangers, way back in a corner, and pulled down a box. Turning toward Russell, he flipped the lid open and smiled.

"These your keys, Russ?" he asked, holding up a ring of keys that did look familiar.

"You shouldn't have those," Russell said. "She took them for a reason." Though, he couldn't remember what the reason was. "Put them back. Put everything back."

"Now, now," Chuck cajoled and walked toward Russell, the key ring dangling from one finger. "Don't go and get yourself all upset. We still need to take a little ride."

Russell couldn't remember why they were supposed to take a ride, but he knew he didn't want to go with this man. Not now, not ever. "I'm not going," he said. "I have things to do."

"Oh, and I was so looking forward to your company," Chuck said softly.

He'd gotten closer than Russell realized, and moved faster than Russell expected. With one swift motion, Chuck spun him around and pinned his arms behind him. The pain that radiated from his wrists to his shoulders made Russell bend forward, and he knew there was no way he could break away from the man's iron grip.

"You," Chuck snarled near his ear, "are coming with me, whether you like it or not. You are my revenge for what your sweet little granddaughter did to me; for the years I spent in that ridiculous hospital, being shocked and poked and forced to sit through therapy session after therapy session."

"You're hurting me," Russell moaned, his knees starting to buckle beneath him.

"Tell someone who cares," Chuck said, then whispered, "Remember The Beekeeper, Grandpa? Well he's back, and you've just been stung."

CHAPTER FIFTY-NINE

Katherine started for the parking area and Vince followed. He knew she didn't want him tagging along, but he also knew she was his best bet of finding Misty. "If you're not checking on the Graysons, where *are* we headed?" he asked when she reached her Tahoe.

"*We* aren't headed anywhere," she said and made a "go away" gesture with her hand. "Don't you need to take care of your plane? Get new tires or something?"

He smiled and walked around to the passenger-side door. "Already taken care of. I called the mechanic at the airport, and he's ordered new tires that are being flown in this afternoon."

"Must be nice to have enough money to simply call and get what you need."

He heard the derision in her voice. "Hey, I work hard for my money. I'm paying to have those tires rushed so if we need that plane—for any reason—it will be available. Now, I believe you said you had somewhere you wanted to go. Do you have an idea where Bell has Misty?"

She stared at him for a moment, then shook her head.

"You're sure? No idea?"

"Yes, I'm sure," she nearly shouted. "Why would I know? You people act like I've been in touch with him. Well, I haven't been, not since the trial when I testified against him."

She took in a deep breath, and Vince watched her struggle to gain control. He waited, and saw when she was back in her police officer mode.

"We—" she went on. "—all of our officers, have been calling people, trying to find out where Charles might be staying, where he might be keeping two girls. We—" She stopped talking, her gaze focused up the street. "Oh, shit," she swore. "Get in the car."

Vince looked that direction and saw a van with a TV station logo on the side coming toward them. Quickly he opened the cruiser's door and slid in. Katherine had the engine started and the vehicle moving before he had his door completely shut. With a squeal of tires and lights flashing, she headed off in the opposite direction, as if in pursuit of a criminal or on her way to a crime scene. Vince finished shutting the door and clicked his seatbelt into place, then looked back. The TV van pulled into the parking lot they'd just left.

"Someone must have told them," Katherine said, giving him an accusing look as she turned onto the next street.

"Hey, watch it!" he yelled as a woman stepped out in front of the cruiser.

Katherine slammed on the brakes, propelling both of them forward. Vince's seatbelt tightened across his chest as the Tahoe stopped only inches from the pedestrian. The woman glared at them and yelled something. Katherine started to undo her seatbelt, swearing when it didn't immediately release.

Vince placed a hand on her arm. "Calm down."

She shook off his arm. "I will not calm down. She shouldn't have been in the street. Why don't they listen? What do they think we have these sirens for?"

"You need to pull over. Take a deep breath."

"I don't need your fuckin'—" she started, then nodded and took a deep breath.

Katherine turned off the siren and lights and eased the cruiser forward and into the nearest parking spot. "God, I almost hit her," she said, leaning back in her seat and closing her eyes.

"But, you didn't." He gave her a minute to unwind before he went on. "It wasn't me, Katherine. I didn't contact any news media. But I'm not surprised they're here. Lately they've been following everything Tom does. His rapid departure from China must have alerted someone."

"Well, they just made finding Misty more difficult."

"But not impossible?" He hoped not. "You said there was something you wanted to do . . . ?"

She looked at him, and he could tell she was debating whether to tell him anything. He knew he'd lucked out managing to get in the cruiser with her, but they were still close enough to the police station for her to order him out.

"The Explorer," she finally said. "The one that pushed the Bane kid's truck off the road. They've brought it here. I want to see if there's anything Gordon missed when he looked at it. Anything besides that tuft of fake fur. We know it was here in Skagway, on my street, yesterday afternoon and parked in Dyea shortly after that. If Bell picked up Sarah after I left home, he had to take her somewhere and then return the Explorer to the campground. That doesn't give him a lot of time to be driving around."

"Think he has them at that campground?"

Katherine shook her head. "It's been checked. No signs of them. Rangers have scoured the area. We—"

The ring of her cell phone cut her off. She frowned and glanced at it, then immediately answered. Vince couldn't hear what was said, but, before Katherine clicked off, she had the cruiser in gear and was backing out of the parking spot. Once again she hit the siren and lights.

"What's up?" he asked as she steered away from the police station.

"Damn TV people," she grumbled and turned onto a cross

street. "Damn all of you."

"What happened?"

"Your boss's idiot wife told one of the media people that I was involved in Misty's kidnapping, reminded them that Bell had kidnapped me seventeen years ago. Once they figure out where I live, they'll head there. My poor grandfather . . ."

CHAPTER SIXTY

The rain had stopped by the time they reached her grandfather's house. There was a tan Chevy Tahoe parked in front, but no vans with TV logos on their sides and no newspaper reporters lined the sidewalk. Quickly Katherine pulled up in front of the garage.

"I need to get my grandfather out of there," she said, barely putting the cruiser in Park before opening her door.

Vince exited from his side almost as quickly. "Where are you going to take him?"

"I don't know." She jogged toward the side door. "Just somewhere where they won't bother him."

"Poppa," she called the moment she entered the house. "Poppa, it's me. We need to go somewhere."

The drip of the sink faucet and the hum of the refrigerator were the only sounds she heard.

That he didn't answer didn't worry her, not at first. Quickly she walked through the kitchen and into the living room. That he wasn't in his usual easy chair did surprise her, and she turned back toward Vince. "He isn't outside, is he?"

"I'll look," Vince answered, turning back toward the side door.

Katherine checked her grandfather's bedroom, then knocked on the closed bathroom door. When he didn't answer, she tried the knob. The door opened easily, but there was no sign of her grandfather.

Although she didn't expect to find him in her room, she opened her door. For a moment she simply stared into the room, seeing the open dresser drawers and the box of ammo, and cans of pepper spray and mace spread across her bed. Slowly her brain absorbed each item, her gaze finally locking on the box she usually kept on the top shelf of her closet.

"He's not outside," Vince said, coming up behind her.

"He's been in here," Katherine said, understanding the significance of that box. "Darn him."

"What?"

"He found his car keys." She shook her head and turned to leave, nearly running into Vince. "Move it!" she yelled and pushed him aside. "He might still be in the garage."

She didn't remember hearing a car's engine when they pulled up, but she'd been so intent on getting inside and getting her grandfather out of the house, she hadn't really listened. Would he remember how to start his Durango? Would he remember how to open the garage door? He wouldn't be trying to kill himself, would he? Just yesterday morning he'd mentioned not being around when his roses bloomed. Was he trying to tell her he was going to take his own life?

Every negative thought she could imagine flashed through her head as she rushed to the door that opened to the garage. She was afraid of what she might find . . . but she wasn't prepared for what she didn't find.

Her grandfather's Dodge Durango was gone.

"Where?" was all she managed to say.

"Maybe he heard about the TV guys," Vince said, also looking into the empty garage. "Maybe he realized they'd come here and decided on his own to leave."

Katherine shook her head. "I don't think he could figure that out, not on his own. Not even on his better days."

She stepped back, closing the garage door as she did before

turning toward Vince. "I'm even surprised he went through my things to find the car keys. He's always respected my privacy, even when I was little."

"Maybe someone helped him," Vince suggested. "Perhaps a neighbor. The owner of the Tahoe parked out front?"

"I don't—" she started, then stopped herself and edged past Vince to head back to the kitchen. "It's a Chevy Tahoe," she stated, more to herself than to him. "A tan Chevy Tahoe."

Katherine wasn't sure if Vince understood what she was thinking, and even she forgot what she was getting at when she looked out the kitchen window. The Tahoe was still parked in front of the house, but, while they'd been inside, a van with a TV network logo on the side had pulled in front of the SUV and another SUV, this one with a Canadian station's logo, had parked behind it. Two other SUVs were parked across the street, and a half dozen men and women, some holding microphones, others carrying large cameras, were heading for the patch of grass that made up her grandfather's front lawn. Neighbors were coming out of their houses, some standing in the street, all looking toward her grandfather's house.

"The sharks have come to feed," she muttered, remembering back to after her rescue, when the media had swarmed around, looking for sound bites, for any titillating morsel of information to print or broadcast about her abduction.

"You want me to go out and talk to them?" Vince asked. "Send them away?"

"No." She knew how futile that would be. "They're not going to leave, not until they have pictures of me, and can once again broadcast my past to the world." Katherine stared at the group on the lawn. A man motioned toward the kitchen window, and others looked her way. "Damn," she swore and stepped back so she wouldn't be as visible.

It was then she noticed the slip of paper on the counter, half under the base of the telephone. Forgetting the reporters outside, she picked up the note and read the short message, the scribbled words bringing back memories.

I've got him, you Judas.

Come alone or he dies.

They all die.

Revenge is almost as sweet as honey.

Charles didn't sign his name, but the smudge of ink with what looked like four wing shapes was as good as a signature. Katherine read the note twice. Charles's audacity angered her. That he had her grandfather petrified her.

Hand shaking, she picked up the phone and dialed. The moment the dispatcher answered, she asked to be put through to Gordon, her voice strained.

When he answered, all she said was, "He's got my grandfather," then hung up.

CHAPTER SIXTY-ONE

Vince had read the note over her shoulder. He could see the tension in her body, the way her hand was shaking, and the tremor in her voice. When she turned toward him, he automatically put his arms around her to comfort her.

Katherine stiffened and reared back, pulling away from his embrace. "What the hell are you doing?" she demanded, the look in her eyes definitely not appreciative.

"Trying to comfort you."

"I don't need any comforting." She stepped away. "I'm fine. I can handle this. I'm a police officer. I'm in control."

Except, she didn't look in control, not to him, and, when the phone rang, she startled and stared at it as if it might bite.

But she didn't reach over and answer it.

The phone rang again.

Vince watched her take in a deep breath, her gaze locked on the phone.

"Aren't you going to answer it?" he asked.

"No. No, I don't think so." She looked at him. "It's probably Gordon. He'll tell me to stay here."

"Which you probably should do." Vince wouldn't argue with her statement that she was a police officer, but she certainly wasn't in control.

Her cell phone rang next.

"In the police academy," she said, checking the phone for the caller, and then slipping it back in its holder without answering, "we were trained that a uniform always followed the orders of a commanding officer. For years I've done that, but I know what Gordon is going to say. He's going to tell me to step down, not to do anything, to let him handle the matter." She looked back at Vince. "But how can I just sit by when my grandfather's life is at stake?"

"You're not going to do him any good the way you're shaking right now."

"I am not shaking, I'm . . . I'm—"

She closed her eyes, and this time when he put his arms around her, she didn't pull away. Instead she leaned into him, resting her head against his shoulder. "Poppa's done so much for me, and now that monster has him."

Vince felt her take in a ragged breath, felt the tremble of her body. He wasn't sure if she was crying or not. He wouldn't blame her if she did. He wished he could tell her it would be all right, but he had no idea how they were going to find her grandfather or Misty or the other girl.

"I don't want to cry," she managed, a catch in her voice. "I cried enough those nine months he had me. But Poppa . . ."

Her voice trailed off, and Vince simply held her close.

The phone on the counter rang again. Looking over Katherine's shoulder he could see the reporters outside. A car drove by, going slowly to avoid the people in the street, then pulled in front of the network vans. A woman got out. With so many people gathering in front of the house, Vince could barely see the hood of the Chevy Tahoe, but so far Katherine's cruiser hadn't been blocked.

"This is all my fault," she said, bringing his attention back to her. "If I'd been here—"

"What?" Vince angled her back so she had to look up at his face. "Do you really think by being here you could have stopped him? Killed him? From what I've heard and seen, Bell has had this all planned out. He knew you wouldn't be here. He's trying to torture you. If you'd been here, he might have killed your grandfather in front of you. Then killed you."

"I wished he'd killed me years ago." She squeezed her eyes tight. "You don't know how it feels going through life knowing you're the one who caused your parents and brother to be murdered. Charles told me if I ever tried to escape, he'd kill anyone who helped me. Now he's here, and he's killed Phil and that college kid, and has taken my grandfather, Misty, and Sarah. Everything that's happened is because of me."

"Katherine." Vince gave her shoulders a shake, and she opened her eyes and looked at his face. "He is the villain, not you. Even if you were in love with him when you were a teenager, you didn't cause him to kill your family or kidnap you. And, unless you invited him here, and told him Misty would be getting off that ship yesterday morning, you're not responsible for anything that's happened in the last two days."

"I didn't love him," she said, barely above a whisper. "How can you love someone who kills your family, who forces himself on you, and makes you do terrible things?"

Vince didn't want to think what those terrible things might have been, and he knew letting her think about it wasn't what they needed. He gave her one more hug, then released his hold. "Okay, enough feeling sorry for yourself. If Bell took your grandfather's car, why? How did he get here? You said he kept you just two houses away from your home. Do you think he's in one of the houses near here?"

He saw her frown as she wiped away the tears on her cheeks. She stepped back toward the counter and looked out the window. The reporters were still on the lawn, cameras aimed at the house. They had moved closer, away from the tan Chevy Tahoe. "That SUV," she said and looked back at him. "That's how he got here."

CHAPTER SIXTY-TWO

Katherine headed toward the side door. Although most of the reporters and photographers were hovering in front of the house, one lone female had stationed herself at the side door. The woman practically had her nose pressed against the glass, but Katherine didn't hesitate. She unsnapped the flap on her holster and rested her hand on the pistol's butt as she reached for the door knob. The woman got the message and stepped back, allowing Katherine to exit without running right into her, but it didn't stop the reporter from firing a barrage of questions her way.

"Miss McMann, how long has The Beekeeper been in Skagway? Have you been keeping in touch with him? How did he know Tom Morgan's daughter would be here?"

How indeed? Katherine wondered but didn't answer. To her relief Vince exited right behind her and wedged himself between her and the reporter.

She sprinted toward the Tahoe, hoping she'd reach the vehicle before the other reporters and photographers realized what she was doing. Vince also ran with her, arms held out in an attempt to shield her from the others. Nevertheless, more reporters appeared from behind their vans, stepping in front of the Tahoe.

"Out of my way!" she demanded, again resting her hand on the butt of her Glock.

"What? Or you'll shoot us?" one of the men asked.

"When did The Beekeeper first contact you?" another asked.

"When was the last time you visited him?"

"Is it true you're still in love with him?" a third reporter shouted, coming up behind her.

Katherine stopped no more than four feet from the SUV and turned to face the man who'd asked the question. Several reporters had their microphones pointing her way, waiting for her response. Waiting to crucify her with her own words.

Words will never hurt you, her mother used to say. Well, her mother was wrong. Words could hurt. Did hurt.

Before she could think of a response, Vince caught her by the shoulders and turned her back toward the Chevy Tahoe. "You heard her. Out of our way," he commanded.

The two reporters stepped aside, but a woman's voice from the side stopped Katherine from moving forward. "How could you do this to my baby?" Sarah's mother demanded, pushing her way passed a cameraman.

Though small in stature, every inch of Mattie Wilson radiated anger. "You said you wanted my daughter to help your grandfather, but what you really wanted was to give her to him, to this monster these reporters are calling a beekeeper."

"No. Oh, no. I would never do that," Katherine insisted, facing her. "When I hired Sarah, I had no idea he was here, that he would take her."

"I've heard what they've said about you," Mattie fumed. "All these years you've acted so high and mighty. I tell you about when a white man rapes me, but do you tell me you understand, that you know what it's like? No. And why? Because you've been waiting for him, waiting for him to come back to you?"

"No. That isn't true."

"Do you think my Sarah is a slut?" Mattie demanded. "Do you think she's like you?"

"No. Not at all. I—" Katherine looked beyond Sarah's mother, to the reporters with their microphones all pointed her

273

way. They'd crucified her seventeen years ago. No matter what she said, they would broadcast what they wanted, whatever they felt would draw the most viewers.

She stopped herself from trying to explain and glanced back at the Tahoe. She couldn't tell if there was a pink cancer ribbon on the back, but, even if it had one, she wanted definite proof. "I've got to get inside, see who it's registered to," she said to Vince.

"My Sarah is a good girl," Mattie continued, her voice becoming hysterical. "If anything has happened to her . . ."

"You!" Vince said, pointing at Sarah's mother. "If you want your daughter found, stop bothering Officer Ward. She needs to get into this vehicle."

He half turned toward the men and women behind him. "That means you, too. Stay out of her way."

Katherine hesitated, surprised to see the reporters and cameramen step back. Mattie, however, stepped forward, not back, putting herself directly in front of Katherine. Her open hand hit the side of Katherine's face with a slap that snapped Katherine's head to the side.

"Okay, that's enough," Vince yelled, grabbing Sarah's mother's arms and pulling her back before she could do anything else.

Katherine shook off the effects of the slap and grabbed the passenger-side door handle. To her relief, the SUV's door opened and she slid inside, quickly opening the glove compartment and looking through its contents. Looking for anything that would identify the owner of the car.

She found what she needed, not in the glove compartment, but in the console between the front seats. A stamped and addressed opened letter was wedged between a bag of cough drops and a pair of dark glasses. Katherine grabbed it and slid back out of the SUV.

Vince continued to act as a blockade between her and the reporters, but the moment she was back on the lawn, the questions began. "What did you find? Whose Tahoe is this? Why did you want that letter?"

She ignored them all, and, keeping her voice low, spoke to Vince. "I need to get to my cruiser."

"Done," he said, and turned to face the reporters. "Okay, everyone, out of our way."

He barged forward and Katherine followed, staying close and ignoring the questions and complaints the reporters threw their way. She saw Mattie try to step closer, but Sarah's mother was blocked by a cameraman, as Katherine passed.

Never had the distance across her grandfather's small front lawn seemed so far, and Katherine's nerves were on edge by the time Vince stepped aside to give her access to her cruiser. She jerked open the driver's-side door and slid in, then groped in her trouser pocket for the ignition key. She'd barely had time to look into her rearview mirror before shifting into reverse when the passenger-side door opened. "No," she automatically responded, even before she realized it was Vince getting in.

"No," she repeated. "You can't come with me. Charles said I had to go alone. If he sees anyone with me, he'll kill my grandfather and the girls."

"And, if you don't kill him, and he gets you, he'll still kill your grandfather and the girls," Vince said, just as forcefully. "Get us out of here."

Katherine saw the reporters behind the cruiser, blocking their way. Stepping on the brake the same time she revved the motor, she hoped they would get the message. Still, she backed out of the driveway carefully, hoping there wasn't an idiot in the crowd who placed a news story above his life. Only when she was on the street and driving away from the house did she give a sigh of relief.

Although she could see several of the reporters scrambling for their cars, once Katherine reached the corner, she put on the brake. "Out!" she ordered, looking at Vince.

"No." He shook his head. "One thing I learned in the service: you don't go into a danger zone alone. When we get there, you can let me off down the street. I can keep out of sight and work my way around to the back of the house."

He might be right about the need for backup, but he had no idea what he was getting into. At least, she didn't think he did. "Do you know where we're going?"

"No, but I take it you do."

Two of the reporters' cars were pulling away from her grandfather's house, making U-turns to follow her. Katherine handed Vince the envelope she'd taken from the tan Tahoe and again drove forward, making a quick turn to the left and then a right at the next corner. Although she kept watch for the reporters following them, from the corner of her eye she saw Vince's expression as he read the address on the envelope. Saw when he understood.

"He's at the Graysons' place?"

She nodded and made another turn, hoping to shake the remaining car following them. "I'm afraid Cora's right. Something has happened to the Graysons. I just hope he has them tied up and not—"

She couldn't finish. She didn't know John and Martha Grayson well but her grandfather did. She'd been to their house a couple times, once when Martha called the police because she thought John was having a heart attack, another time to deliver John's wallet after a tourist found it and turned it in at the police department. They were nice people. Warm, welcoming people. The kind of people who would innocently welcome someone like Charles into their home.

Katherine hated what she was thinking. "The Graysons'

house is a perfect place for Charles to have the girls. It's set back from the Dyea Road and hidden behind a stand of trees. Even if the girls yelled for help, I doubt anyone would hear them."

"Stop the mail and cancel the newspaper and everyone would think they were away," Vince added. "And they evidently have a fax machine, which would allow Bell to send those faxes to my office in Seattle." Vince pulled out his cell phone. "Bob should have tracked that down by now. I wonder if he called Tom. Your boss, Gordon, may also know Bell's at the Graysons' place."

"Which means we need to get there first." Katherine stepped on the gas. This was one case when the arrival of the cavalry would not be good.

CHAPTER SIXTY-THREE

Bob didn't answer his phone, and when Vince called the office number his call was diverted to leaving a message. He didn't bother, put his cell phone away, and tightened his seatbelt. The way Katherine was driving, siren on, lights flashing, he hoped there weren't any more stupid people thinking of crossing the street. Only when they were sure they'd lost the reporters did she slow down and turn off the lights and siren. As she drove along Dyea Road, she described how the Graysons' driveway not only went back a long ways from the road but also curved slightly to the south.

"If you work your way straight back," she said, "you should end up behind the house, but if you notice you're starting to climb, you've gone too far."

Katherine stopped the Tahoe at the side of the road, and Vince looked at the wooded area in front of him. Ground cover made it difficult to see the slope of the land, but it seemed to him the terrain immediately angled upward. "When you say climb . . ." Using the flat of his hand, he indicated a gradual tilt upward.

"I mean climb," she answered, showing him with her hand an angle of thirty degrees or more. "Once you get behind their house, you will be mountain climbing. And, watch out for bears. I heard one's been hanging around here."

Just what he didn't need to hear. "And, if I see one?"

"The best way to avoid bears is to make noise so they know

you're coming." He could see when she realized what she'd said. "But—"

"But, be quiet so Bell doesn't know I'm there. I understand." Vince crossed his fingers. "Let's hope I don't see any bears."

"Be careful," she said.

He nodded. If he'd thought it would work, he would have changed places with her, but he knew neither Katherine nor Bell would allow that. All he said was, "Same to you. Now give me a bit of a head start."

Vince realized his idea of a head start and Katherine's weren't the same when he heard the Tahoe slip into gear and a moment later the crunch of tires on gravel. He also realized she'd been right about the density of the underbrush. Surrounded by Sitka spruce and shore pine, he had to work his way through devil's club and yarrow and over jagged granite rocks. Rain soaked branches dripped water on his head and down his back, and he wished he were wearing a hat.

He found hurrying actually slowed him down, and, if he didn't keep watch, the wet, slippery underbrush would trip him, but, after a while, more light seemed to penetrate the trees, and he thought he saw a corner of a house up ahead. He figured if he angled slightly to the right, he could work his way around to the back of the house without being seen. Most houses had a back or side door. With luck, this one would be unlocked or easy to enter.

A few feet closer, and he realized luck wasn't going to be with him.

At first Vince didn't understand the thump he heard or the blur of off-white he saw near the back of the house. Cautiously, he inched his way closer, then stopped, his stomach lurching into his throat. The owner of the house, in order to keep bears out of his garbage, had built an enclosed stockade just a few feet away from the back corner of the house. Logs set vertically into the ground, their skyward ends topped by a slanted roof, were being attacked by a bear.

For a moment Vince thought it was a polar bear, but, when it turned its head toward him, he realized, in spite of the white coloring, the size and shape of the animal weren't right for a polar bear. Not that it mattered. A bear was a bear, and, at the moment, this one was between him and the house.

Vince gave a start when he heard a door open and a male voice from the front of the house yell out, "Get away from there!"

Although Vince couldn't see the shouter, he wasn't sure if he could be seen or not. Was he the one being yelled at? Or the bear?

Vince took a step back, moving slowly to avoid stepping on a branch and alerting the bear or the man. "Go!" the man shouted, coming around the corner of the house, waving his arms. "Scat!"

Hello, Charles Bell, Vince thought, the moment he got a clear view of the man. Although the quality of the photos the hospital had faxed to Katherine wasn't great, the man standing by the corner of the house, waving his arms and yelling, had the same facial features and body shape as Charles Bell, aka The Bee-keeper.

Go get him, Vince mentally urged the bear. It would certainly make rescuing the girls and Katherine's grandfather easier if the bear in front of him eliminated Bell as a threat.

The bear didn't cooperate. With a grunt, it moved away from the log structure and headed for the woods.

Headed directly toward Vince.

Bell stood where he was, watching, and Vince didn't dare yell or wave his arms. He didn't dare move.

With each lumbering step, the bear came closer. Vince could see spots of dirt on its fur, a briar caught in the ruff near its head. He also saw Bell turn around and again disappear from sight.

Vince had no idea where Katherine was. Had she reached the house?

God, how he wished he had a gun.

The bear stopped and began sniffing the air, its beady, black eyes scanning the woods in front of him.

Vince didn't move. Stopped breathing.

The bear was looking directly at him.

Chapter Sixty-Four

Katherine left her cruiser out of sight of the house and slowly walked up the driveway. Still out of sight of the house, she heard a man shout, "Get away from there."

Katherine stopped where she was, her right hand automatically going to her holster. Pistol at the ready, she scanned the woods and driveway ahead of her and tried to suppress the memories flashing through her mind. Once again she was fourteen years old, trembling with fear.

Closing her eyes, she remembered the feelings. How she didn't want him mad at her. How, when she made him mad, he punished her. How he made her do things she didn't want to do, did things to her that she didn't want to remember.

Bile rose in her throat, and she fought back a surge of nausea. For years she'd experienced nightmares, dreamt he was out of the hospital and had come after her. And, here he was. Outside of the house. Once she made it around the corner, made it past the trees blocking her view, she would see him.

So move, she told her legs, but they didn't move. Her breathing had turned rapid and shallow, her limbs lead weights. Her therapist, during Katherine's sessions, had told her to visualize herself in control of the situation, to see herself as the victor, not the victim. And, Katherine had, sometimes picturing herself shooting him. Sometimes stabbing him with a knife. And, sometimes beating him to a pulp using a board or a baseball bat. She always made him beg for mercy before she killed him.

Made him apologize for killing her family, and for everything he did to her.

In those images, she was in charge, empowered. Bold and brave. And, if this were simply a visualization, she wouldn't have had any trouble closing the gap between them and putting him under arrest.

But, this was reality, and she was shaking, unable to move.

She heard him yell, "Go! Scat!" and knew he was chasing something away. She half expected a dog or cat to come running toward her. But, nothing appeared, and she next heard a door slam shut.

He'd gone back inside. She'd lost her advantage.

"Damn you," she moaned, cussing herself as well as him. It scared her to realize how much power he still had over her.

"Are you a wimp or a woman?" she asked herself, the Glock in her hand becoming unbearably heavy. Either she walked up to that door and faced him, or she called Gordon . . . and jeopardized her grandfather's life, as well as the girls'.

Keeping her weapon out and ready, Katherine made it around the bend in the driveway and sprinted to the side of the house. Drapes had been drawn, allowing the living room's plate-glass window to reflect the cloudy sky and swaying tree tops. Although she couldn't see into the house, if Charles was peeking out, he would have seen her. She waited, every nerve ending on edge.

She heard a sound, but couldn't tell what it was. Maybe Vince. Maybe one tree branch rubbing another. All she knew was it came from the opposite end of the house, out towards the woods. From inside the house, she heard nothing.

Creeping forward, she ducked below the window's ledge, and made her way to the front door. She kept her body flat against the side of the house, her gun in her right hand, and tried the door knob with her left.

To her surprise, the knob turned.

The door creaked as it opened, and Katherine moved forward just enough to look inside. She could see most of the living room and part of a dining area but little else. No sign of Charles.

Her grandfather sat on a kitchen chair directly across the room from the front door. Strips of material had been wrapped around his ankles and tied to the legs of the chair. She assumed similar strips of sheeting bound his wrists behind his back. His head was tilted down, his chin resting against his chest, and she could see a wide strip of duct tape covering his mouth. His eyes were closed, but she sighed with relief. The slow, rhythmic rise and fall of his chest, accompanied by a soft, guttural sound, told her he was asleep.

Katherine knew Charles had placed her grandfather on that chair as a trap, and hoped Vince had found his way around to the back of the house. She stood where she was, listening for any sound that might indicate where Charles or Vince might be.

Still nothing.

Cautiously, she stepped into the house, scanning every part of the room she could see. In the three years she'd worked in Skagway, she hadn't had one instance when she or her fellow officers had needed to enter a hostile environment. Mentally, she practiced the drill, silently announcing "Clear."

She would have moved on to the next room, but her grand-father woke at that moment. His head jerked up and his eyes widened when he saw her. He started to twist about in the chair, and she feared he'd tip it over and break a bone in his efforts to free himself.

"Don't move," she mouthed, holding up a hand to still him.

He made a sound, and she cringed, glancing around as she moved closer. Charles had to know she was in the house. Where was he?

Katherine had her gun in one hand and a knife in the other

by the time she reached her grandfather. Alert for any noise, she crouched behind the chair and made a quick slice through the sheeting strips holding his hands together. She was about to move to the front of the chair and free his legs when she felt the barrel of a gun press against her head.

"Put the gun and the knife on the floor," Bell said, "then stand up slowly and face me."

She did as he ordered, and he pushed both her gun and knife away with the side of a stocking covered foot.

No shoes, no noise. Why couldn't a floor board have creaked? She switched her gaze from his feet to his face. His smile was triumphant. He'd lured her into his web . . . no, into his hive. Once again she'd played the fool.

"You, stay where you are," he ordered her grandfather, then took her by the arm and led her away from the chair. "Want to see my girls? Maybe join them for a while? It'll be just like old times, Kit Kat."

What she wanted to do was puke.

CHAPTER SIXTY-FIVE

Vince fought back the urge to run—he knew he wouldn't have a chance if he did—but he couldn't stop the adrenaline from pulsing through his body, and he realized he was clenching his fists. Time slowed, every second dragging into an eternity as the bear sniffed the air for his scent.

Thoughts collided in his mind. Was Katherine in the house? How long would the bear simply stand there? If he yelled softly, would Bell hear him? If he stood perfectly still, would the bear go away? If he waved his arms, would that be enough?

The summer before, Vince had flown to Alaska's interior for a fishing trip. The guide for the trip had also given instructions on how to avoid encounters with bears. Whenever they traveled from one spot to another, they talked and made noise, and the only bears Vince ever saw were on distant slopes or the opposite sides of the lakes. Last summer, he'd spotted both grizzlies and black bears, admired their size and wild beauty. Standing less than a hundred yards away from this bear, all he noticed were its long teeth, massive muscles, and lethal claws.

Dammit all, he was a computer tech. He should be back at his office, decoding spyware programs and stopping hackers, not debating how to save his own life. None of the self-defense maneuvers he'd learned during boot camp or in the martial arts classes he'd taken dealt with fighting a five-hundred-pound bear.

Go away, he willed.

"Girls, I've brought company," Charles said, dragging Katherine into a darkened bedroom.

She could make out two beds against the far wall with a nightstand between the two. On each bed, a blanket covered what looked like a body.

Charles released his hold on her arm and a light came on, allowing Katherine a clearer view of the room. She recognized Misty from the picture Crystal had given them, though the girl's hair was a tangled mess of curls and a bruise was forming on her right cheek. Sarah looked a little better, except for the haunted look in her eyes.

Both girls were tied like animals, strips of sheeting binding their wrists to opposite sides of old-fashioned, wrought-iron headboards. With their arms above their heads, the blankets covering the girls stopped just above their breasts and under their armpits. The only differences in how the girls looked were that Sarah's blanket didn't completely cover her bare feet, and she had only a single strip of sheeting connecting her wrists and ankles. Each of Misty's wrists and ankles was tied using two strips of sheeting.

Katherine remembered the first week of her confinement. Like this room, the cell Charles Bell had created in his basement had been totally dark. The only time she saw light was when he appeared. Stripped naked and tied to a cot, she'd been at his mercy. For days he controlled when she could eat, drink, or use the bathroom, and, in time, she stopped yelling for help and stopped begging him not to rape her.

Physically weak and mentally defeated, she'd actually thanked him when he began allowing her a little freedom. Never sure when something she did might displease him and result in punishment, she learned to obey his every command, and the more compliant she became, the more freedoms he allowed.

She learned how to fake pleasure when he invaded her body, how to move and say the words he wanted to hear. He never knew the techniques she employed to distance herself from what was actually taking place. After her release, she used those same techniques in an effort to lead a "normal" life. She doubted the boys she slept with ever guessed she was faking, but she knew, and she finally gave up the sham.

"Katherine," Sarah said, her eyes brightening. And then she saw the gun in Bell's hand, and her look of hope disappeared. With a whimper, the girl closed her eyes and turned her head to the side.

The blonde said nothing, but Katherine could tell she was fighting back tears.

Katherine looked at Charles. "Do you realize what you've done to them?"

He shrugged. "I've only pollinated one."

Her gaze returned to the girls. "Sarah?"

"One for the money, one for the honey."

Katherine understood what he meant. "How did you know Misty would be here, in Skagway?"

"Don't you want to know how I knew you'd be here?"

"You're smart. I'm sure, once that damn hospital let you out, you tracked me down through my grandfather."

He smiled. "Ah, Kit Kat, you always did appreciate my intelligence."

"And your cruelty." With her, he'd used that as a weapon. "Did you have to kill Phil? Or that boy she was with?" Katherine nodded toward Misty.

"I needed Phil's radio. And his gun." Charles moved his hand slightly, letting her see the gun was still pointed at her. "You should know by now I'll kill anything that gets in my way. I'll kill that guy you have outside, if the bear doesn't get him first."

So much for Vince coming to her rescue. Katherine didn't doubt Charles would do exactly what he'd said. He was a sociopath. During those therapy sessions, Mary Elizabeth had tried to explain to Katherine why someone could be so heartless; that, for a sociopath, hurting people or taking their lives meant nothing.

"Did you kill John and Martha Grayson?" she asked, fearing the bodies of the sweet, old couple might be lying somewhere in the woods. It would explain why a bear had been seen hanging around the area.

"Ah, the Graysons. They were so friendly until I told them why I wanted their house; then they became quite hostile." He smiled. "I'm letting them cool off."

Which meant they were dead. She wasn't sure what to do next, other than keep him talking. "So you saw Vince?"

"Vince?" Misty spoke for the first time. "He's here?"

The girl smiled, and Charles glared at her. "Don't go getting your hopes up, sweety. Your hero isn't going to have any more success than you have."

Katherine watched the look of hope on the girl's face disappear, but she knew from Charles's anger that Misty Morgan had tried to escape. *Good for you, girl,* Katherine thought and smiled at her.

Russell Ward had watched his granddaughter being pulled out of the room by the man who'd brought him to this house and tied him up. He'd been told to stay where he was, and normally he did what he was told. But, staying where he was didn't seem right. The chair wasn't comfortable, and he didn't like having his legs tied to it. Katherine should have untied the cloth around his wrists, not just cut it away from where it was tied to the chair.

Darn it all, he was going to untie his legs. Besides, who did that guy think he was, telling them what to do? Katherine didn't seem to like him that much.

He pulled the tape away from his mouth, giving a groan as some of the hairs on his chin left along with the tape. He then leaned over and started working on the strip of cloth tied around his right ankle. Try as he might, his arthritic fingers couldn't loosen the knot. He tried the knot on the left ankle. Same problem. Pulling didn't help—didn't tear the material, only tightened the knot.

Damn old age.

Winded, and a little lightheaded, Russell Ward sat back up. The knife Katherine had used was on the carpet, a few feet from the chair. Too far to reach. Her gun was even farther away. Not that he was going to try to shoot himself free. He never was a very good shot. Would probably shoot himself in the foot if he tried that.

But a knife . . .

If he could get over to that knife, he could cut the cloth.

He grasped the edges of the chair's seat, pushed himself slightly up with his feet and shifted his weight and the chair to the side. The chair thumped, but it also moved. Just a little, but a little was better than not at all.

He repeated the maneuver.

Again the chair thumped and moved.

Inch by inch, he was getting closer to the knife.

Step by step, the bear drew closer. Vince held his breath, forcing his body not to move. Stretching his head forward, the bear sniffed, a guttural sound coming from deep in its throat. And, then it reared up on its hind legs, its head higher than Vince's. Staying still ceased to be an option.

Raising his own arms, he yelled. He jumped in the air. He whistled. He clapped his hands. He did anything and everything he could think of to make himself appear larger and more menacing than the creature in front of him.

He even laughed.

Who was he kidding? He was dead meat. No way were his feeble gestures going to scare this bear.

Nevertheless, he kept at it. If Charles Bell heard him, so be it. The way things were, there was no way Vince was going to be coming to Katherine's rescue. With luck, Bell wouldn't know Katherine was in or near the house, wouldn't already have her, and would assume Vince was alone.

"Fuck you!" he yelled at the bear, and then stared in amazement as the bear dropped back down on all fours, turned, and ran.

Ran right into the side of the house.

Katherine heard the thump against the outside of the bedroom wall. She'd also been hearing quieter thumps coming from the living-room area. Charles aimed his gun toward the wall.

A louder thump came from the living room, accompanied by a cuss word.

Charles turned that direction.

Katherine used his confusion and the momentum of his half turn to her advantage. She shifted her weight onto her right leg and executed a low karate kick to his ankles with the side of her left foot. With his feet swept out from under him, Charles Bell went down on his side, the gun going off as his arm hit the floor. Katherine jumped back and kicked again, this time at his hand, dislodging the gun from his grip and sending it flying under Sarah's bed.

Before she had a chance to regain her balance, Charles had her by the leg and pulled.

Katherine managed one hop forward, then fell across his body. With a twist, he was on his back. She didn't see the fist coming at her face, not until his knuckles hit her cheek. Pain radiated from the point of impact to her eye and down to her jaw. For a moment she couldn't see, couldn't think. And, then she grabbed for his arm.

She was stronger than she'd been at fourteen, and maybe he was weaker. She deflected his next blow, sending his fist past her head, but her moment of triumph was short-lived. He wrapped his arms around her chest, squeezing her against his body until taking a breath became impossible.

"Bitch," he growled near her ear. "What I am going to do to you now is going to make anything I did before seem like a pleasure fest. And, then I'm going to make you watch me do them, over and over again."

He released her as quickly as he'd grabbed her, but before she could scramble to her feet, he pushed her to the side and was on top of her, turning her and pressing her face against the carpeting. She felt his hands grabbing for her wrists and knew she couldn't let him get a hold and twist her arms behind her back; couldn't let him get the handcuffs off her belt and onto her wrists.

Sliding her hands as close to her body as she could manage, she arched up, raising her head and bucking him onto her hips. For balance, he tightened his thighs around her pelvis, but that was fine with her. She grabbed his right hand and twisted his fingers back. With a yelp, he loosened his knee grip and slapped at her head. She let her head go with the blow, and reared up on her knees at the same time, pushing Charles onto his knees.

"Katherine?" she heard and recognized her grandfather's hesitant voice.

Charles growled, rose to his feet, spun around, and lunged for Katherine's grandfather.

"No!" Katherine screamed, afraid of what would happen next.

"You left this—" her grandfather started, but didn't finish.

CHAPTER SIXTY-SIX

Vince entered the house through the front door, not the back. He still couldn't believe the bear had actually run from him. Not only run from him, but ran into the side of the house. He might still be there, at the edge of the woods, bent over laughing at the sight of that bear stepping back from the house, shaking its head, and then lumbering off, if he hadn't heard a gunshot.

He didn't worry about Bell seeing him as he ran to the house. A gunshot meant subterfuge was a waste of time. Either Katherine had shot at Bell or Bell had shot at her. He hoped it was the former.

Vince heard Katherine yell "No," the sound of her voice coming from somewhere down a hallway to his right. He'd barely taken a step when he saw Bell stumble through a doorway and into the hallway. Bell was looking down at his stomach, his hands gripping something, his mouth agape. Only when Bell moved his hands away from his middle did Vince understand the man's shock.

In his hand, Bell held a knife, its blade covered with blood. Almost immediately, blood began to ooze from Bell's stomach, staining the front of his shirt and trousers. He dropped the knife and pressed a hand against the wound, color draining from his face. His next step was wobbly, a desperate look in his eyes when he spied Vince.

"Help," Bell said. "I need help."

"What have you done to Katherine?"

"I can't stop the bleeding." Bell stared at his stomach, blood oozing out between his fingers.

"Katherine?" Vince repeated.

"There." Bell motioned with his head back to the doorway he'd just exited. "I need an ambulance."

"You need a firing squad." Vince moved past him to the doorway.

He saw Katherine kneeling over her grandfather's prone body. "Is he . . . ?"

She looked up, an area on her cheek red and puffy. "Vince," she said. "Charles got away. He ran right into my grandfather, knocked him against the doorframe, then kept going." She looked back down at her grandfather. "Poppa, can you hear me?"

"Vince," another voice called, and he saw Misty, an army-style wool blanket covering her body.

"Untie me," she begged, then looked at the girl on the other bed. "Untie both of us."

Vince glanced back down the hallway. Bell had made it to the end, but Vince didn't think he'd be going far. Near his feet, he heard a confused, "What happened?" and noted Katherine's grandfather was coming to. "I'm going to cut the girls loose," he told her.

"No, get Charles," she demanded, before turning her attention back to her grandfather.

"Charles," Vince assured her, "isn't going anywhere."

"Okay, if you say so." Katherine helped her grandfather sit up. "Poppa, take it easy. You bumped your head."

Vince used the pocket knife he always carried to slice through the strips of sheeting binding Misty's wrists and ankles. There were spots where her skin was worn raw, and he knew she hadn't been a compliant prisoner.

The moment she was free, she sat up, holding the blanket in front and as far around her naked body as she could manage. Although he heard no sound, tears slid from her eyes to her cheeks. He wanted to hug her, but he wasn't quite sure how she would react. Misty was the one who initiated contact. She reached out and took his hand in hers, squeezing until her nails cut into his palm. He ignored the pain, and ran his fingers through her tangled curls, drawing her head close to his side. "It's okay," he said. "You're safe now."

He felt her nod, but she still didn't speak. He waited until, with a shudder that racked her body and a voice rough with emotion, she managed, "I knew you would come."

"Thank *her*," he said, moving to the side so Misty could get a clear view of Katherine. "It was Officer Ward who figured out where you were."

"Sarah said the police would find us." Misty leaned back, away from his side, and pointed at the girl on the other bed. "Cut her free, Vince. He did terrible things to her."

Misty released her hold on his hand, and Vince moved to the next bed. The dark-haired girl was crying, softly saying, "I want my mama."

"We'll get you to her just as fast as we can," he promised as he cut through the cloth binding her wrists and ankles.

"Where are your clothes?" he asked Misty once Sarah was free.

"I don't know where he put them. When I came to, I was this way." She shrugged and held the blanket closer.

"I'll look for them."

It was then that Vince realized Katherine and her grandfather were no longer in the room. Cautiously, he went down the hallway. He saw Russell Ward first, seated in a recliner similar to the one the old man had in his own home. He then saw Katherine standing by a table, a radio-phone pressed close to her face.

She was asking someone to send an ambulance.

Charles Bell had made it into the kitchen and back into the living room. He now sat on the floor, his back against the wall dividing the living room from the kitchen, a dish towel pressed against his belly. His breathing ragged and his skin pale, Bell watched Katherine.

"We'll be here," Vince heard Katherine say and saw her put down the radio-phone. She looked at him and gave a feeble smile. "Gordon's not real happy with me. I think I may be looking for a new career."

"Your grandfather okay?"

She nodded. "Just a little shaken up . . . and confused." Her attention turned to Bell. "He must have walked right into the knife Poppa was holding. In a way, he did this to himself."

"Just too bad the knife didn't hit a vital organ."

"Yeah, it would have—"

Katherine stopped talking the same time Vince saw Bell look away from her and back toward the hallway. Both Katherine and Vince turned that direction. Sarah and Misty stood at the end of the hallway, facing the man who had held them captive for almost two days. Sarah held the wool blanket around her body like a shield, but Misty had let hers drop to the floor. In her hands, she held a gun, and it was pointed directly at Charles Bell.

"Misty, don't—" both Vince and Katherine said at the same time.

Vince doubted Misty heard them over the gun blast.

CHAPTER SIXTY-SEVEN

"I'm sorry. I'm so sorry," Misty sobbed.

"It's all right," Katherine soothed, carefully taking the gun from the girl's hand. "It's over now."

Katherine bent down and picked up the wool blanket Misty had dropped. She handed it to the girl and then stepped back. The gun she'd taken from Misty had to be the one that went under the bed when she was struggling with Charles. It was probably Phil's gun, taken by Charles after he killed Phil. Her gun should be somewhere in the living room. She'd put it down with her knife, and Charles had kicked both the knife and the gun aside.

The kitchen chair was now lying on its side, not far from Charles. Her grandfather had obviously picked up the knife and used it to free his legs before coming back to the bedroom. But where was the gun?

"Poppa," she asked, turning to where her grandfather sat in the recliner. "Do you know where my gun is?"

Her grandfather looked at the holster on her hip, where she normally carried her weapon, then started to shake his head. Just as quickly, he put his hands to his forehead and winced. She had a feeling more than just his head would be hurting in a few hours. He'd taken quite a hit against the doorjamb when Charles rammed into him and probably should be checked over by the paramedics when they arrived.

Her gaze switched to Charles Bell's slumped body. No need

for the paramedics to rush. Sarah and Misty would need to be examined by a doctor, but the DA wouldn't need the results for a court case. She wouldn't say it aloud, but silently she thanked Misty. The sixteen-year-old had eliminated the possibility of Charles once again finding a lawyer and jury that would believe his lies. The Beekeeper was dead.

Vince crossed in front of her view. He stooped down next to Charles and reached forward. "Don't touch him," Katherine ordered. "Nothing should be touched until Gordon arrives."

"It's here," he said, pointing instead of touching. "Your gun. He must have picked it up while you were helping your grandfather into the chair."

"My gun?" Holding Phil's gun by her side, she walked over to where Vince was crouching. Sure enough, she could see the butt of her Glock just under the edge of the towel Charles had been using to stop the bleeding.

"I don't know how you feel," Vince said, keeping his voice low so the girls couldn't hear, "but I'd say she shot him in self defense."

Katherine looked down at the gun in her hand. Her fingerprints were on it now.

She smiled. "Or maybe I did."

They heard the sirens, and Katherine opened the front door and waited. Her career as a police officer was about to end. From her first day at the police academy, she'd been taught the importance of chain of command and following orders. It was bad enough in a large force when an officer didn't obey. In a force the size of Skagway's, it was a major error. Whatever Gordon or the chief decided, she deserved.

Katherine heard a low, moaning sound and looked back into the house, afraid it might be her grandfather. To her relief, he looked fine. Sarah, however, was bent over, crying.

Misty tried to hug the girl and hold up her own blanket at the same time. She was struggling with the effort when Vince went over and put an arm around each girl, holding them close to his side. Speaking softly to the two girls, he stood like a bastion against the tide of people about to barge into the house.

The noise of tires on gravel and brakes squealing made it difficult for Katherine to hear what he was saying, but Sarah stopped crying and Misty nodded, and Katherine knew Vince was providing the first step in the months of counseling the girls would need to overcome what they'd experienced.

You bastard, she thought, looking back at Charles Bell.

He'd called her a Judas the day the police rescued her. Seventeen years hadn't lessened his desire for revenge. That he'd found her in Skagway wasn't a surprise. Anyone who didn't appreciate Charles Bell's intelligence was a fool. His taking Sarah also made sense. Not only did the girl resemble both his daughter as a teenager and also Katherine, but taking Sarah was a way of hurting Katherine.

But, why had he taken Misty? How had he known she would be here in Skagway, getting off the ship yesterday morning? And, why ask for so much money?

Misty had eliminated Charles Bell as a future threat, but she had also taken away the answers to those questions.

CHAPTER SIXTY-EIGHT

The news media was forced to stay back on the main road to Dyea as the police, state troopers, FBI, a medical examiner, crime scene techs, and the assistant district attorney took over the house and yard. The Graysons' bodies were found in the freezer in the garage. Since this was both a kidnapping and a murder, Vince knew everyone involved, including himself, would be separated and questioned. But, after a while, it seemed to him the questioning would never end. He kept looking for Tom and Crystal, asking if they knew Misty was all right. He kept getting the same answer: they would be along soon enough.

Doug Pierson, who was introduced to Vince as one of the seasonal officers, took Vince's statement. At first Vince wasn't sure if the officer believed his story of being stalked by a white bear or what happened when the bear turned and ran, so Vince showed him the claw marks on the poles surrounding the garbage cans. Closer to the enclosure they could smell the rotting meat Bell had evidently pulled from the freezer to make room for the Graysons' bodies. The tuft of white fur still stuck on the house's siding, and the spot where the ground was torn up as the bear regained its balance and tore off around the back of the house, confirmed Vince's story. Officer Pierson was laughing when he walked Vince back to where the vehicles were parked and told him to stay there.

Vince did stand around for a while, watching men and women go in and out of the house, but something kept bothering him.

Although he'd seen only the living room, dining area, hallway, and the bedroom where Bell had held the girls, he'd noticed a lack of electronic devices. There was no television in the living room, just a radio and a tape player. No computer on a desk or laptop on the table. No scanner or copier.

No fax machine.

Curious, Vince walked back into the house. He avoided the officers in the bedroom where the girls had been held and CSS techs in the living room. He didn't want to get in anyone's way, and didn't want to spoil any evidence. Besides, he'd seen all he needed in those rooms.

As unobtrusively as he could, Vince opened the other doors along the hallway and discovered there were two bathrooms and three bedrooms in all. The master bedroom and bath looked like it hadn't been used recently, but the other, smaller bedroom had obviously been used by Bell. The bed was unmade, clothes had been tossed on the floor, and a man's wallet lay on top of a chest of drawers, set on its side so a picture in it could be seen.

Vince was looking at the picture when he heard Tom's and Crystal's voices. Without hesitation, Vince picked up the wallet and headed back to the living room.

Sarah had already been sent to the Skagway Clinic, accompanied by a police officer. Vince assumed her mother would go there. Misty, however, was still in the house, sitting in the kitchen with the park ranger Katherine had called that morning. Someone had found the girls' clothes, and Misty was wearing a t-shirt and miniskirt.

Vince reached the end of the hallway in time to see Misty being hugged by Crystal. Although Vince couldn't hear exactly what Crystal was saying, it sounded like she was asking Misty what Bell had told her.

Tom was standing back a ways, awkwardly staring at his daughter. *Don't let her down,* Vince thought, knowing how important the next few minutes would be for Misty. The girl had just gone through an experience no one—female or male—should face. She didn't need to be questioned by her step-mother. She needed her father's uncensored acceptance.

"I asked what he said to you," Crystal demanded, her voice rising. "What did he tell you?"

She'd used the word "said." She hadn't asked what Bell *did* to Misty. Vince might not have picked up on that difference if he hadn't seen Bell's wallet. Crystal's insistence helped solidify his suspicions. "Tom," he said, walking over to his friend's side. "I hope you didn't transfer that money."

Tom looked at him, then back at his daughter and wife. "I okayed the transfer with my bankers, but I told Bob to wait for my call." He looked back at Vince. "You don't think Bob would have . . . ?"

"No, I'm sure he didn't," Vince said. "Go to her, Tom. Tell her you love her. She needs you, not Crystal. I'll call Bob and make sure everything is all right."

Tom started to say something, then nodded and stepped toward his daughter. Crystal was still questioning the girl, but Tom stopped her and opened his arms to Misty.

Father and daughter were in an embrace when Vince turned away and started outside. He'd left his satellite phone in Katherine's Tahoe and was walking toward the vehicle when he saw Katherine. Changing directions, he headed toward her.

"Take a look at this," he said, handing Katherine the wallet he'd removed from Bell's room. "Tell me what you think."

Katherine opened the wallet and flipped through the pictures. There were only two: one of a young girl, maybe ten or eleven; the other the picture that had drawn Vince's attention. "That's Crystal. Mrs. Morgan." She looked up at him. "Whose wallet is this?"

"I found it in the room Bell was using."

303

She looked at the picture of Crystal again, then flipped back to the picture of the young girl. "Oh, my God," she said. "I remember this picture. He had a larger one in his house in Michigan. It's his daughter, Sisi."

"But, why the picture of Crystal?"

Katherine flipped back to that picture, then to the one of the girl. "Look at the eyes, Vince," she said, showing him first one photo, then the other. "The shape of the mouth."

He understood. "She told him Misty would be here. She planned this whole thing."

CHAPTER SIXTY-NINE

Katherine took the wallet with her when she went into the house. She could see Crystal standing just inside the doorway to the kitchen. Misty and Tom were slightly to the side. "Sisi," Katherine called out as she started toward the three.

Tom and Misty frowned, but Crystal looked directly at Katherine, the expression on the blonde's face confirming Katherine's suspicions. Now she knew why she'd thought Crystal Morgan looked familiar. It wasn't because of that picture in *Fortune* magazine; it was because of the picture she'd seen seventeen years earlier.

Even with makeup, Crystal Morgan's eyes were the same as the teenager's who'd testified that her father had never molested her. The acne was gone from her skin, she'd lost a lot of weight, gained a more impressive bust size, and changed the color and style of her hair, but the woman standing in front of her was none other than Sisi Bell. "How could you?" Katherine asked, shaking her head. "No matter what you said, I know what he did to you."

Vince grabbed his satellite phone from the Tahoe and punched in the numbers for his office. This time his secretary answered. "Edith, I need to talk to Bob."

"Bob's not here," she said. "I think he's on his way to see you. He said he had to catch a plane."

"Here?" Vince wasn't sure why his partner would be flying to

Skagway unless he, too, suspected Crystal might be involved in Misty's kidnapping. "Did someone call and tell him Misty's been found?"

"You found her?" Edith's response was laced with relief. "Oh, thank goodness. Was it because the ransom was paid?"

Vince wasn't sure he'd heard right. "What ransom?"

"The money Bob transferred just a while ago."

"Bob made the transfer?" A sickening sensation invaded Vince's stomach. "Transferred money out of Tom's bank accounts?"

"Yes," she answered, sounding surprised that he didn't know. "He said it was necessary."

"But, he wasn't supposed to do that until . . ." Vince wished he could stop the thoughts racing through his head. "Edith, one of those faxes Bob received last night had a routing number on it. It was for the off-shore bank that Bob just sent the money to. I need the name of that bank and those numbers."

"I don't know what you're talking about," she said.

"Routing numbers. They'll be on one of the faxes," he repeated, then remembered what Bob had said. "They came in after you'd left yesterday."

He could almost hear his secretary shaking her head. "Vince, I just received a summary sheet for the faxes we sent and received this week. Nothing has come in to or gone out from this machine for the last two days."

"But, Bob said . . ."

Vince closed his eyes and leaned against the side of the Tahoe, a sinking sensation filling his gut. Bob had told him once that he thought Tom's wife was hot. And, more than once in the last few months, Bob had made trips to the Morgan house. "Mrs. Morgan screwed up her computer again," Bob would say.

Vince had a feeling it wasn't a computer that got screwed up.

"Do me a favor," he said to his secretary, still hoping he was wrong. "Go into Bob's office and check everywhere you can think of to look for a fax. And, while you're doing that, see if you see anything that looks like a routing number. Or the name of an off-shore bank."

"What's going on, Vince?" Edith asked, her tone concerned.

"I'll let you know as soon as I know."

He glanced toward the house. "What the heck?"

CHAPTER SEVENTY

Katherine didn't expect Crystal to push her aside and run out of the house. The blonde almost ran into Ranger Susan Lange, dodged the assistant DA, and dashed by Gordon, heading for the cruiser he'd just left. "Stop her!" Katherine yelled.

Susan, the ADA, and Gordon all stopped and turn back toward the cruiser, but it was Vince who moved first. He dropped the satellite phone he was using and made a dash for Crystal. He reached her just as she opened the door of the cruiser. Katherine saw him grab the blonde by her hair and give a jerk back. Crystal screamed, her arms flailing as she fell backwards toward him. And maybe it was purely an accident, but Katherine had a feeling Vince purposely let go of Crystal's hair and stepped to the side so her butt ended up on the gravel drive.

Susan and Gordon reached Crystal before she had a chance to scramble to her feet. Susan helped her up, but Gordon grabbed her arm, stopping her from escaping. Frowning, he turned and called to Katherine, "What's going on?"

Katherine took her time walking from the house to the cruiser. "She's Bell's daughter," she said. "I'm not sure exactly what part she played in this, but she was in on it. Before Charles was released, she visited him."

"Two months ago, she flew back east to visit a sick uncle," Tom Morgan said from behind Katherine.

She glanced back at him. "That would be about the time

Charles was released. She must have met him and given him whatever money and paperwork he needed to get here."

"How could you?" Tom asked, looking at his wife.

Crystal gave a shrug, and, with her free hand, brushed at the mud and gravel on her slacks.

"You said you wanted to take this cruise to get closer to Misty."

Crystal Morgan scoffed. "Why should I bother getting closer to her? I heard you talking to your lawyer about a divorce. Months ago you and that weasel of a man were gloating over that pre-nup you made me sign and how it would keep me from getting to your money. I needed security."

"But, to ask your father to take her . . ." Katherine said. "After what he did to you when you were a child? After what he did to me?"

Crystal looked at her. "God, he hated you for putting him in that hospital. He was more than willing to help me if it meant he could get to you."

"So, for money, you had your stepdaughter and a fourteen-year-old kidnapped and raped, and four other people killed."

Crystal shook her head. "I didn't think he would kill anyone. And, he promised me he wouldn't hurt Misty. How was I to know he would take another girl?"

"You have the right to remain silent, you have . . ." Gordon began reciting the Miranda warning as he handcuffed Crystal.

CHAPTER SEVENTY-ONE

His secretary was still on the phone when Vince picked it up from where he'd dropped it. He wasn't surprised when she said she'd found no faxes. Crystal Morgan was smart, but she would have needed help in getting money transferred to an off-shore bank.

"I'm coming back to the office," he told Edith. "Whatever you do, don't touch Bob's computer."

Vince found Tom Morgan back in the house. Father and daughter were in the kitchen, seated next to each other at the table. Misty had her head on her father's shoulder, and Tom had an arm around her back. Neither said a word, but their body language displayed a closeness Vince hadn't seen before.

As he neared the two, Tom looked up. "I'm taking her to the medical facility here in town in a few minutes. She says he didn't do anything to her, but she rubbed her wrists raw trying to get loose. And, she did get loose," he said proudly, pointing at the scratches on Misty's arms and legs. "The bottoms of her feet are a mess."

"I almost got away." Misty straightened and grinned. "Twice. I used some of those techniques you showed me, Vince."

"She's a fighter, all right," Tom said, and brushed a kiss against his daughter's forehead before looking back at Vince. "But, that bastard kept her naked. Raped that other girl right in front of Misty. How could anyone . . . ?"

He stopped and pressed his forehead against Misty's.

"My own wife," he said, the agony of Crystal's betrayal clear in his voice.

"And my partner," Vince added.

Tom turned his head slightly to look at him. "Bob?"

"Looks like it. He didn't wait for your call. Your money's already been transferred to an off-shore account, and Bob's left the office. I'm going to fly back to Seattle. With luck, I'll get that transfer of your money reversed before he can get to it."

"The money's not that important. Not as long as I have Misty."

"My reputation is," Vince said. "I'm sorry, Tom. You were right. I didn't do a good job protecting your daughter . . . or you. I just never thought he . . ."

It was Vince's turn to be at a loss for words. "I should have realized Bob was involved. You were right. Why would Bell contact our office and not you, directly? I just . . ."

He stopped. Tom didn't need excuses; he needed results. "I'll get that money back for you."

Chapter Seventy-Two

Katherine was talking to Gordon when Vince approached them. "Can someone drive me to the airport?" he asked. "I need to get back to my office."

Gordon frowned. "We may need you here. I'm sure the assistant DA will want to talk to you."

"I've got to go," Vince said. "It looks like my partner is in on this. If I'm going to get Tom's money back, I need to get to Seattle right away."

"And, what about you? What's your role in this?" Gordon asked, clearly suspicious.

"Let him go, Gordon," Katherine said, remembering Vince's persistence in finding Misty and the way he'd talked to the two girls while waiting for the police to arrive. "He's not involved."

"I'll come back if you need me to," Vince promised. "I just don't have a lot of time to stop Bob from getting away with the money."

"I'd take you," Katherine said, "But, I need to make sure my grandfather—"

Gordon cut her off. "Take him. I'll see to it that your grandfather gets to the clinic. You can head there after you drop him off."

"If you're sure. Poppa's kind of confused." She looked toward the house.

"He's doing quite well, actually. He'll be fine, Katherine. Now, get Mr. Nanini to the airport."

★ ★ ★ ★ ★

Vince asked her to wait until he had a flight plan filed and was sure he had clearance to leave. They talked as he went through his preflight check of the King Air turbojet. "Gordon had Doug Pierson take Crystal back to the station," Katherine said. "I don't think she's going to like her lodgings there."

"Did she mention my partner?" Vince asked, glancing at her from under the fuselage. "Bob Lilly?"

"Not by name. She did say the money better be waiting for her when she got out of jail." Katherine had found that amazing. "I don't think she understands how serious these charges are. If she thinks she's going to get off with just a slap on the wrist, she doesn't know our DA."

"Well, if I have my way, there won't be any money waiting for her, no matter how long or short a time she's in jail."

He put the clipboard he was holding down and came toward her. "How are you doing, Katherine? I'm sorry I wasn't more help."

"You were fine." She laughed, remembering the thump she'd heard and Vince's story about the bear running into the side of the house. "I guess Cora was right, a white bear is a good omen."

"I thought that critter was going to be my demise."

"Well, between that bear hitting the house and my grandfather tipping his chair over, I had a chance to get that gun out of Charles's hands. That made a big difference in how things turned out."

"I hope Misty and Sarah keep quiet about who actually shot Bell. But, what about you? When this is all cleared up, will you still have a job, Officer Ward?"

"I don't know." When Gordon arrived at the house, he'd been angry enough to fire her on the spot. Only after he saw the girls and heard their stories did his mood seem to change. Even so, it wouldn't really be Gordon's decision. The chief would be back soon, and Gordon's report would be on his desk. She'd acted against orders, and that wasn't something either man could overlook.

"Will you be here when I come back?"

"I can't leave my grandfather." But, without a fulltime job, she wasn't sure how they could stay in Skagway.

"I can understand that." Vince touched the side of her face, and Katherine liked the feeling. "I think your grandfather could probably teach me a thing or two about fishing."

"At least until his mind completely goes," she said, hating what Alzheimer's did to a person.

"Which means I'd better not waste any time." Vince leaned closer. "Katherine, I'd like to get to know you better."

"I'm . . . That is, I—" She started to back away, then stopped herself and looked into his eyes. Maybe it was because she knew Charles was dead, or maybe because she'd seen how Vince treated the girls, or maybe it was the tingle that ran through her whenever he touched her, but her usual reluctance to get involved wasn't there. "I'd . . . I'd like to get to know you better, too."

She knew he was going to kiss her, so she wasn't surprised when his lips touched hers. What did surprise her was the warmth that flowed through her body, the sense of elation that filled her. She wrapped her arms around his shoulders—his broad, wonderful shoulders—and kissed him back.

He looked as shocked as she felt when he drew back. His gaze intense and his voice husky, he said, "I don't know what's going to happen in the next few days or weeks. What do you say we make a date. One month from today. Five o'clock at that saloon this town is famous for."

"The Red Onion?"

He nodded. "If for any reason I can't be there, I'll let you know. You do the same. But, if you simply decide this isn't a good idea, don't come, and I'll understand."

"And, the same with you," she said. "One month from today. Five o'clock. The Red Onion."

CHAPTER SEVENTY-THREE

5:00 P.M., one month later

So here she was, sitting on a bar stool in The Red Onion, calling herself a fool. She hadn't seen or heard from Vince during the past month. No phone call, no letter. Not even an email.

He's not going to show, she told herself, once again glancing over the crowd in the bar. Nervously, she turned the stein of beer she'd ordered around in her hands.

Vince had flown into Skagway once that she knew of. Both Gordon and the chief told her they'd talked to him. But, that was the day she'd been in Juneau with her grandfather, seeing a specialist that had given her little hope regarding Russell Ward's deteriorating memory.

Of course, she hadn't contacted Vince, either. Oh, more than once she'd started an email, but, each time, she'd hit the delete button rather than send. Everything she wrote seemed so trivial.

She saw no sense in writing him about Crystal. Katherine was sure Vince, with his connection to Tom Morgan, knew everything she knew, if not more. And Gordon had told her Vince was able to reverse the money transfer that Vince's partner had initiated, and that Vince's former connection with the FBI had gotten them involved in the search for Bob Lilly.

So what could she write about? The alarm at the jewelry store downtown that kept going off, but always proved to be a malfunction? The campers at the RV parks who'd been drinking too much and had to be told to keep the noise down? She was sure Vince would be thrilled to know she'd made one DUI arrest during the month and drove Cora to the clinic after she fell while leaving the police station.

Vince might have been glad to know the white bear was finally found and tranquilized, and had been carted off to a more remote location, hopefully never to return to Skagway. Being a police officer in Skagway was not that exciting . . . not since the demise of The Beekeeper. But hell, she was still on the force, albeit on probation, and she'd had enough excitement to last a lifetime.

Katherine checked her watch. Five fifteen.

He wasn't coming.

Damn him.

Not that she cared, she told herself. Not that it mattered. She wasn't interested in romance. She didn't need a man.

She looked at her watch again.

"Sorry I'm late," she heard behind her, and felt her heart leap in her chest. Holding back a smile, she slowly turned on her bar stool.

Vince stood before her, feet slightly spread apart and hands on his hips to counter the press of the patrons that clustered near the bar. His head had a newly shaved shine, as well as his face, and she saw a flash of appreciation as he gave her a quick up and down, very male look.

"Couldn't get a taxi from the airport," he said, as if answering an unasked question. "I had to walk."

"If you're looking for sympathy, you're not going to get it," she said, not quite sure how to react. "It's only three blocks."

"Got in late, too. With Bob out of the picture, I've really been busy." He smiled. "Damn, you look good."

Katherine was glad to hear that. The dress she had on had cost her a small fortune, but somehow she didn't think meeting him in jeans and a sweatshirt would be any more appropriate than being here in her uniform. And, she'd needed a new haircut, something a little more feminine. Getting dressed up and wearing makeup didn't mean she'd spent all day praying he would show up.

Oh, who did she think she was kidding?

"You look pretty damn good yourself," she said and slid off the bar stool and into his arms.

ABOUT THE AUTHOR

Maris Soule majored in art in college, but her love of books led her to writing. Although she grew up in California, a redhead with blue eyes talked her into moving to Michigan. (For just two years, he said.) Way too many years later, she's still living in Michigan with the same man, not too many miles away from their two grown children and two granddaughters. (But she and her husband do sneak down to Florida for the winter.) In addition to her twenty-six published romances, romantic suspense, and suspense novels, Soule has had three mysteries published by FiveStar/Gale/Cengage. Several of Soule's books have won awards and many are still available as e-books, and in other forms. For more information, check out her website: http://www.MarisSoule.com.